SHARK TOOTHED GRIN

DOUG GOODMAN

SEVERED PRESS
HOBART TASMANIA

SHARK TOOTHED GRIN

This book is dedicated to everyone who lives on salty streets and sandy beaches.

PART 1: YIG THE DESTROYER
CHAPTER ONE: OVEREXPOSED

The day was as bright as an overexposed photo. It was the kind of brightness that sucked the color out of the world and blurred the line between the sky and the water.

"Did you feel that?"

Ed put his hand on the small fishing boat's gunwales to balance himself. He and Jubal were off the coast of Galveston, fishing for redfish and dolphinfish, when the boat bumped up against something. The impact was strong enough to reverberate in the flesh, but not in the bones. It was the bump of hitting the dock after returning from a long, full day of fishing. A bump like that had no place out on the great grey Gulf.

"It's just the sun getting to you, old man. Get your ass away from the edge of the boat before you fall in," Jubal said. He was snacking on chips. Doritos were his favorite. He sat with his back against the pilot's cabin and his belly extended over his balls. He was hoarding the only shade within miles of their boat. Strapped above him, bolted to the back of the pilot's cabin was a tiny old wooden rod. It was a kid's rod, but the reel was long gone, lost to time and memory. The rod could have been salvaged and the reel replaced, but it wouldn't have mattered as much to Jubal and Ed if they fixed it. They kept it as a reminder of two best friends' first fishing trip together.

Ed laughed at his co-pilot in life, but he still thought the boat had hit something, like a sea kayak. He leaned over and looked into the thick Gulf waters. The weak wind made the waves puff upward like the top of a thick quilt.

The Gulf was empty. There was nothing there.

"Thought we hit a canoe."

"Who the hell is going to be canoeing out here? Nothing less than twenty feet should be on these waters."

"We're twenty feet," Ed said.

He looked overboard again. He thought he saw something under the water, a moving shape maybe? But the Gulf water was so thick, it was impossible to see anything more than fleeting shadows.

"You LSU types like to state the obvious, don't you? I know we're twenty feet. It's my damn boat."

"Oh, listen to that little Cougar roar. How are things at U of H? I mean, 'Cougar High?' You still enjoying the No-America conference?" Ed reached out with his right hand and touched his fingertips to the edge of the water. It was June, and the water was warm as fresh blood. Probably 75 degrees. Hurricane season could be bad with water that warm.

Jubal smiled broadly. "You always gotta make it about football when I start to out-fish you."

"Out-fish? I've got at least ten pounds in the cooler. You and your scrawny-ass minnows may outnumber me, but I'm the one bringing home dinner."

Jubal chuckled. He liked getting under Ed's skin. Their wives liked to say that Ed and Jubal bickered like an old married couple. Well, the pair had been inseparable since they were buds growing up in Houston back in the sixties, so they might as well be a couple. They had that special relationship. Two friends who grew up together and would probably die together.

Ed left the water and went back to his chair. Just then, something powerful slammed into the boat.

"Holy…" was all Ed could say before he was tossed overboard.

Jubal watched Ed flop out of the boat with the grace of a cow tipped in a wet field. He could make a joke (and in the back of his mind, he saved a mental screenshot of this so he could tease Ed for the rest of his life about the day his ass fell out of the boat), but for now, he was just concerned about his old friend. Fishin' with Ed was one of the true joys of his life. Never fishing with a "g" on the end. You either fished or you went fishin'. "Fishing" was something rich people did.

None of that mattered now. All that mattered was getting Ed back into the boat.

"Come on!" Jubal shouted. He grabbed the throw ring with a rope attached as he looked over the gunwales.

The water seethed like a thousand tiny, bubbly fish eggs were foaming at the surface.

Ed had a wild-eyed look. Jubal had seen this look many times in the fish that he plucked from the Gulf. It was the grandmaster of WTF looks, the look of a fish suddenly transported to an alien world where they can't breathe 'cause all the water is gone. Jubal hurled the ring at Ed, hard enough to bounce off his head. Ed didn't react to the hit, even though it was bad enough that it'd leave a three-day bruise. Instead, Ed kept screaming, loud and shrill. It reminded him of rabbits. Jubal once heard rabbits being slaughtered. His auntie went out to the hutches, plucked them from their wire cages, and chopped off their heads with an old axe.

Pretty soon the rabbits were all screaming. Just thinking of those screams made Jubal break out in goose flesh. Ed made those same screams now.

"I'm coming, Ed!" Jubal yelled as he thrust the fishing rod overboard where his buddy should be. Instead, all he saw was black liquid, almost like oil, rising up out of the churning water, and Ed's hand slowly being pulled under. Jubal grabbed Ed's hand, but his best friend's fingers slipped in his grasp.

"Ed!" Jubal screamed at the black pool. The waters became still.

"Ed!" he screamed once more, as loud as he could. Then he said, "Fuck that," and jumped into the pilot's cabin, which was mostly a plywood and plastic number nailed to the bottom of the boat. He turned the engine on with his left hand, then realized that in his right hand he'd grabbed the old fishing rod. When did he do that? He placed the rod on the floor and shoved the engine into high gear.

"Motorboat, motorboat go slow…"

The voice was as smooth and dark as obsidian.

The engine popped and stuttered. Jubal glanced back over his shoulder. Seeing nothing, he throttled the engine again. Red splayed up between the twin engines.

"Motorboat, motorboat go fast…" came the smooth voice again, but more energetic this time.

"Ah, Gawd damn me," he moaned as he turned the engine off.

Jubal looked from the engine to the throttle. Something was caught up in his propeller. He had to find out what, even if he already knew.

Cursing the engines for ever working that morning and bringing them out on the Gulf, Jubal edged to the back of the fishing boat. He looked over, and what he saw disturbed him on a level that hadn't been shaken since Vietnam.

He turned and threw up into his boat and backed away from the engines that were snagged on human intestines. An arm was completely twirled around one motor blade. An eyeball was floating in the Gulf.

Jubal retreated to the front of the boat, sinking down on the floor. He reached into the pilot's cabin for his old fishing rod. Those were good memories. They could anchor him in this nightmare.

The boat began to bob as something large plopped in.

"Motorboat, motorboat go slow…motorboat, motorboat go fast…"

Jubal remembered the old game from when he was young. It was a game like Ring Around the Rosie. All the kids would hold hands in a circle, and the speed of the circle would change depending on what you chanted. The goal was to see who could last the longest without falling over. He'd really enjoyed that game.

He could smell the thing. It stank like fish that'd been left out to rot on the beach all day.

Quickly, Jubal removed his LSU watch and wrapped it around the fishing rod. He clutched the fishing rod close to his chest and thought of the first crappie Ed and he had caught together as kids. That had been a good time. That was a good memory to die on.

"Motorboat, motorboat step on the gas!"

Jubal looked up, and that's when he saw her teeth. All those amazing, serrated teeth. So flashy and white. All covered in blood.

Ed's blood.

And now Jubal's.

CHAPTER TWO: THE RAINBOW IS ME

Doctor Lynne Carter poured coffee first into his Styrofoam cup, then emptied the canister into Doctor James Talbot's cup.

Dr. Talbot cracked his neck. "What a morning. It's been a feeding frenzy of psychoses."

"Sugar?" Dr. Carter asked. He wore the stuffy professorial look as easily as his seal brown sports jacket with elbow patches. Between his scruffy salt-and-pepper beard and his tiny spectacles and derby hat, he looked like he belonged on an English moor chasing ghosts.

"No. Black is fine." Dr. James Talbot was young and ex-military. His suit was neat, pressed, and he wore nothing on his face except the kind of demeanor that always took and never gave.

"This next visit will be very special, James," Dr. Carter said. "There are very few people like her on earth. It will be good to meet someone of her unique capabilities."

"Capabilities? Does she suffer from Paris Syndrome?"

"No, she isn't Japanese. The woman who is about to enter into my office is much rarer. She is a true DID. I worked with her for years to learn to recognize and co-exist with her separate identities."

Dr. Talbot took a sip of his coffee. "I've met schizophrenics with identify disorders before, but a true Dissociative Identity Disorder patient? I thought they weren't real."

"They are exceptionally real, and exceptionally complicated. This woman, Yig Slaton, has three alters who would step in and take over in times of extreme duress, usually when Yig was challenged socially or mentally. Cautious Clara was her first alter, who helped her in class. Cautious Clara is a smart, Southern belle. The other two are Nadia, who takes over at parties and clubs and such, and Petra Powerful, who is her shield against all transgressions."

"So what is the descriptor for Nadia?"

There was a knock at the office door.

"Pay attention now, James." To the door, Dr. Carter said, "Come in."

The secretary, a thin, 30 year old mother of two, opened the door. In limped Yig behind her, and behind Yig, her cousin Emily.

"Good morning, Dr. Carter," Yig said.

Yig shook Dr. Carter's hand.

"Good morning, Yig. This is Dr. James Talbot. He is joining me from Harvard University. He is learning my patients and techniques, and will be sitting in on this session if that is alright with you, Yig."

Yig and Emily shook Dr. Talbot's hand.

Yig said, "Sure. I understand. How are you going to learn all the world's psychoses if you don't get out there and meet some crazy people, right?"

"Language," Dr. Carter said. "Let's not start the session badly."

As Yig sat down, she leaned into the back of the chair as if she was going to push the front legs up, then remembered otherwise. She rubbed her leg. An orthotic boot covered her ankle and shin.

"How is your leg?" Dr. Carter asked.

"It's been worse, but the pain killers do a lot."

To Dr. Talbot, Dr. Carter said, "Yig's leg never fully developed, so she has a rare form of peripheral neuropathy. She's endured much pain and trauma from her leg all her life."

Dr. Carter nodded to the tall blond leaning against the wall. "And how are you, Emily?"

Emily smiled from behind her dark sunglasses. "Life is good, Dr. Carter. Thanks for asking."

Dr. Carter pulled up his tablet and pen. He said, "First of all, Yig, have you had any symptoms? Any fugues or dropped time?"

"No, nothing like that." Yig paused.

"You are free to speak your mind here. We have confidentiality. What brings you in?"

"I just wanted to come in because work is stressful. Emily said I should talk to you."

"Your cousin is right." Dr. Carter turned to the younger psychologist and said, "Yig has a very supportive, forward-looking family. I wish more families took their approach."

To Yig, he then said, "What is stressing you?"

"It's not any one thing. I mean, not a single thing, Dr. Carter. You know I work for Cerberus, right?"

"Yes. Congratulations. I hear they are very selective."

"And very competitive. But if you can make it 18 months, the rewards are big. Like, seven figures big, so it's worth sticking around. Do you know how much good I could do for my family with that kind of money? My parents could quit working, my cousin and I could travel the world and never have to work again. It'd be paradise. The problem is, I've been placed in charge of this project."

"Oh?"

"Don't get me wrong. The project was my idea, and I'm very happy with it, but that's just it. It was my idea, so I really want to see it succeed. If it works well, this could be huge for me. Monumentally huge."

"You cannot put a price on mental health. This sounds stressful, perhaps too stressful. Are your alters helping?"

Yig hesitated to answer. She picked at her skin nervously. Out in the streets, a car horn blared.

Dr. Carter placed his pen in his mouth. "Yig, in order for this to work, you're going to have to talk to me."

"I don't have alters the way I used to, Dr. Carter. That hasn't changed. I can still be a little Petra Powerful at work, but I know it is me at all times. I'm mostly concerned with what will happen if I get too stressed."

"That is entirely up to you."

Emily's phone buzzed. "I'm so sorry," she said, ushering herself out the door.

Dr. Carter pointed to the painting of a rainbow over his desk. It was a kid's drawing, made with bold swaths of vivid colors and thick-walled borders. Two clouds bookended the rainbow, a white cloud, and a dark grey cloud. "Do you remember the mantra? Will you say it for me now?"

Yig took a deep breath. "The rainbow is me. I am a many-colored thing with beautiful sides to who I am. I am one person made up of many personalities, but I am the sum of my parts, and I am stronger as one than I am apart. I am one person. One person."

"Good," Dr. Carter said. He jotted down a note and shared it with Dr. Talbot, who nodded but said nothing. When Dr. Carter looked back to Yig, he knew instantly she was gone. The woman sitting in front of him wore the same outfit and had the same haircut. She had the same strange color of skin that made her seem curiously ethnic, and she had the same brown eyes. But her back was stiff, her shoulders tight, and her legs were crossed. Her jaw was set, and those same eyes that were so languid before had transformed into intense onyx jewels. Dr. Carter knew who this was.

"Petra, this is unusual."

"I know, Dr. Carter. Dr. Talbot, good to meet you. I am the one who got Yig to come here. She doesn't know it, but I put the earworm in her brain. There is something I needed to talk to you about. There is a problem, Dr. Carter."

Dr. Carter leaned over to his colleague and said with an air of wonder, "If you were to take her blood pressure right before, and right now, you would find it had dropped as much as 20 points. While Yig is nervous, Petra has always been calm and steady. Like a grandfather clock."

"Dr. Carter?"

"What is the problem, Petra?" His voice was so calm it was almost syrupy, and a hint of his East Texas upbringing seeped into his words.

"I can't explain it, but something is different. So I staged it for Yig to set this appointment. I can't take long, or Yig will get scared. I don't want her scared. Right, Dr. Carter?"

"Of course, Petra. That is very thoughtful of you. "

"That's me. Always thinking, always planning ahead. But something is wrong. Not down here, at least not yet. But something is coming. We can all feel it. We've been absorbed for so long. Yig hasn't needed us. But she is going to need us now more than ever."

"Why?"

Petra leaned forward. "Monsters, Dr. Carter. Monsters are coming."

"You are a very professional, courteous woman, Petra. Can you use a more concrete word than monsters?"

"They're circling us. I can feel them near."

The door slammed open, and Dr. Carter jumped.

It was Emily. Her sunglasses were off. Her eyes were red with tears. She shook Yig by the shoulder.

"Yig, something's happened. We need to go home."

Yig uncrossed her leg and dropped her shoulders as she turned in her seat and asked, "What happened?"

Both doctors noticed the almost immediate change. Yig was back, and never the wiser that she'd been gone.

"Your grandfather, Yig. He's gone missing."

Dr. Carter looked at Dr. Talbot darkly.

CHAPTER THREE: NO HELL LIKE THE MISSING

Yig's phone buzzed. She checked it, saw the text from her supervisor, Malik, that he was looking for her, and then she silenced the phone. Cerberus and all the chaos of that world would have to wait.

Leaning into her cane, Yig stood with her parents, Emily, and Uncle Jeremy and Aunt Tilly at the end of the dock and watched the Coast Guard Cutter, Manowar, come ashore. Manowar was an 87-foot patrol boat that specialized in search and rescue operations. Its bold white paint stood out in stark contrast to the brown bay waters. Already one of the Dolphin helicopters (the workhorses of maritime search and rescue) had landed and returned to base.

As the Manowar circled around the eastern tip of Galveston Island, it turned toward the setting sun. The windows of the pilothouse reflected the bright, savage summer light. Everyone watching the boat held their hands up against the reflection. Then the cutter docked and the crew went ashore.

For the third day, Yig's parents searched the faces of the crew for any sign that would tell them the outcome. The crew gave no indication one way or another.

Her father said, "If they found your grandfather, they'd be smiling and shaking each other's hands. Or they'd be rushing into the station."

What the family did not know was that the Coast Guard was very aware of the family's presence, and the crew of the USCGC Manowar were trained in how to react when coming ashore. There were no jokes, no smiles. They exited the Cutter professionally and entered the Galveston Station without allusions. Once they disappeared, Yig's mother, a frail woman with sunken cheeks, moaned softly. The sound was gone as quickly as it appeared, like a pressure release valve of emotion.

Her brother-in-law, Uncle Jeremy, put his hand on her mother's shoulder. She did not respond to his touch, but wiped a tear from her face with her paper napkin.

Turning, Yig's mother looked down upon the black cane. A silver Cthulhu head sat on top of the cane, dreaming his dreams. "You shouldn't be standing so long, Yig."

"I don't mind," Yig said, though the pain was welling up inside her leg, and she limped when she walked now.

Yig's father thanked the Army Corps of Engineers for continuing to allow them to use their dock. Then the family walked to their cars to go home. Coming up over the curb, Yig slipped and jammed her bad foot into the concrete. Immediately, an intense flash of pain shot up and down her leg.

She clenched her boot as she crumbled to the ground. Her family circled her.

"Yig, are you alright?" her cousin asked.

Yig didn't say anything. She held her hand up to show that she was okay, but internally, the pain was spreading out, finding new paths along her neural pathways to terrorize. She rocked back and forth on the curb. The behavior helped her absorb the pain.

"What is it like?" her father asked.

Yig would have laughed if she wasn't concentrating on meditating the pain away. Her whole life, her leg had been in pain. Some days her whole leg seemed to throb and other times it was more like an electric sliver shooting up one side. Each pain meant something different to her. It was like the Eskimo word for snow back when everyone believed that the Eskimo had hundreds of words for snow. But Yig did have hundreds of words for pain. Pain was her vocabulary set.

Sharp.

Blunt.

Raging.

Throbbing.

Numb.

Pulsating.

Rapacious.

Grinding.

Electric.

These are just a few examples of the many kinds of pain Yig had experienced in her 25 years of life. Yig had experienced so many types of pain, she could explicitly distinguish between them. They were like branches of the same giant river, a river that she had explored and mapped to its smallest creek and spring. She knew the vocabulary so well, she had even endured the God-damning awfulness of the pains combined. Throbbing numbness. Sharp grinding. Rapacious electric grinding. They were like Constructicons combining to form one giant Devastor that attacked her leg over and over. Medication could reduce the sensation to a dull white noise, to a merciful afterthought, but just like a ghost standing in the corner of the room, the pain was always there, spreading its white fingertips around her, ready to snatch her once the drugs wore off.

Finally, the pain started to wear off. "I'm fine, everyone. I just need to take some pain killers when we get home."

Her family helped her up. Emily gave her back her cane, which she had lost when she tumbled down. They got in their cars and returned to the family home in Galveston's historic district, where the Slatons had lived since before Yig was born.

Emily followed Yig and her parents into the downstairs living room of their narrow house. Uncle Jeremy and Aunt Tilly had to park down the crowded road. They would be coming past the oleanders and through the front gate in a few minutes. Like many houses in the area, the Slaton's home resided within a block of a restaurant or café. Often customers ended up stealing their parking despite the road signs disallowing parking.

The Slaton's home was over a hundred years old, built in the time after the Galveston hurricane. It was a classic Victorian coastal that had withstood many storms, both nature's and mankind's.

On the wall next to the stairs was an old photo of her very young grandparents standing among the broken boards and devastation of Galveston after the hurricane. The man had survived hurricanes, wars, and epidemics. And now he had vanished like he'd never been there at all.

The first night after her grandfather's vanishing, they had all stood around the house. It was like they were all wearing masks, and nobody really saw the person they were talking to, just the masks they were wearing over their true selves. And when they talked, the sound was muffled, and the intentions were lost in translation because nobody could see the emotions hidden behind their wooden masks. They did not say much, just stood around the room, circling the drain of their shock until somebody suggested they eat. They had forgotten to eat. Emily went to pick up KFC, but it stayed on the table mostly uneaten and was eventually packed away by Aunt Tilly.

Yig stood in the corner of the living room next to an antique table with a small white doily on top. From here, she could watch everyone else. She could also think about her masks and which Yig to show. On the one hand, it seemed obvious. This was the place for Yig the Respectful Who Honors Her Mother and Father, a.k.a., Cautious Clara. She saw room for Petra Powerful, Who Was Helpful and Always Willing To Volunteer For Things, but she thought maybe this was the wrong place for Petra. It was definitely the wrong place for Nadia.

On the second day, they brought the fried chicken to the dock and ordered pizza after returning home. Now, nobody wanted to eat again, and fast food and delivery sounded rotten. The idea that their grandfather would not be found quickly was beginning to settle into their brains. This would be a long search. The Coast Guard had warned them that this was a possibility. They had traveled to the last GPS points taken from her grandfather's cellphone, but after circling the area for a day, they had found nothing. Their search was as void as the darkness spreading across the island.

"I'm going to contact some people," Yig's father said. Oscar Slaton was a tall, gaunt man with an ever-widening patch of bald spreading across his head. Except for a couple of interviews he gave the day that his father went missing, nothing seemed to be moving forward. A pragmatist, he knew better than to assume his father was okay, or even in trouble, but it had been three days. Oscar's hell needed harrowing. He wanted a body to bury.

"Dad, we should let these people do their job," Yig said. The pain killers she'd taken when she first walked into the house were starting to calm her leg, but she thought she sounded a little snappish with her father, and that made her feel guilty.

Yig sat in the leather chair with the little claws on the end of it. With her cane and black dress, Yig looked more ready to discuss gothic prose than search and rescue operations.

"I don't want to stand in their way, but we know people with boats. We can use that. We can get out on the water and look for him."

"Dad," she protested.

Oscar looked to his wife, who sat in a recliner next to the window, staring out into nothingness. Moreso than ever, Yig's mother looked twenty years older than her father. The fatigue of the vanishing was clawing at her insides and stripping her of flesh and form.

"Your mother has hardly eaten since Dad went missing."

Yig made a mental note of how quickly her father reverted to calling his father "Dad" and dropped the more familiar names the grandchildren used. Her grandfather wasn't missing; his dad was.

"You know she loved him very much. She never had a father of her own, so when she came to us. When she came to us…"

He could not finish the words, so he changed course. "I have to go looking for Dad, or I will never forgive myself."

Yig shook her head. She reached up to her father, who leaned over and hugged her. They didn't cry. A flood of tears had already been shed between all of them.

"We will help," Emily said. Oscar looked at his niece, then back to Yig. "Okay. Call who you can. We'll meet at the boat ramps over on 61st."

Yig sat in her Civic outside of her parents' home. She was thinking of her grandfather and the games he used to play when she was little. He had always been very fit for his age, so even when she was eight, she remembered him chasing her around his house. He also liked to play magic tricks with her. Grandfather always had a quarter behind Yig's ear, even when she was a teenager and WAY too old for his tricks.

"Why do you like to play magic tricks, Granddad?" she remembered asking him when she was little.

"Oh, I don't know. I guess when you have a granddaughter as special as you, you just try to keep up."

That was Granddad Slaton in a nutshell. You always left his house feeling extra special.

Yig's phone vibrated. It was Malik. Yig dried her tears before answering.

"Hello?"

"Hello, is Yig there?"

"Malik, this is Yig."

"Yig, sorry. You sounded different. How you been?"

"As good as I can get, I guess."

"Yeah. Again, I'm real sorry about your grandfather going missing. I hope y'all are alright. It's all anyone talks about."

"Thanks."

"But Yig, you have to understand. People are talking about your loss. That can be a good thing, and it can be a bad thing. You haven't been to work in three days, Yig. We're really missing you."

"I know. I'm sorry. It's just that this whole thing…"

"You don't have to explain a thing to me, Yig. And the CEO, Riggs, he is behind you one hundred percent. But I have to be honest with you, Yig. You want me to be honest with you, right?"

"Yes."

"Work is falling. You have that project with the boats. We've got to remain customer obsessed. It's competitive in our line of work. You know what I'm saying?"

"I do."

"So do you think we will see you tomorrow, Yig?"

"I need one more day. We're going to go out and search the Gulf ourselves."

There was a pause. She could hear Malik's frustration on the other end.

"This puts us in a bad position, you know? But you know we are behind you, Yig. Take care of yourself. Just don't get trampled in the dirt. A lot of people have burned themselves out here in six months. You've got yourself into a good position, a profitable one with a lot of potential. We've got to dive deep, and you can't do that…" his voice trailed off. Malik cleared his throat. He said, "You can't dive deep when you're burning through vacation hours, no matter how you're using it. That sounds harsh and makes me an asshole, I know. I'm embarrassed to say that, and I can hear it in my voice. But I'm looking out for you, Yig. You're one of the good ones. Cerberus isn't your typical company. You knew that when you came on board."

"I understand. One more day, Malik. I still have the vacation time."

"You know it isn't about that. Will you have cell coverage tomorrow?"

"I don't know. We'll be out in the Gulf."

Malik hung up.

CHAPTER FOUR: SUNK IN THE GROUND

When Yig parked her Civic in the short lot off of 61st Street, she found a small armada of fishermen and recreational boaters floating off the boat ramp. Yig parked her Civic next to her father's Silverado with her eye to the veritable flotilla anchored in the bayou. Her father and Uncle Jeremy had pulled up moments before Yig, so they were seeing the immense show of support at the same time.

"Where did all these boats come from?" Oscar asked Uncle Jeremy. Meredith, Yig's mother, had gone to the dock with Aunt Tilly.

"Galveston may not be the biggest island, but it is big in heart, Oscar. I called a few, they called a few."

For the first time since her cousin entered Dr. Carter's office to say that her grandfather had gone missing, Yig's heart felt a little less heavy. They had easily doubled the manpower that the Coast Guard was putting into the search effort, and added dozens more vessels into the search vicinity.

Oscar took off his ball cap as he stood in front of the searchers. A camera crew had appeared, though nobody could remember them being notified of the search.

"My family would like to thank you for your time," Oscar said. "For three days now, we've felt lost and alone with our father and patriarch missing. This is the first time in three days we haven't felt so alone. We appreciate everything you all are doing." Then he made the sign of the cross as people removed their hats. "Father, we thank you for this showing of support in our most troubled time. Please watch over the searchers and watch over my father. Let him know that we are looking for him and that we miss him. Amen."

After the prayer, they spent the better half of the morning trying to set up a search strategy, but by 10am, with the sun raining its terror on them and the water only making life more miserable by reflecting up the heat, they all decided to head two miles offshore where Granddad Slaton's phone last gave a ping.

As her father boarded a twenty footer called *The Electric Ride*, he turned to his daughter. "Yig, are you sure you want to do this with your leg and your job? Most of these boats won't be back for hours, if not most of the day."

"Dad, finding Granddad is the most important thing in my life. How could anyone expect anything else from me? When I woke up, I took the high-end pain blockers and I'm wearing proper footwear. See?" For emphasis, she kicked the dock with her boot. She did not jerk away in pain. "I'm fine, and you need people. I can take care of myself."

Her father didn't say no, but he didn't say yes either. He looked at her as if trying to decide how to handle the situation. One of the fishermen coughed, and that brought Oscar back to the surface waters of the situation. It also reminded him that looking for his dad was more important than arguing with his adult daughter who was only trying to help.

"Be careful. You've got your phone?"

Yig held it up for him to see. "Never leave home without it."

"I will call you if we find anything. You do the same."

She watched him climb into a boat, then scanned the waters for her own boat to join.

"Ma'am?"

The man in the boat was about her age, curly-haired, and his unbuttoned shirt exposed sun-tanned abs. She held her hand over her face as if to block him out of her life, but really she was blocking out the sun. She was also covering her sunglasses.

Yig exhaled slowly, but inside, she was trembling. While most people would have seen a handsome spectacle of a man, her anxiety showed her a social situation she was not prepared for. This man outclassed her in beauty and social status. She was clearly out of her water with him. Yig actually thought of changing to Nadia. This was Nadia's area after all.

But that made things worse. She'd been looking forward to being Petra Powerful for the day. Not converting to Petra, but being like her. *I am the sum of my parts, and I am stronger as one than I am apart*, she thought. She didn't want to play the New Girl today. She needed to take charge.

Amid a storm inside her, she rolled her shoulders back and leaned into her Petra Powerful, saying, "All I need to know is whether or not your boat functions."

He thumbed to a single console, twin engine waiting at the dock.

"I can get you out there as good as the rest of them. My name's Duane, by the way. You're Yig, right?"

She nodded for her name, but examined the boat. The boat had no more than a narrow awning to shield her from the sun. And it looked kind of small. She examined the boat warily.

"Did you bring enough gasoline?"

"I've brought extra."

"I appreciate you coming out and helping my family."

Duane jumped on his boat, saying, "I just wanted to help. I got a call from a buddy of mine last night. We were down at Jamaica Beach when I learned what your dad is doing."

The beautiful man held out his hand to her. Yig wanted to hesitate, but the Petra in her knew better. Held out her pale hand. Duane steadied her while she boarded the boat.

"That's a tight grip," Duane said as he let go of her hand and shook his own. Yig smiled. Petra always had a tight hand grip.

Once she was seated (he made sure she had a life jacket), he drove the boat, the *Susannah*, around the island, in line with the other searchers. The line of boats took a bearing between South Deer Island and Galveston Island, then gunned past the many coves and bayous that made the ragged northern edge of the island.

Traveling at high speed along West Bay with the wind whipping into her face and singing through her hair, the only way to communicate was to shout. Yig didn't want to shout. So instead, she examined the impressive electronics console on the *Susannah*. She did not know much, if anything, about boats, though she had been on her fair share of them. She was an island girl, after all. She was pretty sure she could turn the key to turn the motors on and steer the boat, if necessary, but only if necessary. Boating wasn't her thing. Fishing from the shore, yes. But going out into the Gulf to fish? When she was a kid, sure, but now? That was all Granddad.

Duane clearly had all the latest gear. Most of it looked brand new and right out of the box. GPS, multifunction displays, CHIRP sonar, thermal display, and long-range radio. Duane pointed to a passcode that was taped under the Wi-Fi. Thinking of Malik and Cerberus, she knew she could make good use of the Wi-Fi. For a small boat, the *Susannah* had big capability.

The bay lay like a dead body sunken in the ground. Discolored and dirty, it was an unsolved case now covered in a coat of sediment, oil, and the excrement of a thousand migratory bird species. Branches and oyster reefs pockmarked the once beautiful body. Seagulls had long ago plucked out her eyes, and worm-slithering fish were all that remained in the thick, warm water of the bay. The unabashed sky pressed against the bay. The sun was the serial killer salaciously gazing upon his work with the kind of demented mix of pride, regret, and necrotic love that only the most twisted mind could inhabit.

Once beyond the San Luis Pass, the small armada of searchers gunned their boats into the open water, making straight to the GPS coordinates. As they crossed out into the shelf, the waters turned blue as the sky. Yig felt lighter out there. That's when the Dolphin helicopter veered down at them. It swept low over the boats, close enough to feel the thrum of the helicopter's blades.

"What the hell?" Duane shouted as he shot a middle finger to the Coast Guard helicopter.

The helicopter continued on its way. Yig noticed it was following a near straight line down the coast.

"Did you see that?" Duane yelled at her over the rush of water and spray.

Yig did not respond. She was watching the boats in front of them. They were all slowing down. That, combined with the appearance of the Coast Guard's helicopter, meant they had arrived at the last GPS point. Boats were already turning east. Duane pulled back on the throttle, and the *Susannah* churned to a slower speed lower in the water.

"I guess this is us," he said.

They spent the afternoon slowly crawling along the coastline while the Dolphin flew overhead in its extended grid search. The Dolphin was like a silent little bug on the horizon that grew into this loud roaring monster, then turned and retreated back to the horizon, a tiny muted bug again.

Yig used Duane's binoculars to scan the waters while Duane studied his instruments. He showed her how to look for fish and how to distinguish debris or anything that wasn't a fish.

"Can I ask you something?"

"Yes."

He hesitated. She looked back over her shoulder at him. From behind her sunglasses, he seemed darkened by the sun.

"What is it?"

"I don't want to come off as racist or anything, and I don't mean to be offensive, but I have to ask: are you Middle Eastern?"

"A little." If Yig was a celebrity, her IMDB profile would list eight to ten races and ethnicities in her family tree. Three religions, too. As a teen, she got used to being asked by white kids if she was Hispanic or Middle-Eastern or "Arabic." To anyone of a minority race, she was white. Ethnic white, but white. With an unconventional name like Yig, she had come to accept her status as some kind of mysterious ethnicity that even she did not understand.

"I thought I saw something there. Do you speak, you know, Arabic?"

"Do you?"

"No."

"There you go."

She could feel the coldness between them. Her Petra had been too Powerful with a side of Angry.

"Iye eakspe Igye Atinlye, though." She smiled. She had to smile. The poor kid looked like he felt he'd really put the white slam on her. They continued searching, and Duane didn't ask again about her ethnicity, though she caught him watching her a couple of times, which felt warm and awkward inside her belly. She wasn't used to a guy that handsome looking at her that way.

Later in the day, she caught him stretching his legs.

"Do you need a break?" she offered. Petra Powerful could be helpful, but it had to be tempered. It was like a function diagram. Is the person needing help above you on the totem pole? If yes, then help. If the person is equal to you, then do you gain by helping them? If yes, then help. If the person is below you, can help today be used to help you later, especially against a common goal? If no, then suggest a way they can help themselves. That way, you aren't the bad guy. Duane was lower on the org chart of life, but he was helping her search for her grandfather. So the function diagram aligned with help.

"Thanks."

Yig took the wheel and Duane sat down on the floor with his back against the center console. For a while, she steered the boat ever eastward, then westward, as much in a grid-like search as she could keep. Then she got a message. She grimaced at the text and put the phone away.

"Can I ask you something?" Yig asked.

"Mm-hmm," he grunted.

"Do you work?"

"Sure. UTMB. I'm a tech."

"Do you like the people you work with?"

"Sure."

Yig chose her next words carefully. "Do people there throw each other under the bus to get ahead?"

He chuckled. "No. Work isn't supposed to be like Big Brother or Survivor. It's life, not a reality competition."

Yig sighed. "Where I work, we have this tool called 'The Forge.' It sounds very intriguing, but it really isn't. The Forge is a way to keep everybody pushing forward. It is supposed to be a tool that helps you always improve yourself. Hence, 'The Forge.' But it is really a way for everyone to undercut each other. I just got a notice that I have seven new reports in The Forge."

"Is that bad? It sounds bad."

"Reports on you are not good. I don't like the break room, which is where my boss holds these supposedly fun competitions between co-workers, but really they're more like corporate dogfights."

"The only competition I have is playing hoops in the back lot after work. But then again, you work for Cerberus, don't you?"

She nodded.

Duane said, "Everybody was happy when they moved into Galveston. 'Silicon Valley Comes to Galveston,' you know? But I've heard horror stories from friends of mine."

"Well, it has great stock options, but you have to make it two years there. According to Forbes, if you can survive ten years there, you can retire wealthy. And I've met people who cashed out in less than ten years."

"How long have you been there?"

"Eighteen months." The words were like a heaving sigh coming out of her mouth, like Atlas setting down the world for a minute's rest.

"Eighteen long months. I hope it's a good pile of cash."

"Lupe and Jaime Maldonado."

"Who are they?"

"The Maldonados live off of Avenue P. I was having a hard time when I was younger, and so I was wandering the street at night. They could have left me alone, but they brought me in and watched over me and called the police, who called my parents. Jaime works at the meat market, and Lupe is a hotel maid. On the weekends, they clean offices. They have three kids, two dogs, and a hundred things that need fixing at their house. When I make it at Cerberus, I'm going to use the money to fix their house up."

"That sounds real nice."

"I've got a whole list. When I feel bad at Cerberus, I repeat it like some kind of weird fairy tale mantra: Lupe and Jaime Maldonado, puppies, 9th Street Park, pay off Emily's student loans, buy my parents tickets to Europe. They've always wanted to go."

"Nothing for you?"

Petra Powerful stiffened.

"Why do you do that?"

"Do what?"

"Stiffen up all of a sudden. It's just me and you out here, and we probably won't speak to each other again after this."

"Why wouldn't we see each other after this?"

"Well, I mean, I thought…you know?"

Petra smiled, then looked away.

"There's something different about you that I like, Yig. You've got layers."

"*Onions have layers.*"

He laughed. "It's not that. Something else. I don't know, maybe I'm wrong, but it seems like there's something else going on, like there's something inside you trying to break out."

Duane was going to say more, but something caught his attention on the electronics.

"That's a large animal." Duane pointed to the multifunction screen. It showed a lot of noise.

"A dolphin?"

"Too slow. Maybe a pygmy whale. We sometimes get those out here. Could be a tiger."

Yig felt her skin break out in gooseflesh despite the mid-summer heat. "As in shark?"

"Yeah." Duane looked overboard. That made things worse for Yig. She didn't know why. She looked at both sides of the boat, which to her seemed much smaller and more exposed than it had two minutes ago.

Duane checked the multifunction display again.

"Of course, it could just be a large group of schooling fish. Which makes sense 'cause whatever it is, it seems to be following us."

Yig felt compelled to look overboard, no matter how bad of an idea her head told her it was. But looking into the Gulf was like staring into the darkest shadows: the water revealed nothing.

Duane explained: "The *Susannah* is great shade for the fish. Even for sharks, something about the electronics has always attracted them. You know sharks can detect electricity, right?"

She seemed to have heard that before, but she wasn't sure where. Perhaps on television. She kept an eye out for the shark/fish/whale. After a while, the noise receded away. Whatever it was, it had left, or moved out of the scanner's range.

"So tell me," Duane said, his interest in their stalker waning, "where does a girl get a name like Yig?"

They traded places, and Duane returned to the console. She took the binoculars and scanned the waves. Nothing.

"How weird are your parents?" she asked.

"They're pretty weird."

"I'll bet they aren't as weird as mine. See, my parents were always dark and twisted. They travel to horror conventions for fun, they like to watch those shows where doctors operate on people, and they named their one and only after a Lovecraftian god."

"Lovecraft, huh? I don't know much about that, but your name's better than Duane, I guess. Every time I hear my name, I think I should be chewing tobacco or walking in pig shit or something."

"Are you kidding? Dwayne "The Rock" Johnson?"

"Yeah, but that's spelled differently. He's Dwayne. I'm Doo-wayne."

Yig laughed. "I could have been Meredith, after my mom, or Amy, after my grandmother. My family tree is rooted in all these normal-sounding names. But no, my parents decided to name their ONLY child Yig."

"It's unique. Kind of cute."

"Is the father of serpents cute? It's not even gender-appropriate, and it's a made-up name."

Duane chortled involuntarily.

"What is so funny?"

"I'm sorry, but I just think that's the most badass name ever. I wish my parents had the balls to name me something like Yig."

"It gets worse." She was about to say something more, but then she noticed something floating in the water behind Duane. She ran to the side of the boat and pointed.

"It looks like debris. It could be anything," Duane said, though he didn't sound confident. Duane called *The Electric Ride*, then turned the boat toward the debris. Something was definitely floating in the water.

Yig reached over the boat and grabbed the debris.

"Careful!" Duane said.

She turned around and held out for him the old, dripping fishing rod. It was a kid's fishing rod.

"Maybe some kid dropped his rod out here?" Duane suggested. It was the Gulf. There was trash everywhere.

Yig peered closer. Something shiny dangled from the rod.

"Duane," Yig croaked. "That's a Rolex."

CHAPTER FIVE: STARVATION COVE

The Texas Game Warden boat floated next to the *Susannah*, with four or five more search boats nearby, yet far enough away not to be affected by the undulating waves. The game wardens were tagging the fishing rod and the watch and placing them in bags.

The sun was starting to descend. Most of the search boats had already returned home. Even the Coast Guard's Dolphin had stopped its grid search of the area. There was promise from the boaters to start again the next morning.

"We'll identify the watch once we're back on dry land," Jerome Mullings said. He was a tall, handsome man with a kind smile and a love for the water. "In the meantime, how's the search going?"

"Nothing yet," Yig said.

"I'm sorry about your grandfather."

"Thank you. We loved him very much. But can you be honest with me about something? Are we fooling ourselves being out here?"

Jerome hesitated so that he could choose his words carefully. Yig was getting used to officials of any kind slowing down and choosing their words carefully while around her or her family. She wished they would just come out and say what they were thinking.

She said, "Be honest with me."

"Well, there is a lot of Gulf. Part of me wants to tell you that the Coast Guard are professionals and do this better than anyone else, so if they have not recovered your grandfather…"

Yig clenched her fists. This was the first time she had heard the word "recover" in reference to her grandfather. The word exploded in her like a bolt of lightning.

People were found. Bodies were recovered.

"Are you okay?" Jerome asked.

"It's just my leg. Old injury." She rubbed her leg. While the leg was starting to buzz, the leg wasn't her problem.

Duane grabbed a water bottle from the cooler and offered it to her. She accepted it, nodded her thanks, and leaned back against the center console.

She was aware of Jerome speaking. He was recommending some coordinates outside of the Coast Guard's search area, but he was doing it in such a way as to not make it sound like the Coast Guard would definitely recover (there was that word again, like another jolt to her heart) her grandfather if he was located in their area.

"And the watch?" Duane asked.

"It's not my Granddad's," Yig said.

Jerome said, "This might turn up as something. It might not. Most likely, some people were fishing out here. They put their watch and fishing rod down on the edge of the boat, and it fell in without them ever knowing. The good news for them is that this is an expensive watch with a serial number on it, so I'm sure we can track down the owner and return it to them. For you all, it's probably time to head back to the island for the night. It'll be dark by the time you dock."

"Thanks." Duane looked at Yig, who looked like she had just walked over a grave. "We'll do a little more before we turn in. We won't be far behind you."

"Don't stay out too long. When it gets dark, these waters get dangerous. I'd hate for you to run into another boat or run yourselves ashore."

"Don't worry, sir," Duane said. "I've come prepared with the proper equipment."

Duane and Jerome shook hands, then Duane shook hands with the Cajun behind the wheel. The game warden's boat made a careful U-turn in the water and headed for land.

Duane started the boat and began searching again, but Yig stayed pressed against the console.

For Yig, all the color had drained out of the world. The sun had turned white and the Gulf black, and everything else in creation had faded into shades of gray. She wanted the color to return, wondered if this was the world her mother had lived in since the report came out that her grandfather was missing. God, it was a horrible world. No blue sky, no green palm trees, no purple blossoms on the oleander bush in the front yard.

Yig reached for the top of the console and pulled herself up. She had to get out of that world or succumb to it. She focused on the blueness of the water, but the evening sun was fading, and the water was turning black as oil.

From her leg, crimson pain throbbed. She focused on the redness of the pain as she stood up. The pain was real and that made everything else real. She found that it was almost night by the time she fully recovered from the shock of hearing the new word in her pain vocabulary.

The sun was almost down. Purple and red flared like warning lights shot far from the west.

Low on the sky, opposite the dying flares, a fat full moon rose, like a bloated, severed eye. They had turned toward land. She would sleep at her home tonight. She had already made arrangements with her folks.

She needed time away from the search and the tragedy and the endless tears.

She needed to take a shower and wash all the stink and sand out. The Gulf had a way of seeping into your skin, and if you weren't careful, it would stay there like a parasite, feeding off you for the rest of your life. She had met many water people on the island who had long ago stopped fighting back the tide. The women, especially, were drawn-out strings of leather with a certain crustiness and nicotine-salty smell that followed them wherever they went.

Maybe after a long shower, she would watch something light and colorful on television. Comfort food for the brain. She needed a good laugh to restore some color back into her life. Then she would sleep only as long as necessary before returning to work, to the Forge. The word made her tense up in her shoulders. Yig forced her shoulders to relax, then listened to the sound of the water being churned up by the motor.

They had come around to the northern side of the island now. The coves here had oddly unsettling names like Snake Island, Carancahua, and her favorite, Starvation Cove. Soon, they would pass South Deer Island, and then they would be minutes away from her Civic and then home.

Duane slowed the boat and watched his sides. "There are a lot of sand bars around the islands. It's tricky, but I know them pretty well." He picked up a long pole and stuck it in the water. It went down and dipped outward. Nothing. "Just to be safe, though, do you think you can help me check the sides? It's dark and I don't want to get stuck."

"Of course." Yig took the pole, which was padded on one end, and stood at the front of the boat. She prodded to either side. On the left, the pole struck dirt.

"You hit dirt on the left."

"How far down?"

"Six feet?" She was guessing.

Duane steered to the right. By using this method, they rounded two sandbars. In the distance, she could see the lights of Galveston blurred by the hazy, humid air that was settling in for the night. In West Bay, a tugboat was pushing its load to port.

"Five feet." He turned away.

"Nothing."

"Good," he said, and kept heading in that direction. Looking out across the water, she felt she was slipping into some dark ethereal plane that was punctuated by orange and white lights dancing in the distance. Land mixed with water mixed with sky. Or better yet, Galveston and

Gulf and night all together. Like her, all the identities absorbed together. The rainbow, muddied.

Out of the muddy blur, she recognized Hoecker's Point because it looked like a bunch of rings in the water. On the map, Hoecker's Point was a gruesome geographical outline, like the skull of a sinister bird with way more cavities than should ever be possible. Duane and she were near the entrance to Starvation Cove.

She pressed the bar down into the water. Felt the push back of sand and silt.

"Six feet right."

Duane stayed right.

"I said six feet *right*," Yig yelled over her shoulder, but the boat kept moving right. She checked the right side again. Maybe four feet.

"Four feet!"

He didn't change course. Hoecker's Point rose up out of the water, its grasses waving in the breeze, cilia to filter dirt and piss and boater's trash out of the Gulf. The Petra in her was getting really pissed. She was about to say something when the bottom hit the rod. Three feet.

They were going to run aground quickly if Duane adjust course immediately. She turned to give him a nasty look and correct him as she shouted, "Three feet!"

Duane was gone.

Yig rushed to the back of the boat, tripping over the cooler and bashing her knee into the pilot's console. Lances of pain charged up and down her leg. Rapacious electric grinding. She pushed the pain down. She looked to the left and to the right of the boat but didn't see him.

"Duane!" she yelled, a little more fearfully than the Petra in her wanted.

Nothing.

"Duane, this isn't funny!"

A couple of dirty seagulls yelled back at her angrily as they flew overhead. They didn't like their nighttime flight interrupted by piddling land creatures.

Yig was thrown into the center console and cried out in alarm. The *Susannah* had struck the sandbar. A new wave of pain burned up and down her leg. A bloody gash seared her skin. Once Yig got her balance back, she chastised her stupidity, shut off the engine, and called out for Duane again. She was tired of whatever game he was playing. Falling overboard was the sort of thing that happened to drunks and very old people, and he was neither.

A flashlight! She needed to find him in the dark waters. Yig kneeled down and scrounged through the pilot's console for a flashlight. She tossed aside a few waterproof cases. There was some wire, a coil of sailing rope, and a paddle, but no flashlight.

"Shit." She used her phone's flashlight instead. She waved it like a torch in a dungeon, but really, it was as effective as using matchstick to illuminate a darkened auditorium. The light of the full moon was much better at creating shapes and silhouettes, most of them appearing much more dangerous than they were minutes ago.

Yig didn't want to back out of the sandbar because she was afraid of hitting Duane. She grabbed the pole she had been using to prod for sandbars. She used it now to search for Duane's body. Gently, she pushed the pole into the abyss, hoping she didn't strike him.

"Please don't be Duane. Please don't be Duane," she repeated every time she slid the pole into the bay waters. The pole never found him, and eventually, she decided she had no choice. She had to escape the sandbar. She turned the motor on and put the engine in reverse.

Something bumped up against her hull. She thought it must be another sandbar, but maybe it was Duane. (Hoped it was him and feared it was him in that abhorrent dichotomy of all missing persons' events.) She stopped the *Susannah* and fished for him in the water. Again, nothing. Then she remembered the multifunction. She switched it on and toggled through the screens while she wrapped her shawl around her shoulders. The night was bringing a cool wind scraping across the water, and she wanted no part of it.

"What the hell is that?"

The fish finder was indicating another large body, like a small whale or large school of fish.

Or a shark.

Yig could feel the dread spreading along her spine and the gooseflesh breaking out on her arms and the nape of her neck. First, she scanned the dark water for a fin. Seeing no shark fin, she then took the pole and slowly pushed it into the water underneath the boat. There was nothing there but the pull of the waves and the sand.

The silver moon reflected in the salt water off Hoecker's Point. Here, there were only slowly rolling waves. Casual waves without a care in the world.

She limped down the length of the boat and checked again. Nothing. She tried to pull the pole out, but it would not come out of the water. The pole was jammed into something, like concrete. (Or a body. Please, God, not a body.) Trying not to imagine the pole caught in Duane's ribcage, she jerked hard on the pole, but it didn't budge.

She left the pole in the water and checked the fish finder. Behind her, the pole jerked to one side. It wavered, then darted side to side, then was sucked down quickly and disappeared.

According to the fish finder, whatever was there had disappeared.

Turning around, Yig saw that the pole was gone. A coldness swirled in her gut. A lesser person would have balled up in a corner of the boat, or worse, gone to look for the pole.

The Petra in her had a different plan.

She slammed the boat into reverse and if that meant running over whatever the hell was out there, so be it. (Whatever it is, you're about to get cut into little pieces!)

The boat hit something hard, like another boat. The whole back of the *Susannah* lifted up, then made a giant splash as it dropped back into the water.

Yig grabbed the gunwales and screamed.

A dark fin surface from below. It appeared underneath the light of the moon, its shape silhouetted in the moon's reflection on the water. Yig felt cold, wet fear shooting through her body, like a poisonous vine out of the pit of her stomach. Her pupils widened, and she choked down her scream. Based on the size of the fin, the shark must have been longer than the boat.

The fin cut across the patch of water lit up by moonbeams and disappeared into the darkness. The spell of fear that had kept her frozen in place broke. Yig rushed to the pilot's console and steered the boat away from Hoecker's Point. She knew she was playing to the shark's strengths by moving into deeper water, but that damn thing hadn't just rocked the boat, and she did not want to be stuck out on the water with no ability to control where she could go.

The *Susannah* cut a deep wave as the boat retreated back into the bay. Yig imagined the shark jumping out of the water, seal-attack style, and landing on her. She thought it was big enough to crush the boat into pieces, and if that happened, she would be left to its mercy. For a microsecond, she imagined herself like Captain Hook knocked overboard and the giant crocodile Tick-Tock chasing after her. She had to escape to land.

But with only moonlight to guide her, Yig quickly ran the boat aground again. Sand spit up on the side of the boat.

"Come on!" she yelled at the sand bar and the fates and anything else that would listen to her.

The boat sagged and swayed as if a bear had crawled into the boat. Yig broke out in a fear sweat. Petra forced her to turn and face whatever was happening to her.

It was an image she would remember for the rest of her life. NO amount of therapy sessions would convince her mind it was all a hallucination.

Somebody was in her boat, but it was definitely not Duane. The person in her boat was taller by at least a head or two and much broader in the shoulders than Duane. She was strong and smooth, and her muscles rippled in the moonlight. She had jet black eyes as shiny as obsidian. Doll's eyes. She had never seen eyes like that before. And her mouth was full of rows of wicked, triangular teeth.

The woman with the shark's teeth opened her mouth, and as the mouth opened it was like the mouth of a giant jack o'lantern, carved impossibly long by an untrained and demented hand because the child who carved this pumpkin decided to fill it with angular teeth and foul odors instead of square blocks and candlelight. Yig could distinctly make out the bloody hand of a man wedged between the sharks' teeth.

The mouth dropped open, like the bottom jaw was connected to the top jaw by silly putty that was being stretched to its limit. Inside the shark's mouth, she saw Duane's face. It was impossible for Duane to get in there, Yig thought. But there he was, being eaten alive.

"Run," Duane's head said between convulsions.

Yig screamed as she scrambled backward. Her left hand fell on a small case. She popped it open and found her hand resting on a flare gun. Instinctively, she aimed the gun at the shark thing.

The creature smiled wickedly. With a final crunch, it swallowed the rest of Duane whole.

Yig grimaced and fired the flare gun. A bright red ember shot through the night and careened off the wereshark's temple. Her face lit up like a devil's red face in hell. It batted the flare away, and the flare fizzled into the water.

"I can smell your blood," the creature said. Yig looked down at the gash in her knee from moments ago. She wanted to scream.

The shark took one step closer. Its wet, clawed toes sprawled outward on the deck of the small boat.

Yig had no choice. She jumped overboard. Hit the water swimming and never looked back. She expected any second for the shark monster to grab her by the foot and pull her down into the abyss.

Instead, she felt a collision from below her. It was like being hit by an F-150. Her skinny body was thrown like a bundle of sticks held together by cloth.

For a brief moment while she was being shoved, she saw everything in the moonlight. Her body was at least five feet in the air. The massive bull shark was erupting out of the water below her. She wouldn't have believed that this shark and the creature on the boat were one in the same, except that she distinctly saw Duane's hand still wedged in the creature's teeth.

Fortunately for Yig, the angle the bull shark took was from the side, so instead of falling into her ever-widening mouth, Yig was flung twenty yards across the bay and up onto dry land, where her body rolled uncontrollably before coming to a rest.

The large shark fin darted to land. Beneath it was the moonlight, big and thick as cream. The moonlight surveyed her like the lewd eye of some demented killer, and as it made its second arc, Yig fell unconscious.

CHAPTER SIX: GETTING WARMER

The new word in her pain vocabulary was Impaling. She had felt Sharp, but not Impaling.

Yig woke in the hospital, rolling in her bed because the morphine had worn off and the pain was sudden and instant, like giant summer fireworks exploding in her chest and sending its burning spider's legs spreading out across her body. She gasped. The sensation was like somebody had wrapped her chest in a tight band of metal spikes.

"Yig, you okay?" Emily asked. It was the dumbest question Yig had heard. Of course she wasn't okay. She was pretty much the opposite of okay. What was that? Yako?

"Nurse!" Emily called out. Then, to Yig she said, "You broke three ribs when your boat crashed into a sandbar. Some fishermen found you out at Hoecker's Point."

Yig took a shorter breath, and it didn't hurt as badly. Her eyes rolled as she took in her environment. Pin-pricked square tiles on the ceiling. Cold bed rails. Bleached floors and latte-brown linens. Blinds holding back the sand-blown night air. Curtains separating her from other patients. This room was a sanctuary for cleanliness, a bunker to keep out germs and bacteria and viruses. If the Gulf waters were infection and the streets were violence, then the hospital was the safe zone.

A female nurse in burnt orange scrubs pushed back the privacy curtain and took Yig's wrist in her hands. She checked Yig's pulse.

"Do you need anything, Yig?" Emily asked while the nurse shot her a dirty look that said, *Don't mess with my patient.*

"Water," Yig's voice cracked in her throat like hundred-year-old paint.

Emily handed Yig a small cup with a sippy straw. Yig drank until the cup was empty despite the pain she felt in her chest when she swallowed.

"I'll call your dad," Emily said, raising her cellphone to her ear. Yig nodded and watched the nurse take her vitals. She felt a little pain in her chest that was not from the broken ribs and the attack. Large brown monsters full of teeth snapped at her from the edge of her mind. She thought again of her father and mother, so transposed by her grandfather's loss that they could not come to the hospital and watch over her. While she couldn't belittle them for choosing to search for her missing grandfather, or at least, get some sleep, Yig felt a twinge of betrayal by their absence.

"She's awake," Emily said into the phone. "Yes," she said, then "okay." Then she hung up.

"They are coming straight over, Yig."

"Look at me," the nurse said, commanding Yig's attention. She was a middle-aged woman with the piercing eyes of a nurse who had experienced many traumas and was not to be crossed when she gave direction. "You have three broken ribs. You are lucky your lungs weren't punctured. It is going to take some time to heal, but fortunately, you do not require surgery. We have wrapped your chest. You need bed rest. The doctor will re-evaluate you in the morning. I expect you will be released then."

The nurse patted Yig's wrist. "Press the red button if you need us. Otherwise, try to rest."

To Emily, the nurse said, "You look like a nice girl. Help your cousin out and go home. She needs sleep, and so do you. She will be here in the morning." Then the nurse walked out of the room.

After the nurse left, Yig asked about the search.

"I shouldn't say," Emily said.

"Come on, Em," Yig said. Emily seemed wary. Yig thought she knew why. "Look, if it's bad, it's just bad. And if it's really bad, I can handle it."

"The coast guard suspended the search. Since nobody's found anything, and since there isn't any evidence of a boat wreck, the cost of the search couldn't be justified."

Yig's heart sank, and she felt guilty for wishing her parents were with her. She couldn't be mad at them for wanting to find their parents instead of being by her side. How would she react if her mom or dad was missing? And Yig was a grown woman, capable of taking care of herself. Right?

As if reading her mind, Emily said, "Your mom and dad left only an hour ago. Your mom was so distraught, they nearly admitted her to the hospital. Her blood pressure skyrocketed, but it came down on its own once Uncle Oscar started soothing her. He took Aunt Meredith home. This stress is more than her body can take. Not that you should feel guilty about any of this, Yig. This is about how your mom's dealing with stress and nothing else. You want some pudding or something? I can get you some food if you're hungry."

Yig smiled. Good old guilt-ridden Emily. If she gave you bad news in one instant, she'd look for a way to help you in the next.

"You wouldn't steal to save your life. You're my Rory Gilmore." It was true. Emily was the Girl Scout, the Homecoming Queen, and the President of the Student Council all wrapped into one southern beauty.

She believed in the three F's of Texas: Faith, Football, and Freedom. She was as opposite as you could get from Yig. Yako.

"If I'm Rory, who does that make you?"

"Paris?"

"Don't be mean. You're probably Krysten Ritter's character."

"Also, I would steal for you." Yig knew Emily would demand pudding from every nurse until she got what she wanted. But she wouldn't steal.

Emily changed directions. "Yig, what happened to you on the water?"

Flashes of teeth and salt and grit danced in her mind like a ballet dancer spinning on a tightrope. The images slipped and fell from her mind and disappeared.

"Honestly, I don't remember. Something hit me."

"Yeah, it's called a sandbar, and you hit it head-on. You were lucky there were fishermen nearby. They heard you screaming. I guess you got hit pretty hard."

"I guess so." But there was something still there. She couldn't quite make it out. A popping motor? Shards of boat hull exploding? She felt like an action hero flung over the side of the cliff who finds himself suddenly grasping at roots and grasses to not plummet to his death. That was her, grasping at roots and grasses of images that would not stick in her head. She was thrown from the fleeting images back to the real world by the buzzing of her cellphone.

"Ignore that," Emily said. "It's been going all night."

"Probably Cerberus."

"You should really quit your job. They aren't good people."

"And do what? Give duck boat tours the rest of my life?"

"There are other things you can do. There's the conservation, and historical restoration."

"I could work the Strand as a street performer at Christmas Time. Put on a bodice and sell Victorian trinkets to the little darlings." Yig's voice, shallow as it was, mocked a false Cockney accent. "I want more from life." She reached for the phone.

Emily grabbed the phone before Yig could get it. When she wanted, Emily had unbelievable speed. She shook the phone playfully at Yig and said, "Get some rest. I'll find your pudding."

Emily left with Yig's phone in her pocket, which meant that Yig could not check her e-mail. She really wanted to check her e-mail. What if they e-mailed her? How else could she respond? She checked the room to see if Emily had left her phone or if there was, by some miracle, a laptop lying around. There wasn't.

Feeling lost and incapable, Yig reached up to reposition her pillow and winced. Her chest hurt when she raised her arms.

"You got hurt in the water, eh?" an old woman's voice said from behind the curtain.

"Yes. I guess my boat hit a sandbar." Again, the flash of images: shredded boat, popping motor, gaping jaws. Five slits.

"You don't sound so sure."

"No," Yig admitted. "It all makes sense that that's what happened, but...I don't know."

"The mind has a hard time...remembering after an accident."

As the woman spoke, she paused, and Yig heard a strange dripping sound behind the curtain. She realized she had not heard the dripping until the woman spoke, after Emily left. She leaned over to see her better, but her chest pain restricted her.

"What brought you here?" Yig reached out for the curtain, her own arm no more than a thin curtain rod of flesh and bone. She could not touch the curtain without drawing a racking pain along her arm and chest, so she pulled back and listened for the woman to continue. She had an accent. It wasn't the typical clip of people from Northern Mexico. Maybe it was Honduran or Salvadoran or Peruvian. Yig was no good at accents, so she couldn't pinpoint its origin, just its difference.

"Oh, this island brought me here many years ago. I guess I never really left. I leave sometimes, but I always come back. I never truly escape."

"I know what that is like. My leg keeps me tied close to home. Chronic pain."

The woman chuckled. "I remember the first time I heard my condition categorized as chronic. God, I used to wish for acute."

"What is that dripping sound I hear? Are you—Are you bleeding?"

"Listen, I can't talk for very long. I run out of breath. Your accident. Tell me more. Try to remember."

Yig inhaled deeply. Lightning flashed outside. She hadn't known it was going to storm. The weather here was always swift and merciless.

"I remember being out on the boat with this guy. He was pretty cute, and he just wanted to help me search for my Granddad." The boat, she remembered. The *Susannah*. It was becoming clear now. Oily bay water, thick like black honey. Out on the bright Gulf. The Coast Guard helicopter. An expensive wristwatch and an old rod. And something else.

"I was dismal. My leg wasn't hurting, but I was in pain."

"Go on," the voice cooed between drips.

"We were coming back home, back to the dock. I was going to take the night off. There was..."

"Yesss?"

Then she remembered.

"There were teeth."

As Yig spoke, the lights flickered in the hospital room, then went out. A moment later, the backup lights blinked on. Though it was still dark inside, Yig could hear the nurses exclaim about the turn of bad luck. They started going around the rooms, checking on patients.

Lightning flashed again, and Yig saw the shadow of the woman. She raised a withered arm, as narrow and feeble as Yig's, but with flesh hanging loosely from her arm bones. A skeletal form raised up in her bed.

"I am going to tell you something..." the woman said as she sat up in her bed. Liquid dripped into a small black puddle underneath her feet. She could hear the metal-against-metal sound of the woman pushing back her own privacy curtain. Her feet slapped against the linoleum. The slapping of her feet made Yig uncomfortable.

"You don't have to get up," Yig said. The woman ignored her.

Yig felt suddenly cold. She reached for her cellphone, then remembered Emily took it, so she reached for her brown blankets, but her arms hurt.

"There is a saying on the island...an old saying." The old woman took a deep breath and stood up next to Yig's curtain, her scarecrow form exaggerated by the shadows. *"When the silver of the moon touches the black of the water..."*

The lightning flashed, and the hag's skeletal shadow grew, reaching to the ends of the curtain. Bony fingers curled around the top of Yig's curtain railing, much too high for a normal-sized person to reach. Yig shrunk to the edge of her bed farthest from the old woman. Everything felt very wrong here.

"The waters will run red with your blood!" the hag cackled.

Yig screamed. In the same instant, the shadow of a second figure, large and bestial, appeared in Yig's room. She could barely make out the second shadow, which cursed the hag in a language Yig did not recognize. The beast jumped at the skeletal figure, and then the curtain was thrown to the side as Emily entered the room, her arms loaded with pudding.

"Holy shit!" Yig shouted at Emily.

"What's wrong with you? The power went out for a little, that's all. I found pudding. They even have butterscotch."

But Yig was inhaling sharply, to hell with the pain, and looking beyond Emily to the empty beds in the room. Her monitor was alerting the nurses to her high blood pressure.

"I want to leave."

Yig leaped out of her bed. The adrenaline coursing through her body held the pain at bay while cold fear was gripping her.

"You can't leave." Emily tossed the puddings on Yig's bed.

"This is America, right?" Yig's eyes searched the corners of the room for haunted shadows, but all she caught was the staccato gunfire of lightning flashes.

"But you haven't been discharged. What's going on? You look like someone walked over your grave."

Yig pulled on her shorts and her boot. She tried to pull her shirt over her head, but the pain in her chest kept her arms down. She decided to go with the bandaged look.

"I can't stand to be here another minute. I've got to get out."

Under the cover of darkened halls, they snuck their way past the nurse's station, through the wide corridors, down the stairs and out the front door of the hospital. Yig looked over her shoulder once more at the hospital. She was pretty sure she saw the shadow of the hag in one of the windows. A cold dread crept over her. Who was that woman? What was that thing?

As Emily drove Yig home, Yig phoned her parents and told them she had left the hospital, she was okay, and she just wanted to sleep in her own bed. They relented only when Yig promised to take herself back to the hospital the next morning to properly check out.

"Okay, Dad."

"Why don't we stay over at your place tonight?" he asked.

"Dad, I'm fine."

"It'll be no trouble."

"You've got enough on your plate, Dad."

"I've never been a big sleeper. You know that."

"Dad."

Her father paused. "Okay. But ask Emily to stay with you."

"Yes, sir."

Yig hung up the phone, then checked her e-mail. She was glad to not have the e-mails she was half-expecting, though there were twenty from her co-workers at Cerberus. She could feel her time away building to something bad at Cerberus, but circumstances were overriding her just then.

"Uncle Oscar finally gave into you."

"He made me promise that you'll stay over."

"Well, duh. Yea."

They giggled, and their laughter was enough to break the tension in the car and make the bad memories of the past six hours go away.

Yig watched the downtown rising up around her. It was like being transplanted into a Victorian world slickened by rain. Many of the buildings were built after the infamous 1900 hurricane, which was why tourists flocked here for the ambiance and why the island held so many Victorian festivals downtown. There were gothic churches and French Colonial lofts with iron balconies mingling with palm trees and art deco federal buildings. This gave the downtown an otherworldly vintage look. The many shops and restaurants, seeking to cash-in on the attraction, had modified their storefronts to make them assimilate even more perfectly into this Dickens-in-Texas genre smash. As lightning flashed, Yig half-expected the Frankenstein monster to step out from an alleyway or maybe Batman to swing by on his Bat line.

Without warning, Emily pulled over. This late at night, there was no traffic on the roads. Soon, it would be 2am, the killing hour when all the drunks attempted to drive home.

"What you doing?"

"C'mon. You gotta check this out."

Emily got out of her small hatchback. Yig followed. The air felt thick in her lungs as she left the car's cocoon of recycled air conditioning. She could practically feel her hair tightening into thick waves, if not coils. Many women who had migrated here from other parts of the country marveled at the "instant island-perm." Some fought it with a barrage of straighteners and hairspray. Since Yig had grown up with it, she learned to accept it as a harsh reality, as permanent as the sun and the Gulf spray.

Emily ran to the side of the brick cross-street and kneeled down. A short domed shape dragged itself along the gutter. As Yig approached, she recognized the creature as a sea turtle. Turtles sometimes came ashore, but they usually stayed away from the city and never came this far inland.

"What is it doing here?" Emily asked Yig. "Is it lost?"

The turtle was like an old lady late for church, ignoring the two young women blatantly gawking at her. It had dragged itself at least half a mile inland, somehow getting over the seawall and then crossing several major roads. The way it was dragging its one flipper, and the thin drops of blood behind it, Yig didn't think the turtle had escaped the roads without being hit.

"We have to return her."

"It's been hit and is bleeding. We should call somebody."

"At the rate this girl is crawling, she'll be in the bay by the time anyone arrives to help her."

"And why are we going to stop her?" Yig had carried several red sliders back across a road, only for them to go charging head-on back into traffic. "If this turtle is trying to get to the bay, let her. C'mon. I want to go home."

"You're right, of course. Grab a hold and help me carry her to the water."

"Are you crazy? Salmonella, cuz."

"You can bathe when you get home. Let's do the right thing."

"I just got out of the hospital!"

"You're right. I'm sorry about that. Wait here, and I'll move it."

Yig watched as Emily got out of the car and went to the turtle slowly pushing itself along. Emily reached down and struggled to lift the turtle. Yig sighed. A moment later she was outside, helping her with the turtle.

"No, I got it."

"No, you don't." She put her hand underneath. The turtle felt surprisingly light in her arms.

"How much trouble do you think this will get us into?"

They both trucked him down the sidewalk, step by step, under the balcony of an office building. Yig slipped on the slippery bricks only once. The turtle flapped its flippers for a moment, then went still as its head receded into the shell. Yig wished she could do the same.

"I feel naked out here, wearing nothing but a bandage over my boobs."

"Free the nipple, Yig," Emily grunted as they stepped slowly down off the sidewalk and crossed the street. They had only a few blocks more before reaching the bay side of the island, which was where all the cruise ships put in to port.

"I just don't want to be seen by any of my co-workers. That's the Cerberus building over there." Yig nodded at a tall building several blocks away. It was a new construction designed to complement the Galveston skyline, so it used a tiered design with a turret on each corner to harken back to an earlier time it never knew. Pseudo-Victorian.

"Most people I know who've worked there quit after two months. It's a crappy place to work. I still don't know how do you do it."

"The list."

"Ah, the good ole list. There isn't a silver bullet that can get rid of the world's problems, Yig. It takes determination, and doing the little things, like this."

Yig smiled. "The things I want to do aren't that much bigger, they're just bigger to me. Of course, I'm not going to get any of that if I don't get to work soon."

"You were in the hospital."

"I'm scared they may put me on a performance improvement plan, which is another way to say 'we're going to fire you in three months.'"

"You were in the hospital. Nobody gets fired for going to the hospital."

"I do this, it'll pay a lot of bills for all of us."

"You don't have to look after the family. We've survived this long. We will survive without you getting a million-dollar contract."

As Yig walked, she slipped on something wet and smooth. She nearly fell on her butt, but she was able to save herself from an awkward fall. When she looked back, she saw a small crab run off.

"What the hell?"

"Look," Emily said, nodding over Yig's shoulder. "Full moon."

Yig looked at the full moon, drifting between tendrils of rain clouds. Suddenly, it began to drizzle where they were, and Yig would have thought about how beautiful the moment was with the drizzle on her shoulder and the full moon above if her mind hadn't remembered teeth.

She remembered the full moon laying in the sky like a bloated eye, and that reminded her of the thing in the water only a few hours ago (or was it technically yesterday since it was past midnight?). She also remembered the dark shape, the *Susannah*, and Duane's body being gnashed to death. Yig nearly dropped the sea turtle as all the memories came back to her.

"Emily, we have to get out of here! There's something out there, and it attacked me in the boat. I think it's out here."

"I think Cerberus has rattled your head with their nonsense."

"No, really." Yig stopped. She looked around, hunting for haunted shadows or strange shapes in the night. Emily lowered the sea turtle. Once the turtle could touch the ground, it gave the two cousins a nasty look, then continued its bloody charge to the bay.

"This isn't funny, Yig."

"I know." She grabbed Emily by the wrist and ran back toward the car. As they ran, Yig noticed more creatures of the sea floor flocking down the street. An exodus of blue crabs, mud bugs, shrimp, and turtles moved down the street.

"Seriously, Yig. This is crazy. Where the hell are they all running to?"

"Not to. From."

Yig saw the creature before Emily. It stood at least six feet tall despite being hunched, and it was broad-shouldered. It walked slowly down the street, uninterested in the small creatures fleeing its path. It was hunting much bigger prey.

"What is that thing?" Emily asked as Yig pulled her around the corner.

"That is what attacked me on the boat!" Yig hissed.

Emily peeked out from behind the old hotel's sandstone wall and watched the creature. Its body seemed oily in the drizzle as it slowly moved up the street, casting its blunted head from side to side.

"It has a dorsal fin!" Emily exclaimed.

Yig shushed her.

"It looks like a shark."

Yig shushed her again.

"Sharks can't walk on land!" Emily countered.

They ran down the back of the alley and around the corner onto another street. Yig could barely keep up with Emily when she was healthy. She had no chance of keeping up with her in this condition. Yig's lungs were on fire, crisp and all fireworks, and her leg was a block of ice. Yig had to stop her cousin.

"C'mon. We can get around this thing," Emily said.

Yig shook her head and motioned with her arm. "You go. Circle around to your car, then come get me."

"Let me pick you up. I work out. I can do it. I can carry you."

"I'd slow you down."

"No, you wouldn't. I don't want to leave you, Yig."

"You're not leaving me, Emily. You're saving me. There's no way my broken ribs or my fucked-up leg is going to allow me to keep running to your car. Even if I did, I'd probably slip and break a kneecap on the pavement. You're fast. You run back to the car and come get me."

Emily ran down the street, arms pumping at her side. She looked back over her shoulder once, then disappeared around the end of the street. Yig looked for the monster, then limped away. She didn't want to be seen if the thing followed them down the alley, so she hid out of view behind a garbage container and a Galveston Daily News self-serve. She sat down behind the self-serve and on the gutter. The concrete was wet, which made her pants sag. Her left leg was in too much pain to curl up next to her, so she extended it down into the gutter and hoped the darkness would hide her leg. The garbage bin and newspaper self-serve happened to be sitting between two cars.

After a moment of dead silence, her ears attuned to the quiet and started picking up the smallest sounds, like a piece of a container bag tumbling down the street, "THANKYOU! THANKYOU! THANKYOU!" printed on the side. She heard palm fronds gently flapping in the wind. Her heart pounded in her chest with a power that seemed loud enough to wake the hardest sleeper in the high rises around her. Just when she thought she was clear, she heard a sound like somebody large walking slowly up the alleyway. Fear clawed at her neck with cold fingers. Yig thought to run, but to where? There was no better hiding place, and to get up now would give away her position. No, better to stay here and hope that Emily returned with the hatchback.

A crab (she knew not which kind) crawled over her leg and out into the street, where it was suddenly crushed by a Yukon full of college girls drunkenly blurting out songs. They seemed to have come out of nowhere, like phantoms from a mist.

"Help!" Yig yelled to them as she ran up to the truck. The girl in the passenger side seat saw Yig and smiled, pointing to her and sang out louder her favorite Erasure song. "I'm so in love with you! I'll be forever blue! That you give me no, that you give me no, Soul I hear you calliiiing, oh, baby pleeeeease!"

The driver honked at Yig jubilantly and swerved a little as she turned down a street, taking with them all sense of pop music karma and sound. Yig was once again completely alone and enshrouded in dark quiet.

She retreated quickly back to her hiding spot behind the garbage can when she saw the creature emerge from the alleyway. By peeking between the can and the newspaper self-serve, Yig could see the creature.

At first, all she saw was the silhouette of a tall woman with a large shark fin jutting out of her back. The shadow stood in the alley and did not move. Yig waited and watched the black shadowy form. She hoped it would turn around. Or at least turn to go down the other side of the street.

Then the shark monster stepped under the fluorescent traffic light, and its body was bathed in an orange glow.

The tall woman was naked and hairless. She had a wide mouth that was more like a black pit in her head, a pit ringed with little white triangles. She moved her head from side to side as she entered the street.

"You cannot hide from me, little fish," the creature said. "I can feel your heart beating." The creature took another step out of the alley. Its feet had thick claws on the ends of its toes. "It is getting louder, little fish. Louder and faster. Would you like to hear it?"

The creature quietly clapped its clawed hands together. Yig choked as she realized that this was no ruse to try to get her to expose herself and run. The hand clapping perfectly mimicked Yig's beating heart. Still, Yig could not run.

"I'm getting warmer," the monster said. Her voice was oily.

The creature walked down the sidewalk.

"Warrrrmmmer."

"Oh, I'm hot now." She placed her long fingers on the self-serve next to Yig. Her long nails dangled over the side of the self-serve.

Tires squealed. For a second, Yig thought Emily would come driving up and save her. Instead, it was a car turning down the street and away from them.

As soon as the creature turned, Yig ran as fast and hard as her lungs and feet could carry her. From behind her, Yig heard the creature's wet feet slapping on the pavement. She knew the monster was chasing her, and yet she refused to look back, as if looking at the creature would give it power. Then she felt the creature hit her. Teeth and wide-open jaws reached out to her.

CHAPTER SEVEN: ONCE BITTEN

Yig could not blink the blurry out of her eyes. It was like cataracts had formed over her eyes while she slept. Her mother and father were smudges in front of her. Her father was pacing in front of the bed, and her mother sat in a chair next to the open curtain. Mid-morning light was streaming into the hospital room from outside. Yig wondered if she had dreamed everything from the previous night. Emily would be able to tell her if everything was a dream, but the room was devoid of a bright blonde blur she would have attributed to her cousin.

"Emily's fine," her father said, as if reading Yig's mind.

"Where…is she?" Her words swirled in her mouth like they were caught in a tide pool, the effect of the pain medication. At least her chest and leg didn't hurt.

"She's at home resting. You two had a very busy night." Yig wanted to agree verbally, but her brain felt foggy.

"Yig," her mother said. It was the first time since her grandfather had gone missing that Yig could remember her mother addressing her directly. "Why did you leave the hospital without checking out?"

Because a ghost hag tried to attack me, and a shadow monster stopped it, Yig wanted to say. Instead, what came out of her mouth was, "When you're Yig the Destroyer, I guess you make some dumb mistakes."

"Not my daughter," her father said.

Even with the haze over Yig's eyes, she could feel her mother's eyes focus on her reproachfully. A small cartoonish V seemed to appear on her mother's blur just below her forehead. "They found you lying in the street," she said.

Yig rubbed her eyes, and her parents' images started to focus. Their faces looked cracked and withered like used rope or Christmas decorations that were left out all winter and spring.

"I have to get to work," Yig said.

"Work? You are in a hospital bed. You aren't going into work," her father said.

"I haven't been to work in days. I know everybody must be mad at me."

"I don't care if they hate you. You're not going to work today."

"Dad, I'm not a kid anymore. I'm an adult, and I can make my own choices."

"You have an excuse." He defiantly slapped down the newspaper on her bed. Yig held up the Galveston Daily News and read the front line: *Woman Bitten By Shark.* The secondary line read, *Amid Tragedy, Family Still Searches for Lost Grandfather.* Yig had to finish the first paragraph before she figured out the shark bite victim was her.

"But Dad, I haven't been bitten by a shark. The boat hit a sandbar."

Gravely, her father said, "You're lucky to be alive, Yig."

He held out his hand and helped her out of the bed. She looked to the curtains, but it was too bright to see if anyone was behind them. While her father steadied her hand and looked away, Yig's mother helped Yig remove some of the bandaging. They held up a cellphone so she could see the wound on the back of her ribs.

Underneath her shoulder blades was a large circular pattern of notches, like a crown of triangles on her ribcage. The expression "Oh my God" wanted to come out of Yig's mouth, but her lips did not move. She traced the outline of the bite with her fingers. The pain was one of hard lumps under the skin from inoculations.

"I've been bitten by a shark." The words seemed so strange when they finally came out.

"It is the first confirmed shark bite in two years," her father said. "Between your bite and your Granddad, the story is expected to go national."

Yig was an island girl. Though shark bites were rare, the patina of fear was always there, like the island sat inside a circle of teeth always ready to snap its jaws tight. And when there was an attack, usually on one of the other islands, the fear became something tangible.

"National."

"Those vultures," Yig's mother said. Yig knew her mother meant the news reporters. They'd been trying to interview the family for days now. They would be even more insistent now that Yig had been bitten. And they would want photos.

A flush of something bitter and sour emptied into her stomach and gurgled up her throat. She would have to talk to the police, and she would need to make an appearance in front of the press. She should be the one to speak to them, too. Her mother was clearly not capable, and her father was so focused on patching everything up, he had no mind for anything but trying to fix problems. Yig needed Petra Powerful, but felt like the New Girl.

"How did this happen to me? I don't remember being bitten by a shark." She did, however, remember something dark in the night chasing her.

"I have to leave." She was very confused. Though only a night had passed, it felt like an eternity of information and data had been provided for her to sift through. The boat, the sandbars, the full moon. The mouth with Duane inside. The hag and the shadow. The exodus of crustaceans. The shark woman. Yig felt like throwing up. She leaned over the sink and spit up bile.

Her mother said, "Yig, you are not leaving here until you've been discharged. We're not having another incident like last night. I mean, if you had not been returned to the hospital, the doctors wouldn't have realized their mistake."

So maybe everything about last night was true. "What mistake?"

Her mother waved her off. "You don't need to be troubled, sweetie."

"What trouble?"

Her dad said, "Oh, those bastards didn't see the shark bite last night. We're going to sue the ever-loving shit out of this hospital. When I'm through with them, they won't have enough money to hire a single doctor. They'll have to sell these damn curtains as shower curtains just to get out of bankruptcy. I'm going to make this hospital pay for mistreating my daughter."

Yig's mother put her wrinkled arm on her husband's. He took a deep breath and calmed down.

Her mother sighed. "Yig, they didn't see the shark bite until you were returned to the hospital. They said that you must have gotten it when you left, but how could you possibly get bitten by a shark without ever going into the water?"

Yig had a lot of questions that demanded answers, but one loomed higher than the others in Yig's mind. "Wait. How did I return to the hospital?"

"Don't you remember?"

"Where is Emily?"

"Calm down, Yig."

"Where is she?"

"Not now."

"Where is Yig, Mother?"

Her mother and father stopped and stared at their daughter. It was like lightning had flashed in the room. An internal switch between them had been flipped.

"I'm sorry. It's just a slip of the tongue. It's the drugs, I think."

Her parents did that thing where they talked to each other without using any words.

Yig pleaded. "It's just everything, honest. I'm under a lot of stress from work, and with Granddad, and now this. That's all there is to it. It was an honest mistake."

"Okay," her father said, his silent conversation with Yig's mother over. But as they walked out, Yig knew it was definitely not okay.

CHAPTER EIGHT: DIVING DEEP

Yig spent a few more hours being tested and reasserting her desire to leave. Her parents stayed in her hospital room and waited while she was tested and her blood was drawn. "The doctor will be here soon to speak to you" was a common refrain Yig heard.

Her father said, "They're making damn sure their ducks are lined in a row now, Yig. You're receiving nothing but the best care now that they know they're screwed. How do you miss a shark bite?" They wheeled Yig out for more testing.

When Yig finally returned to her room, a detective was waiting with her parents.

"I'm not with insurance. I can help you file with the station, but I think you should talk to a lawyer first. Missing a diagnosis is bad, but it isn't necessarily criminal, at least not from what you've told me," the detective was saying to Yig's father.

When Yig entered, the detective focused entirely on Yig and asked her many questions about the previous night. Yig told the detective everything about Duane and what happened that night on the *Susannah*. The detective took notes while she spoke.

When she finished, he showed her a picture of Duane. He looked young, almost cherubic. He still wasn't wearing a shirt, at least not one that covered his abs.

"Is this him?" the detective asked.

She nodded. Tears formed on the edges of her eyes.

Quietly, the detective said, "The *Susannah* is registered to the Gunderson family. Their son is Duane and fits the description you gave. He has been missing since last night. While parts of the boat were located, no human remains have been discovered yet. There is a dive team out there now, but I don't expect them to find anything."

"What do you mean?"

The detective looked to Yig's father to gauge Yig's strength. Her father nodded.

"Bodies get washed out with the current, or they get devoured by crabs and fish. We don't have much hope of finding him."

"Thank you, Detective," Yig said.

The detective touched Yig's arm. "There are about to be a lot of people in your life," the detective cautioned her. "Not just press and GCPD, but biologists and ecologists, too. I imagine they're going to want to discuss what happened to you out on the boat."

Yig's stomach sank. She just wanted this over and to return to her life. She didn't want to meet more people and keep rehashing the story. She said as much to the detective.

"I know this is a difficult time for you. Focus will turn to Duane Gunderson. Give it a few weeks, and people will go away. If you ever need to talk," he said, and handed her his business card. He also gave one to Yig's parents, and then he left.

An hour later, the doctor arrived.

"I hope you've got the right diagnosis this time," her father said.

The doctor raised his hands in protest. "I'm not the person who looked at your daughter last night. My name is Dr. Nguyen, Chief of Staff of the Emergency Room. I took this over last night and am the one who ordered all the tests. Your daughter is in the very best of care, Mr. Slaton."

"What'd I tell you?" Oscar muttered to his wife and daughter.

"I am not going to talk about what happened last night, though. My lawyers have told me to leave it to them, and I'm sure your lawyers will tell you the same. I do want to go over your injuries, Yig, and talk about what you need to do to take care of your injuries."

He went over her charts and discussed the bite and the broken ribs. He told her about the antibiotics that he had prescribed for her wound, the side effects she may experience (itching, swelling), and that if they got too bad, to come back. He told her about care for the broken ribs, which was bedrest and not to flex.

"The good news, though, is that you're healing remarkably fast. Have you ever had a broken bone before?"

"No, not really."

"Some people are just born that way. I had a friend of mine, he used to skateboard when we were young. He was always crashing off of stairs and pools and he'd break his leg and be up and skateboarding a few weeks later. Thank your parents because you are healing at a rate I've never seen before."

Her parents looked at each other nervously.

"So can I go home?"

"Yes. A nurse will be in shortly to check you out."

Her parents insisted that they at least drive Yig home, but when they got to her home, Yig insisted she was okay and just wanted to get some rest.

When she closed the door behind her and was finally alone in her house, Yig pulled the bandage off her wound and re-examined the extraordinary bite in the long mirror in her living room. The bite wound stretched from the bottom of her armpit to the top of her hip bone. The wound looked like someone had tried to carve a connect-the-dots sideways smile into her chest. On her back, a small "c" had been punctured in similar connect-the-dots fashion. Each little tooth was outlined with dried blood like mascara around slit eyes. Every individual cut was crisscrossed with stitches that would need to be pulled in two weeks. In the mirror, she counted thirty-two cuts and sixty-six stitches.

Yig reached behind her back and touched the wound with the back of her thumb. The Lumpy pain, the Inoculation pain, was gone. She felt nothing in her chest. She raised her arms up above her head. Last night, she hadn't been able to get her elbows above her shoulders. Now she slowly moved her arms into a Yoga pose, forming an oval with her arms above her head. She expected soreness at least. Tight pain. Hot pain, too, perhaps. She stretched her clasped hands as far as possible. She found no pain and no limits due to pain. Then she leaned to her left and to her right. Still, no pain.

She removed all her bandages and braces.

Yig's living room was sparsely decorated. A couch on one side. Opposite it, instead of a television, stood her long mirror. Her mother had complained about placing what was obviously her closet mirror in the living room, but Yig had only laughed. "When you are young and single, you get to do 'crazy' things like place the closet mirror in the living room, Mom," she had said.

She kept no photos on her walls. On one wall was a local painter's depiction of a kraken capturing a schooner. It was a gift from her parents. This was the home of a person who lived at work. Nothing important was here. It was only a refuge from her job, where most of her life was consumed.

She put on a green sports bra and black yoga pants. She rolled out her Yoga mat. She felt along her calf for the murmur of pain that usually called out to her. Since waking that morning, she hadn't taken any of her pain medication. Sure, there had been the hospital morphine, but that was given to her last night after she returned to the hospital. She had been without any pain meds for at least four or five hours. As long as she could remember, she had never gone this long without *something* calling out from her leg.

She stood straight up, took a deep breath, and slowly entered into a chair pose. For this pose, she held her arms straight up overhead and lowered her hips as if sitting in an invisible chair. Chair pose pushed pressure along her legs down to the lower shin and ankles. This was a position she simply did not do because the pain was too intense. She held the position for five seconds, then slowly stood back up and checked her legs. She smiled. Everything felt fine.

What the hell?

Next, Yig moved into the warrior pose. Feet turned inward, legs widened apart, the pose had always been a true horror of yoga poses for her, a pose that often brought out pain from her leg. This time, she was able to do a full lunge, dipping slowly down almost to the ground, then pulling herself slowly back up.

She paced back and forth on the mat, shaking her hands and convincing herself not to get overly excited. She'd had moments of painlessness in her life, usually following an increased regimen of pain meds. That had to be the cause here. The morphine still had a hold of her. But she did not feel drowsy or groggy in the least. Hell, the hospital had released her, hadn't they? *So how can this be pain medicine*, she wondered.

It was time for the ultimate yoga test, the one pose guaranteed to cause her leg to break out in electric pain. This was, of course, the tree. One foot up, one foot down. The up foot slid against the side of the knee, body posture was maintained, and for Yig, the arms were held out for balance. You don't get a nickname like Yig the Destroyer for having good balance.

To force the problem, she put all her weight on her left foot. Rarely had she accomplished tree pose without pain erupting in her leg. Yig raised her right foot up, pulling it along the inside of her calf, expecting the cries of pain from her leg that would tell her nothing had changed.

The call never came. She pulled her insole up to her knee and stayed in position for seven seconds before toppling over. She landed on her injured side, but with a big grin on her face. She wiggled her toes. They felt fine. In fact, they felt good, like she had more yoga in her.

Yig felt along her leg, smiling.

Rip every page out of the pain vocabulary book. Yig was pain-free.

It was time to go to work. And it was time for heels.

They were neither Italian nor lavish, but they had pointed heels and straps. She'd found them in the back of the closet in a dark corner where dreams went to die (mainly clothes that didn't look like they were bought by a teenager or prepubescent with dreams of what it would be like to be a grown-up). She had bought them for a night out with her friends, back when she first started telling boys at clubs that her name was Nadia and then gave them her cousin Emily's phone number.

Yig had bought them in Houston's lavish Galleria while out with her friends. She had waited until she was home to put them on because secretly, she knew what was going to happen, and she didn't want to endure the pitiful looks from her friends when she put them on at the store and the inevitable occurred. So alone in her bedroom, she had laced the straps, stood up, and immediately regretted purchasing two-inch kitten heels. Five seconds later, the $100 pair of pumps were flung into the back of the closet and she was rubbing pain medicine over her feet.

As she rode the elevator to the ninth floor alone, she thought of the guard who took a second glance at her in her skirt. She hadn't responded. Responding was something that Nadia would do, not Petra Powerful, Who Was Too Good To Denigrate Herself by acknowledging her appeal.

What am I doing?

Yig tugged her skirt down, trying to stretch it lower than half-way down her thighs. This wasn't her. It sure as hell wasn't Petra. More infuriating was trying to figure out where it came from. She had worked with the Dr. Carter to get all of this under control. She wasn't supposed to be inventing new identities. *RA, RA, RA*, she reminded herself. Reduce and Accept, Reduce and Accept, Reduce and Accept.

The elevator dinged and the doors split open. She pulled her jacket close to her chest but stepped out with her right leg first for everyone to see the difference. Right, then left. RA, RA, RA.

Like a flock of flamingos, her co-workers turned to look at her, almost in unison. If she hadn't been Petra, she might have walked out in embarrassment at all the attention. After everything Malik had warned her about, Yig thought maybe the people in her office would say or do something. She *had* been in the paper and on television after all. But this was a predatory salesforce, not a room of comforters, so just as quickly as they stopped to look at her, they quickly turned back to their telecons, their sales calls, their instant-messaging meetings, and their telefacing. This wasn't an episode of Ally McBeal. It was the Forge, and everybody's feet were to the proverbial fire. It said so on the wall in iron letters over a flaming Cerberus insignia, along with countless other mottos.

EVERY DAY IS A CHANCE TO EXCEL.
THE FORGE IS WHERE GOOD CUSTOMER RELATIONS ARE MADE.
IF YOUR FEET AREN'T IN THE FIRE, YOU AREN'T WORKING HARD ENOUGH.
CAN'T STAND THE HEAT? GET OUT OF OUR KITCHEN.
YOU CAN'T DIVE DEEP IF YOU DON'T STAY LATE.

Yig pushed a strand of hair back around her ear and demurely slipped into her cube. Unlike the place where she paid rent, these half walls were her real home. Her photos from her trip to Disney World were on the shelf alongside her Steel From the Forge Award for Individual Achievement and her Smiths of the Forge Group Award. Her computer had every connection to the outside world she could want from Facebook to Netflix to a free cable group account. Even her ergonomic office chair was pricier than any piece of furniture she owned, which was a good thing because she had slept in it on more than one occasion. (Showers were located on the fourth floor.)

Her walls were as she had left them three and a half days ago—covered in charts, Post-It notes, and an artist's rendering of what the drone delivery system (officially labeled "Naval Drone Delivery System" but also called the Cerberus 1) would look like when complete. Next to it was a photo of Cerberus 1's current state: nine rotors (one detached for service), an opened plastic underbelly with lots of exposed wires, and none of the cameras installed. It was a work in progress.

Unlike the picture of the Cerberus 1, her cube was tidy and organized. All the charts and Post-Its were organized by task. Everything on her desk had its proper space. The place looked trim and clean, like a hotel lobby or a model home. This was the Petra in her: organized and functional.

One thing seemed to be missing, though. She hadn't expected a party or a banner. But something? A card? A note?

"Yig, welcome back!" Malik said from an open office door.

"Thank you, Malik. It is good to be back."

Without acknowledging her, he waved her into his office, then shut the door behind her. He hadn't left his swivel chair.

"So do you want to see my shark bite?" Yig asked.

"Naw, that sounds disgusting. I never go near the water."

"Really? You're not afraid of the water are you?"

"I live on land. I leave the water for stupid white people. No offense, but you never hear of a black man getting bit by a shark."

She pulled up the side of her shirt. Malik winced.

His phone rang, and he gladly stopped to take the call.

"Yes, sir. Uh-huh. I understand."

He hung up. "What was that about?"

Malik stopped her. "Look, things aren't as June Bug cool as you think they are. You've been gone for four days."

"Three and a half, actually, and I did have the vacation time."

"You and I both know that isn't the point. This place is like the ocean, right? It looks one way from above water, all bikinis and waves, but underneath the surface..." He pointed to her side. "Sharks."

He had her sit down at the small table in his office. Then he reached into his desk drawer and pulled out a manila folder with Yig's name on it. He took his time opening it and perusing all the files, the commendations, the complaints, and even a few clippings from the Galveston Daily about her father's search.

"You see this file? This is a file of two people, Yig. One is the company woman who has advanced in rank and salary and is now a valued team leader under my supervision. She worked on me team with the silver mines, and now she is head of the Cerberus 1 project. The other is a derelict employee who draws complaints from her fellow workers. You don't have to be a genius to see that one of the people has a future with Cerberus and the other does not. You need to choose who you want to be, Yig."

"I am here for the long haul, Malik. The success of Cerberus is my passion."

Malik continued, his voice low and his tone rigid. This was the formal verbal notice, Yig understood. "You have a team of six working with you on the Naval Drone Delivery System. This is based on a new delivery method that you suggested to me and my supervisors as a way to keep pace with the other dotcom warehouses on the West Coast. That was a real rock star moment for you, even though you seem to be more Mary Kay than Joan Jett. 'We can deliver goods to boaters,' you said. Upper management loved your bright thinking. Even gave you a bonus check and a "Light of Prometheus" trophy, which hangs from your cube wall. But it also means you are in charge of making drone delivery services to boats happen. You. I've received several recommendations from your team that you be removed from leading them due to a lack of commitment."

"What? Who sent them in?"

Malik opened the file folder on his desk. "Most companies wouldn't tell you, but lucky for you, Riggs believes everybody should know where everybody else stands. Five complaints from Alison, three from Brad, two from Ethie, and one each from Keiko and Steve."

Yig's heart sank. That was bad. If it were up to Yig, she would run out of the office and never come back. That's where Petra came in, and where she helped her. Petra could take blows like this and power through them. Petra protected her from the possibility of failure. Petra steadied the ship. She immediately went for the pertinent question.

"Am I being put on a performance plan?" She knew a performance plan was the kiss of death in the Forge. It was the company's way of saying they would give you a chance to redeem yourself, but really, it was time to start sending out résumés.

"It has been suggested. But Riggs likes you, and there is obvious beneficial PR in your family's predicament. In fact, Riggs wants you to authorize a statement saying how well Cerberus is helping you in your trying times."

"I release a statement, and this all goes away."

"I didn't say that."

"No, you did not. I did."

"There's no way that is going to happen."

"Why not? Isn't that how compromise works?"

"It's not that easy is all, Yig. This is a place of business. Everybody's a shark. You've lost your position."

Yig's heart sank.

"Fine. I want a sales bonus, then."

"You're not in sales."

"When the drone to boat delivery system works, and it will work, Cerberus's sales will increase. We will gain national recognition for it."

"It's just a drone landing on a boat, Yig."

She winced.

"No, it's not. In the field of online warehousing, it is as good as Sputnik. Hell, it's better than Sputnik. It will be the first of its kind, and we will be setting the pace in the race to drone delivery. And when that happens, I want the same sales bonus as the top three salespersons."

Before Malik could respond, Petra said, "Make it happen," and walked out of the office.

Bobbi was waiting at Yig's desk, practically bouncing with anticipation. She had brown curly hair and always dressed in a button-up blouse and an earth-colored pencil skirt. Bobbi enveloped Yig with both her arms. It was like being crushed by a marshmallow of positivity.

"I'm so sorry about everything you are going through. Your grandfather, the bite, I don't know how you do it."

Yig embraced Bobbi and accepted her love. Bobbi was like a puppy, always giving and always on. If the Dos Equis guy was the Most Interesting Man in the World, Bobbie was the Most Affable Woman in the World.

She handed Yig an envelope.

"You shouldn't have," Yig said, slicing the envelope open with her letter opener.

Bobbi shrugged. The picture on the front of the card was marigolds in bright yellows and oranges. It was a Get Well Soon card signed by lots of people who were not on her project team.

"I want to talk to you and hear all about everything that's happened in the last four days, Yiggy, but there is something you should know first."

Bobbi's face was scrunched up with pain and doubt.

"What is it?"

"I don't know if I should tell you. Did Malik tell you?"

"Tell me, Bobbi. What is it?"

"Alison. She scheduled a meeting with the team and Riggs."

"She did what? When?"

Bobbi pointed to the digital clocks on the wall. "It started ten minutes ago."

"That little saboteur. Where is the meeting?"

"Riggs' office."

Yig pursed her lips. "I need to send an e-mail first."

"You can use my desk if you want."

"No, I have to go up. I have to. This can't wait." She really felt the urge to send the e-mail though. She went to the elevators and hit the up button. Waited two seconds. Hit it again. And again, and again until the elevator dinged and the doors slid open.

The top floor was the twenty first. The elevator took forever to lift her to the penthouse. While she waited, her jaw began to hurt. While she massaged away the pain, she noticed her reflection in the mirrored walls. From one direction, half her face disappeared. From another, her face split into infinity. Rows and rows of Yig. She took a deep breath. "Reduce and Accept, Reduce and Accept, Reduce and..." She didn't stop her mantra until the doors opened.

The office foyer was lavish enough to make any CEO blush. It opened onto a wide fountain with a giant Cerberus three-headed dog. Water gushed from each mouth of the dog. The dog itself was extraordinary, too. It was see-through and lit up from the inside in red, green, blue, and yellow lights. The dog's heads had strange teeth, too. Yig couldn't figure out why they looked so weird to her, but they always did.

Along the sides of the foyer stood intricate models of Greek warships and Spanish galleons, as well as marble statues of krakens, leviathans, and sea monsters.

There were two conference rooms on either side of the foyer. They both had glass walls so that Yig could see who was meeting there. Her team was in neither room. That meant they were meeting Riggs in the executive suite.

Riggs' secretary, a young and attractive woman with perky breasts and her hair pulled back in the world's most perfect ponytail, stood up as Yig approached.

"Ms. Slaton," the young girl said.

"Don't," Yig growled. She fishtailed around the young woman and pushed open the doors to Riggs' office.

And inside, Yig was screaming at herself to stop what she was doing, turn around, and talk about this later. But she was screaming from farther away than usual. For the first time in a long time, she could feel Petra's presence at the forefront, a hurricane of power and confidence that both scared and aroused her.

"What do you think you are DOING?" Petra growled.

Her entire team was sitting at the conference table: Steve, Brad, Ethie, Keiko, and Devon and Emmett. Her team was typical over-achieving and under-socializing geniuses with an overabundance of caffeine and poor wardrobes. Except for Alison, who always looked about as perky and perfect as Rigg's receptionist. Alison stood at the back of the room. She was talking the presentation to the Cerberus 1.

Everyone turned their heads and looked at Yig, including Riggs.

"I'm briefing our CEO on the progress of the drone system. She asked specifically for us to meet her today. You weren't here, so she gave the task to Steve and me."

Yig glared at Steve, who shrunk in his seat. She said, "Steve and I, not Steve and me. If you can't get the specifics of your grammar correct, what makes you think you can ever know the precise detail of the drone delivery system?"

Yig made sure to look into each and every one of her team member's eyes. She wanted to make it awkward. While she moved from face to face, she came to the only person who wasn't absolutely petrified of her: Riggs. She was leaning back in her chair, a fiendishly satisfied grin on her face.

"You see that, folks?" Riggs said. "That is drive. That is going deep. Look at her. She's been searching for her lost grandfather, been bitten by a shark, been to the hospital, and she is back here swinging for the fences. Oh, I knew I chose well when I told HR *Get me that girl!* Welcome back to the Forge, Yig. You can take the presentation from here."

Yig moved to the back of the room and waited for Petra to sit down. Then, knowing absolutely nothing about the presentation, she began the overview. None on her team dared to contradict anything she was saying, though Alison could barely contain her anger. As she went through the presentation, she found her jaw hurt less and less. She was calming down, too.

At the end of the presentation, Riggs pushed her olive-skinned hand over her bald head and said, "Anything else?"

Alison said, "I have a few comments."

"I don't think that's a good idea," Riggs said. "If you have anything else, we have a system for that. Or you can e-mail me directly."

The team was all too eager to leave. As they exited, Riggs touched Yig's arm.

As the door shut and they were left alone, Riggs said, "I'm an odd duck. I always have been. Everybody thought I was crazy when I said I was going to start Cerberus. 'You don't actually make anything,' they said. But I launched the website and company, and now I have a few billion in the bank. They said a company couldn't run like this. They said it was unfair. They said it was more like a feeding frenzy than an organization. I've read the articles, I've seen the comments. But Cerberus has a higher profit margin than Amazon. You see where I'm going with this?"

"No, ma'am," Yig said.

While Riggs spoke, she walked back into her room. She walked behind a wall and changed into a beautiful two-piece bathing suit. Yig then followed her out onto the balcony. Everybody knew that Riggs kept a swimming pool out on her balcony. This was in addition to the pool in the company's rec room.

"If what I do is so bad, why does nobody report me? Sure, people talk, but when asked to go public, they never do. And I don't buy them off."

Riggs stepped down into the pool.

"Come with me, Yig."

"Pardon?"

"I want to talk to you down here. In the pool."

Yig wasn't so sure. Not even the Petra in her was so sure. The pool seemed to look over the twenty first story into nothing. That, and the balcony pool was see-through. Looking down was looking at cement and concrete. Galveston's downtown.

"Come on."

Yig removed her kitten heels and stepped down into the pool.

"Further."

Yig could feel the warm water soaking through her clothes. Before she could protest, Riggs said she would buy her new ones.

"Further."

She took a few steps and tried not to look down.

"Yig, this company is not for everyone, but for people like you who seek out the extraordinary, who don't want just any old job, it had its appeal. That is why I chose you. You are very special to this company, Yig. You are very special to me. But I want to make this clear: screw up again, and all those dreams and hopes, all those people you want to help on your list? You might as well throw it over the edge of this balcony. Understand?"

"Yes, ma'am."

Yig got out of the pool. The executive secretary was there to meet her with a towel and a credit card. Yig dried off, took the card, and went to her cubicle before leaving to buy the new clothes. As she exited the lobby, another woman watched her. She was waiting for the right moment to kill Yig.

PART 2: FREE STATE OF YIG

Lovin' you has got to be
Like the devil and the deep blue sea
Forget about your foolish pride
Oh take me to the other side
-Aerosmith, The Other Side

Little mayhem never hurt anyone.
-Halestorm

CHAPTER NINE: FALLING TO PIECES

Tired? Yes. Stressed? Beyond a doubt. A sense of satisfaction as refreshing as water in the desert? Hell to the yes.

It was 10pm, past the usual quitting time for Cerberus. By the time Yig finally left the Cerberus building, late diners and club patrons were heading out. She had spent the afternoon reviewing tasks and updating the project schedule. There was drone integration to work out, calls to the FAA to be made, and software to be coded. The goal was to test the first drone deliveries in Galveston Bay. At 5, she'd met with her team, then briefed Malik, who congratulated her.

"The coup d'état failed. That's good for you, which is good for Cerberus. Riggs really likes you."

"Before this, I didn't know she knew my name."

"Well, she certainly does now. Don't forget about the market impact assessment."

Yig spent the rest of her evening with a Monster drink in one hand and cost summaries and market analysis reports in the other. She was the Kali of Cerberus. But as the night wore on, it took its toll.

Ever since stepping into the office, Yig felt she was being watched. Several times during her team meeting, she stopped to look over her shoulder at the other cubes. In her mind, she half-expected to see a giant masked man in black robes hovering over one of the cube walls. But every time she looked for him, he disappeared, always sticking just outside her periphery.

Now she had a headache that she could pinpoint in her frontal lobe. The pain in her head was different from the pain in her leg that she'd known all her life (except for the past twelve hours). Her leg was still miraculously pain-free. Her head, however, felt like there was a tiny cave diver spelunking between the fissures of her brain and shining a bright, flaring light from somewhere deep inside the folds. It was blinding and confusing and retched.

She flexed her jaw, but that didn't help. She put her hand to her head and pressed hard.

Outside, Yig felt more and more like a visitor in her own body. She watched herself walk up to a man on the sidewalk and order him to get out of her head. The man tried to ignore her, but she glared at him. She was inches away from his face. She heard herself say, "I dare you to pretend like you don't know what I'm talking about."

The man was incredulous. This was beyond awkward to the point of almost a threat of harm. Yig was not a tall woman, but she practically loomed over this man. He did what so many people learned to do: he pulled out his cellphone and pretended to take a call as he walked off, glancing over his shoulder at Yig, who watched him leave as she scratched at the itch in her ribs. The silver moon was rising above the gothic downtown buildings.

Her jaw had fallen out of socket when she'd been yelling at him. She pushed it back into place.

In the distance, Yig heard more than voices; she heard a distant buzzing like the crackling hum of electric wires. Like gnashing teeth.

She did not realize what she had done until afterwards.

Yig jumped up with a start. The alarm clock said 4am. She was under the sheets, yet she felt cold. She'd been sweating: fear sweat, like waking from a bad dream. Her bedroom stank of brine and dead fish. She reached for the light at her bedside, half thinking a hand would reach out of the dark and grab her hand.

She flicked on the lights.

Her sheets were soaked in blood.

Yig screamed as she clutched at her sheets. Her hands were also covered in blood, so pulling at her sheets only made them dirtier. She crawled out of bed and discovered she was naked. Her floor was a mottled mess of blood and sand. Beach sand.

Stooping down, she sifted through the small globs of bloody sand. It was thick around her fingers, like amniotic fluid. The stench was unbearable. She slipped on the mess as she bolted for the bathroom and threw up in the toilet. The vomit stung her mouth like battery acid. She wiped her mouth and looked in the toilet. Green and red bits of something she did not eat floated in the water.

She heaved again.

When she was sure she was finished throwing up, Yig checked her body but found no injuries. In fact, the only wound on her was the shark bite. Realization crept over her: this was somebody else's blood.

Pulling herself up, she wobbled into the shower, careful to avoid the mirror. She was afraid of how many faces she might find looking back at her. She washed off, then collected her sheets and burned them in the gas fireplace. The wet sheets burned poorly, stinking up the small condo. Yig had to return to the bathroom and lose the rest of whatever the hell was filling her stomach.

As the flames burned her evidence, Yig grimaced at the warmth. It was the time of year in Galveston for constant AC, not building fires. There was no such thing on this island as extra warmth being a blessing.

While the sheets burned, Yig plopped down into her sofa and searched the local news on her phone. Was there evidence of what had happened to her last night? Was there anything new involving her grandfather? (She doubted the latter since she didn't have any text messages from her relatives. She opened a news report about a grisly murder in Galveston. The video showed a news reporter standing on the beach. The topic of the hour was murder and a body that drifted up on the beach.

"That's not me. That's not me." She reassured herself, but it did nothing to settle her suspicions.

Yig shut the phone off. She stared at the long, black mirror on her wall. In the dark corners of the mirror, a shadow hovered beyond her view. Was it behind the couch? When she leaned closer, it disappeared.

"Who are you?" she yelled. The painting of the kraken fell off the wall.

Yig jumped.

Yig spent the rest of the night cleaning mud out of her carpet and Lysoling her condo to death. She made an early morning run to Wal-Mart to buy Febreeze. After treating her condo, she showered with the curtain drawn back and facing the closed doorway. Something was here. She knew it.

She pulled out her razor and shaving cream and applied the cream to her legs. Despite all the chaos swirling around her, Yig still found time to revel in her pain-free existence. She had expected to need meds when she woke up, but her leg felt as good as it did the day before.

As she applied the cream, though, she noticed that her skin was still soft and hairless. She usually had some little stubble, especially on her calves (a genetic fluke of her familial DNA). Her legs, arms, and even her armpits were as smooth as riverbed stone.

Yig put the razor and shaving cream away.

Horror and fear make for great hunger, so for breakfast, Yig ate six strips of bacon. Then she put the cooked the rest of the bacon and devoured them, too. She scrambled two eggs and ate them. She still wasn't satisfied, so she cooked two eggs over-easy and lapped up the yolk. When she left for work, the cooked parts of the egg were still left on her plate.

While she drove to work, she thought of her grandfather. Emily called. His body was still unrecovered.

Emily was up at 6am at the gym when Yig FaceTimed her from her car's Bluetooth. To Yig's left, the Gulf of Mexico was a giant black void under a night sky that was only starting to peek out from the east. The void was home to many dark, underwater things that stayed hidden beyond the waves and the splashing tide.

"Emily, what happened when I left the hospital? The whole thing is a black hole in my memory. Do you remember?"

"We went driving around 'cause you were seeing things in the hospital. Then we got separated. When I got back to you, you were roaming the streets and delirious, raving about weird things that don't make any sense. Clearly, you shouldn't have left the hospital, so I took you back."

"I must have been crazy insane. Do you remember what I was raving about?"

"It was past midnight. For all I know, you were raving about the Cookie Monster, Yig."

"Okay. Thanks, Emily. For this and for taking care of me that night."

"What else are cousins for?" But she watched her cousin warily. "You'll let me know if you need help, right Yig?"

Yig didn't respond.

"Yig?"

"Yes!"

"Tell you what. I'm going to make an appointment for you to see Dr. Carter again."

"I just saw him."

"And you've been through a lot. I'll send you the appointment reminder once I've scheduled it."

Yig got into work by 6:20am. She used the time to review her team's work and point out where they needed to make changes or provide further information for the 10am review with Malik. At 7am, she went to the cafeteria for some more eggs (she was really hungry) and to meet Bobbi and Devon for breakfast.

"Hey, Yig, you okay?" Bobbi asked. Yig blinked her eyes and realized she was standing distracted in the middle of the cafeteria.

"Oh, sorry. I was just thinking about the upcoming review."

"Hey, don't worry about it. We've all been there."

Yig didn't tell them what was really happening, which was that she'd been distracted by the morning food truck. It had dropped off rib eyes into the cafeteria kitchen, and they smelled SO good.

"Pay attention," she heard a voice say. Clearly Petra. She hadn't heard Petra in a long time. She had heard the Petra in her voice often. That was part of the therapy plan for reducing and accepting. From Dr. Carter, she'd learned to accept Petra as part of her identity and not a separate entity. So why was she hearing her again? Was she disassociating? Maybe it was a good idea that Emily was scheduling the appointment with Dr. Cater.

"Yes, it is," Petra said. "Now pay attention."

Bobbi wasn't on Yig's team, and Devon was not the kind of teammate who undercut her, which made both something of an anomaly at Cerberus. It also meant she could sit back and listen to them talk about the guys in their lives. For Devon, it was all about Emmett and their upcoming nuptials. For Bobbi, it was the guy she wanted to meet. (Meat.)

Yig wanted to do as Petra instructed. Petra was always right about everything. But Yig found her mind wandering to the rib eyes. She could practically smell the blood in the wrappers as the meats were transferred to the refrigerator. Little wine-colored dollops clinging to the juicy steaks. The pockets forming in the packages with all that blood. (Blood.)

"What's with the smile?" Bobbi asked.

"What? Nothing." Yig responded.

"Nothing? You just had a look on your face like Chris Evans walked up to you buck naked."

"Hmmm. Meat."

"If it's man meat you want, sister, let's go clubbing downtown tonight."

"YIG!" Petra snapped.

"What?" Yig asked. Socialization? "I don't know."

Bobbi looked at Devon for support. "Ooohh…" Devon cooed. "A chance to mingle with the singles. I'm game. Come on, Yig. It'll be fun."

A gentle breeze washed over Yig. It was the Nadia in her, a gentle hand on her shoulder, telling her that everything will be okay.

Yig said, "Fun sounds good. Okay."

The 10am meeting went even better than Yig could have predicted. She demonstrated to her bosses that she was in control of the project by correcting all of her team members' statuses and adding further actions for the team. This sounded worse than it really was because that was the traditions of The Forge, which had principles like "Own Your Data" and "No Excuses." If the idea was really good, it would survive in The Forge. It would be smelted into something strong and unbreakable. This was true not only for Yig's drone delivery service, but for all Cerberus projects.

At lunch, Yig ordered the rib eye that she'd been dreaming about all morning. She selected the bloodiest piece she could find. It tasted better than anything she could remember. She skipped the Hollandaise sauce and ate it as-is.

She reached down and picked the bloody rib eye in her hand and opened her mouth wide. This was going to taste good.

"Yig! Don't be gross!" Petra said. "You can't do that in an office. Everybody will see you and then they will belittle you behind your back. You won't be able to move up the ladder if you EAT THAT RIB EYE WITH. YOUR. HANDS!"

Yig sighed and put the rib eye back on her plate. She wiped off her hands with her napkin, and placed the napkin on her lap. But she cut a big piece of the rib eye and shoved it in her mouth, Petra be damned.

(Yes. Damn them all.)

Who is that? Yig wondered. The voices in her head did not respond.

She finished the rest of her rib eye. Then she received the appointment reminder from Emily. Dr. Carter was away on travel, and would return in two weeks. He would see her immediately upon his return. The appointment was set for 7pm because that was the earliest time he was back on the island.

She wanted to get back to work, but there was a pesky salad on her cafeteria tray. She'd always been a salad girl. The minerals and vegetables were good for her leg, and she didn't want the excess of the cafeteria's other meals.

(Until today.) The voice was wet and oily.

(Don't eat that.)

Yig couldn't agree more.

Petra said, "Yig, eat."

"I don't want to," she said aloud. She surprised herself by speaking out loud. She glanced around the cafeteria room. About thirty other employees sat at lunch, talking about projects, schedules, and possibilities. None of them noticed her.

"Salad is good for you," Petra said. "Baby spinach and almonds and feta cheese. Good source of protein *and* good for the digestion. A little balsamic for oils and a hint of sugar."

Yig stabbed the salad with her fork and shoved the meal in her mouth, eating it quickly, like a child being forced to eat his peas to get desert.

She wanted to spit it out.

"Don't you dare, Yig."

She swallowed and shoved another forkful of salad in her mouth.

She felt a twinge of pain when her teeth bit down on a nut. Spiked, needle pain. She feared she'd chipped her tooth, so she held a napkin to her bleeding mouth and dashed for the nearest restroom. She removed the napkin and spread her lips so she could see her teeth better.

In the mirror, her lower cuspid was bleeding below the gum line. The blood drained across her gums and stained her otherwise perfect teeth.

The tooth was not chipped, but it wiggled in her mouth.

"Are you kidding me?" she moaned. She thought of the years wearing braces in sixth and seventh grade. Her parents had insisted. A few thousand dollars ensured she would always have a pretty smile.

Yig knew she should leave it alone, but pushing against the tooth made her feel better. Like pushing against a tension point to relieve stress. So Yig pushed it with her tongue, and then she gently rocked it between her thumb and her middle finger. Inexplicably, the tooth wiggled more.

Yig looked around the bathroom. She was all alone. She knew she shouldn't do anything, but her tooth felt so much better when she moved it. When it stood straight up and down, it was like a bottle rocket incapable of lifting off yet scorching the earth it was tethered to.

She leaned in close to the mirror and wiggled it a little more.

Suddenly, there was a pop and a ping, and her lower cuspid was rattling in the porcelain sink.

"Oh, shit," she thought out loud. *What did I do?* She put the tooth in toilet paper, then in her head made the plans to take the rest of the day off. She needed to see a dental surgeon as soon as possible.

As she pulled up her phone contacts list, her tongue explored the empty socket where once an adult tooth had been.

Yig's tongue found something new that shouldn't have been there.

She put her phone down and washed her mouth out with water and pushed her face real close to the bathroom mirror. She pulled her lip back. There was something white in the pocket where her tooth used to sit. It looked like a little tooth pushing up from under the gum line.

Maybe the tooth broke, Yig thought as she opened up the toilet paper that held her excavated cuspid. She searched for any jagged edge or sign of imperfection, but found none. The tooth was complete. Nothing had broken off.

Yig leaned back in close to the mirror and opened her jaw wide. Tucked between her block-shaped incisors and molars, a sharp little point of a tooth erupted from her gums.

Yig jumped at the sight of the tooth. She grabbed a paper towel and dabbed her gums. Little black splotches of blood soaked the paper towel. She threw out the towel, then called her dentist and made an appointment.

"But I lost a tooth. This is an emergency!" she said after a minute of bartering with the receptionist.

"I understand, but believe it or not, Dr. Landis is already seeing another patient who lost his front teeth from a football accident. Kids are deviants, Mrs. Slaton, but I promise you, he will see you today and we will resolve this. Come by at 3."

Yig returned to her desk, her mind dizzy with questions. She could taste the copper in her mouth. She pulled up her phone and opened her mouth. Blood dripped out and plopped on the carpet. Closing her mouth, Yig looked around to make sure nobody noticed. Then she sucked down the blood in her mouth and patted the carpet with some tissue from her desk.

Malik came by as she threw away the bloody tissue.

"Good afternoon, Yig."

Yig smiled without parting her lips, which was unnatural for her. She had always been the kid with the big wide smile.

"I haven't seen your team's report yet. I need it by one so I can see it before you walk us through during the weekly project review."

Yig nodded. Inside her mouth, she could taste the blood building up. Malik looked at her weird, then went to his office.

By 12:30, she had worked out a system of swallowing blood and wiping her mouth every few minutes. This system allowed her to not look like a B-movie vampire that had spent the last ten minutes feeding on virgin necklines. She'd also lost her other lower cuspid and one molar. Both she kept in a peppermint tin.

More teeth were coming in. In all three spots, a new, triangular tooth had appeared under her permanent (temporary) teeth. The first tooth to erupt was now almost completely out. The tooth was sharp and jagged and hurt when she wiped it with her tongue, so she left it alone. After the presentation, she would excuse herself to go see the dentist...or a veterinarian.

Before heading to the meeting, Yig grabbed a wad of tissues and shoved them in her skirt pocket, then rinsed her mouth out with water.

Unlike the regular conference room, the weekly project review meeting room had no table except for the small one with the laptop and projector. Thirty chairs circled the walls of the room. Malik sat at the far side with the Delivery Team Lead, Innovation Lead, and their assistant leads as well as the meeting's admin support. Yig's team sat in seven more chairs: Steve, Brad, Ethie, Keiko, Alison, and Devon and Emmett.

The meeting started normally enough. Yig led her leads through the team's progress. She Owned the Data, she kept her statuses Customer-Oriented, and she offered No Excuses. She did everything expected of a low-level supervisor in The Forge. Outside, she was the person they wanted to employ, a people-oriented perfectionist with big dreams.

Internally, she was something completely else. A jigsaw puzzle that, when complete, formed an image blasphemous to society. The image could have been of a wolf eating a man through the dead man's anus. Or it could have been of a shark birthing from an unwed mother. The image itself did not matter to Yig. It was something Yig believed was dangerous and embarrassing and shouldn't be shown at all costs.

So she paused between charts, made sure to swallow as much blood as possible, and wiped her mouth every few minutes just to be sure. But the more she spoke, the more her teeth loosened in her mouth. They felt like light bulbs that hadn't been screwed in all the way, or nails on an old fence that wiggle constantly. The nails were waiting for that final little nudge to shove them out of their holes. Yig made sure not to prod her teeth with her tongue, no matter how good it felt.

Finally, the Innovation Lead stopped her and said, "Yig, your mouth. There is blood dripping from your lips."

"I'm sho shorry, Mike." She could barely get words to fumble out of her mouth. "I guesh I go' my 'eeth raddled. I have a cu' tha' seems oo have re-opened."

"Can you finish?"

Yig knew the appropriate answer was yes (one of the tenants of The Forge was Have A Backbone, which was not meant as a statement of physicality but still usually used that way), but she wanted to say no, that she needed to see the nurse. To her side, she caught a glimpse of Alison smiling impishly.

"I'm o'ay." She wiped her mouth again and continued the presentation, describing that the first drone tests to Riggs' yacht would happen in three weeks' time. She didn't sound like herself, though. The pitch of her voice was a little low, and she had to concentrate on making the sounds. Fortunately for Yig, she was Petra, and Petra was Cool and Collected in the Face of Adversity.

But then the horrible happened, and she felt her teeth oozing out of her gums one at a time. She had seconds before all her incisors starting plopping out of her mouth like gumballs from a candy machine.

"Eh-kuse me," she mumbled and ran for the bathroom, her hand over her mouth.

She ran into the first bathroom and slammed the door open. At the sink, she grabbed a paper towel and opened her mouth. Four of her teeth dripped out in a torrent of blood. She coughed, and two more fell out of her mouth. Yig started to cry.

"Why are my 'eeth falling ou'?"

She heard laughter.

"One, two, three, four, who don't have no teeth no more?"

The words echoed in the bathroom. Yig looked up.

She looked under the stall doors. She was the only one in the room.

Back at the mirror, she examined her hideous reflection and cried some more. Bloodstains had ruined her blouse. She wiped away her tears, pulled out another tooth, and looked at her face in the mirror. She cleaned the blood off her chin. Slowly, she opened her mouth. It was like a thick, black void (With Duane's head and hands and feet, right?) opened up in her mouth. Her mouth was ringed with little white, triangular teeth.

"Five, six, seven, eight, that smile is looking really great! Ha! Ha!" the voice laughed. Yig moaned and heaved up more teeth while looking for the source of the voice. She pushed open the bathroom stalls.

"Oh, I'm not there, little girl."

She checked one of the sinks.

"Now you're getting closer. I'm down here. Waaay down here. Ha! Ha!" Yig looked down the sink hole. At first, she didn't see anything beyond the black, wet void of the drain. But then a little yellow film blinked over the void. The eye was as black and glossy as beads. Like shark eyes.

"I seeeee you!" the voice said as the eye in the sink hole blinked.

Yig jumped back and ran out the door, where she bumped into Alison.

"What the hell?" Alison yelled.

Yig shrieked.

"Oh my God what happened to your teeth?" Alison smiled with wicked glee.

Yig backed up and Alison followed her into the bathroom.

Alison pushed forward until Yig's back was against the sink counter. Alison said, "Everybody is giving you a pass because your stupid 'Granddad' went missing and you were bitten by a shark, but I'm not. You have no right to take off time while the rest of us work like slaves for you day-in and day-out."

The door shut behind Alison.

"Alithon, pleash. You don' wanna oo at."

"Listen to you. You sound retarded. You're not the center of the universe, Yig. There are other people on this project. It may have been your idea, but we're the ones building your idea."

"Pleash," Yig begged.

"Pleash," Alison teased back. "It's not fair, and I'm tired of taking your shit."

"Nothing's fair in this world, girlie-girl," a voice said from the stalls.

"Who said that?" Alison's eyes darted around. Her voice trembled with anger and fear. "Who said that? Get out here right now or I'll report you in the Forge."

Water began to spill out of one of the stall toilets by the bucket load.

"Hiding in the stall?" Alison growled.

"Run," Yig said.

"Fuck you," Alison said. She approached the stall.

From behind the stall wall, a monstrous face covered in water and full of teeth and scars rose up and smiled down at Alison.

"A is for Alison, who was eaten by sharks," the monster said and jumped over the stall. It had a large dorsal fin and a broad chest. Its face contorted, and a giant bulging shark's nose formed over the monster's face.

Alison backed away, but tripped over Yig, who was gawking insanely at the wereshark. The wereshark lunged for Alison, attacking her muscled torso with magnificent jaws. Alison squeaked out a scream, and then was silenced by the rending teeth. As the wereshark's long tail swished past Yig, the monster growled. "Y is for Yig who was bitten by sharks." Then it bit down on Alison's shoulder and shook her until her arm popped off. Blood splashed against the mirror.

Yig ran so fast out of the restroom she forgot her teeth. She ran out of the restroom, down the stairwell, and out to her little car. She fled.

CHAPTER TEN: THE MASQUERADE

As Yig drove home, teeth continued falling out of her mouth. The sensation in her mouth was like the tightness she remembered whenever the orthodontist tightened her braces. The only way to relieve the pressure was to wiggle the tooth until it erupted from her gums. Once the tooth came free, she felt the pressure go away, and immediately felt better. She popped off the top of her Yeti mug and used the container to spit out her bloody teeth.

She got home, pulled off her shirt, ran to the bathroom, and checked herself in the mirror. The monster in the mirror was bleary-eyed and tight-lipped.

"You must do it," Petra said.

Yig shook her head. She was scared of what she would see was (or was not) in her mouth.

(Open wide.)

Slowly, Yig spread apart her lips. Half her teeth were completely gone. All she had left in their place were little white nubs like tombstones. Yig howled. The sound was inhuman, or maybe it was more human than any other sound. It was the sound of imperceptible, permanent loss.

She gently pressed her gums together. They made a sickening sucking sound as they touched.

"Everything can be controlled," Petra assured Yig. "There have been many advancements in modern orthodontics."

Yig ignored her. She retreated to her bedroom and crawled under her covers and cried herself to sleep. Even as that last light of wakefulness reduced to nothing like a morphine drip emptying itself into her veins, Yig knew there was someone else in the room with her. It had a hulking, hunched shape and stank of dead fish. It stood in the corner, watching her. Its inhale and exhale mimicked her own deep breaths, and then she fell asleep.

Her phone woke her. First, she looked to the corner of her room where the shadows were darkest. After she found nothing in the corner, she checked her sheets for blood. This was her last pair of sheets. She would need to buy more if she ruined this set. Aside from an abnormal bunch of hair *Am I going bald, too?,* her sheets were clean.

The text was from Bobbi. She knew it from the chiming ringtone she gave her best friend: Sesame Street. When Bobbi learned that Yig's phone rang to the Sesame Street theme song whenever Bobbi called, she thought it was an insult. Yig had to explain that she chose that song for her because everything about Bobbi was sweet and innocent and warm. Nothing bad came from Sesame Street, and she absolutely meant it as a compliment. Bobbi's text read:

Let's go clubbing!

Hell, no!

U need to get out and get away from everything.

There's a club doing a masquerade ball TONITE.

Come onnnn. Let's cut loose and have some FUNN! Devon will be there.

What about Alison?

What about her?

Yig thought of the ramifications of the last text. It circled her guilt like a bad drain in a bathroom. A drain with a glossy black eye at its center.

Is she okay?

I guess. I heard she went home after lunch.

Yig's mind conjured the bathroom and the blood and the gore. A decapitated arm. Blood splashing against the mirror. Had she dreamed it all? She took her phone to the bathroom and turned on the light. She closed her eyes, opened her mouth wide. When she finally looked, all her teeth were in her mouth as they should be, as if they never left. She laughed joyfully. She touched her beautiful incisors and her rough molars. She remembered complaining to her friends that her teeth looked too small. Her legs had too many scars, and her teeth were too small. These were just common surveys of a woman's own body. Now, she was just glad to have her imperfect molars back. She prodded them with her tongue to make sure they didn't wiggle, and she felt a little like George Bailey coming home to his drafty old house with the broken banister and loving every blemish. But then:

Crap, am I having fugues again? She wondered. She remembered what she said to her mother and father not two days ago. *Where is Yig, mother?*

Her phone chimed. *Sunny day, Sweeping the clouds away…*

Shit. Bobbi was calling.

Can you tell me how to get, How to get to…

Yig picked up the phone.

"Yo, homegirl, what's up?" Bobbi asked.

"You tell me. Is everything okay there?" She was happy to hear all the consonants coming out of her mouth.

"Well, except for the bloodbath in the conference room, everything is okay."

Yig inhaled sharply.

"Yig, I'm totally kidding. We have got to get you out. I think the stress is getting to you."

"No, really I can't, Bobbi. I have a lot of work to catch up to, and I am only getting behind on everything."

"Sorry. Doctor's orders. As in Doctor Riggs. She says you're to go blow off some steam. She gave me $150 to take you out tonight, and she insists that it is well spent."

"$150?"

"The perks of working for eccentric billionaires and their think tanks. They spend less every day wooing customers."

Yig thought of her teeth that may or may not have fallen out. She also thought of her personalities, and the identities she used outside of work. All Devon and Bobbi knew was the Petra Powerful side of her. What would they think if they saw another side of her? Would they still respect her identity at work?

"I'm just not right, Bobbi. I don't want to be seen."

"Awesome! That's what masquerade balls are for, dummy."

If she was going out, her cousin was coming with her. She called Emily, who was more than happy to try a masquerade. She picked her up at 7, and together they met Bobbi and Devon at Galveston Rose Boutique to find suitable clothes for the masquerade.

Unlike Emily, Devon, and Bobbi, who chose to wear traditional cat's eyes masquerade masks, Yig decided on a different approach, choosing a thick black scarf to hide her neck and mouth. She didn't want to take any chances. Emily applied dark, smoky makeup to Yig's eyes to give her a very harsh look.

"Ooh, you look dangerous," Bobbi said.

This was still June in Texas with the heat hovering around 90 degrees during the day, so the masquerade costumes had a modern, Texas twist. Long, heavy dresses were out. Spaghetti straps and loose-fitting tops were in.

"Oh, hell no, bitch," Emily said when she saw Yig putting on her shirt. Yig always wanted to laugh when Emily cussed. It was like hearing a Girl Scout leader cuss. "When did you get abs?"

"Those are sick!" Devon gushed.

Yig stuttered.

"So, you don't remember working out?" Bobbi teased, but it was Emily's darkened face and silence that Yig noticed. Bobbi laughed at the awkward silence.

Emily said, "There's no way I'm letting you out of here in anything less than something that shows off your six-pack." Bobbi had a ribbed black diamond halter top that felt perfectly indecent to Yig.

"God, I am so jealous," Bobbi said. "You look like Jillian Michaels and Mina Harker had a baby."

"And I totally get your reference," Yig said with a smile on her face.

"That's why I love ya, baby. Let's go have some fun now, Mina Abs." They high-fived each other.

But it was Nadia who walked out the door with her two friends.

Galveston is an island of two cities. There is Galveston pre-Hurricane Ike and Galveston post-Hurricane Ike. They were light and dark. Ying and Yang. Two sides in conflict with each other and yet building off each other. The post-Hurricane Ike world was evident amid the new condominiums, the reconditioned beaches, and the many sculptures carved from oak trees destroyed by the hurricane. The changes were also evident in new retro buildings like the Cerberus Plaza. Old Galveston, pre-Hurricane Ike Galveston, was there in the 1970s resorts and condominiums lining the seawall. It was there in the art deco style of buildings along Broadway.

But Galveston was a city always dividing itself into new parts. There was the Galveston that existed after Prohibition ended and there was Prohibition Galveston, a city that attracted tourists and celebrities to its nightclubs, speakeasies, and red light district. Outwardly, it had been a town promoting civic morality, but internally, it was a town buttressed by sin.

After the great hurricane that nearly wiped out the city, few of its structures remained. Those that did, like the Bishop's Palace and Moody Mansion, were eerie markers of a bygone, Victorian age. The city had been divided again. But the city that survived echoed back to its roots, and rebuilt new buildings in stark Gothic and Victorian architectures.

Along the shadowy streets of this split-personality city, the four friends paraded between boutiques, art galleries, bars, and tourist traps. They conned a teenage boy into sneaking them some ice cream, they threw back tequila shots, and they laughed at the street performer who tried to get them to join his act. Bobbi and Devon danced, Emily sang, and behind her scarf, Yig flirted. She felt good being out with friends.

Emily and Yig stopped for a minute while Bobbi and Devon checked out necklaces at a kiosk cart.

"Your leg," Emily said. "You seem to be doing really well lately. Is it a new medicine?"

"Yig thought fleetingly of telling Emily the whole truth, about the shark, the bathroom, her teeth, and the missing people she was probably murdering. But she couldn't find it in herself to tell perfect Emily about something so outrageous that it made almost no sense to her. Her grandfather was still missing. She didn't want to pile onto that stack of crap laundry with her own problems, especially because they sounded like she should be sent to a mental hospital.

"I think the drugs they gave me at the hospital are working really well. I need to go talk to them about that because I haven't felt this pain-free in...well, about as long as I can remember!" Yig laughed her comment away.

"Well, I'm glad," Emily said. "You deserve this." They held hands for a minute, and then Bobbi and Devon jumped at them, and they carried on down the street.

Nestled between gas lamps (the city was devoted to its Victorian embellishments), Yig found an art gallery that was both arresting and haunting. Three large candlesticks held candles molded to look like skulls. Each skull was intricately adorned in Spanish etchings. Illuminated on the wall behind the candlesticks was a large painting of a ship sinking at sea. The lighted eyes of shadowy monsters watched the sailors reaching for salvation from the currents' cruel machinations.

Yig walked inside. Her friends did not realize they had lost their fellow party-goer for at least five more feet down the sidewalk. They stopped singing Joan Jett and the Blackhearts when they realized Yig was absent.

"Where is that slut?" Bobbi asked. Devon slapped Bobbi teasingly. Emily chortled to hear her cousin described as a slut.

"You mean Nadia?" Emily asked. The tequila had relaxed her proprietary nature when it came to Yig's disorder.

"Who is 'Nadia'?" Bobbi asked.

"Yig. She's been using that name since college. She gives out the name 'Nadia' to any guy she meets. But be careful. If they ask for a number, she's as likely to give them yours as mine."

By then Emily found Yig gazing at the blackened paintings in the gallery. She was eyeing one in particular, a small one with two sides of a shark. One looked cruel and sleek in the water. The other side seemed to be exploding. It screamed as it blew up into a thousand red and orange streaks of paint.

"I want this one," Yig said.

"Sure, *Nadia*," Bobbi said.

Emily and Devon laughed.

"It's like, four hundred bucks. Do you have that kind of money?" Bobbi asked.

"Not on me, no, but I can get it."

"C'mon! Let's go party, Nadia! I want to meet a good-looking boy," Bobbi said.

Her friends pouted their lips.

Yig said, "There's nothing in the world like a good-looking boy, except a good-looking man." Yig left the art gallery with them.

By nightfall, the club, Dante's, was packed and had a line of people in costume around the building. Once inside, the girls found that the repurposed factory was a wide dance floor ringed with couches and bar tables. Lights flashed from the ceiling to the beat of the rhythm of the songs they danced to. Like so many buildings, though, this one was marked as pre-Hurricane Ike. A fluorescent line was drawn around the room, about four feet up from the floor. "Hurricane Ike September 12, 2008" was written above the line in one corner. Later in the night, foam would spew into the dance floor until it was high enough to reach the water line. A personal "fuck you" to Mother Nature.

All the people in the club were disguised, even the waitstaff and bartenders. Some of the disguises were brilliantly exotic and made to look like bird's beaks encrusted with jewels. Many had feathers. Emily's had long batwings hiding her beautiful blond locks. Bobbi and Devon wore much simpler masks tied off in the back.

Dante's did a good job of not turning the nightclub into a sausage fest. The boy to girl ratio was about 1:1. Dante's attracted the women by giving them what they wanted: danceable beats, surprises, and low-cost drinks. Like the best clubs, Dante's knew that to get the boys in, they had to cater to the women. If the women wanted to be there, that was all the boys cared about.

As Yig danced to the rhythm of the music, she was glad to be out with Bobbi and Devon and Emily. She felt good. She felt alive, like she was absorbing everything. Sucking the marrow out of life, sort to speak. Or at least a Jell-O shot out of some guy's belly button. He giggled when her lips tickled him, and that made her giggle.

"This feels soo good!" she started telling total strangers. This was the Nadia in her, she knew, and she didn't care.

The smell of sex was palatable. Sex and blood. It was weird, but she felt she could smell which dancers had enjoyed a quickie in the bathrooms and which were high. That was a weird one that didn't make much sense. And she could swear that Emily was on her period. That was gross when she thought of how she could smell Emily's blood, but it was there in her nose, salty and sweet.

Damn, this place is beautiful, she thought.

"I feel electric," she admitted to Bobbi, who was grinding up with some beefcake from the docks. Devon was texting her fiancée from a corner, and Emily had disappeared into the crowd.

Bobbi smiled at her. "I feel giddy and squishy."

"Can you feel the electricity in the air? Like, every circuit and every cord, and the electric vibe of every dancer?" Her hands were up in the air as her body swayed.

"Are you high? Did somebody slip you something?"

"I don't need drugs to get high."

"You're a dirty slut."

"So are you!" She kept dancing.

Devon brought shot glasses over to them.

"Where did you get those?"

"Some guy. He asked me if I wanted to make out, so I showed him my engagement ring, and he gave me the shots."

"Men are pigs," Bobbi spat.

"Are you kidding?" Yig asked. "Men are awesome. People are awesome!"

"You are nothing like the Yig From Work, you know that?" Devon asked her.

"You're right. I'm not her. I'm something better." She took a swig of the shot glass.

"You're drunker, that's for sure," Devon giggled. They hugged.

By 11, Yig had settled on a blue-eyed boy wearing a Lone Ranger mask who she found kind of silly. Still, he had good rhythm, and his biceps were some special kind of yummy when she put her hands on him. She found herself doing things on the dance floor she had never done, not even as Nadia.

He reached in to pull her close, and she pushed him away. "Hang on, Lone Ranger. I need to cool off."

She walked away from him and plopped down on the couch next to Bobbi and Emily, who were laughing at her.

"Oh. My. God," Emily started. "The bitch has been unleashed."

"Everybody back off, cause Nadia is here!" Yig said, snapping her fingers.

"What has gotten into you?" Bobbi asked cheerfully.

"I don't know."

"Are you still high?"

"No. Where's Devon?"

"She said she liked us, but she'd rather be home having sex with her fiancée."

"Loser."

"Your ride's cute, Yig," Emily said. "Want to see some photos I took of you and the Lone Ranger on the floor? Y'all were practically doing the double-backed beast. Whoo!"

"He's not my ride." *Was he*, she wondered. He was cute and all, but was she really that far gone that she would go home with a stranger? Usually, the answer was no, but something about tonight felt different. Like things could be shattered, the impossible could become the possible, and maybe she had a thing or two to show the Lone Ranger.

"Hey, where's my phone?" Bobbi asked. "Shit. Did somebody take it?" She started checking the sofa cushions.

"You probably dropped it on the floor while you were going to town with that enchilada out there," Emily said.

Bobbi laughed nervously. "Seriously, my phone has Cerberus info on it. Proprietary."

"Calm down, honey," Yig said casually. "I'll find it for you. Watch this." She waved her hand across the dance floor, then got up and walked into the center of the floor. Emily and Bobbi watched her amble into the middle of the dancers. Yig stopped, dropped her head, and flipped her hair back, popping up with Bobbi's phone in her hand.

"How the hell did you do that?" Bobbi asked after she unlocked her phone, then put it away.

"Magic," Yig said, not sure how it had happened and not really caring. It felt mellow and energetic at the same time.

"You're insane, Yig!" Emily cheered.

"I feel so much. It's weird." She sipped a cocktail. "I mean, it's like I have ten-foot long fingers. It's like I can look at on the dance floor and I see this bright blue electric current everywhere. And it's not just the music. It's you. It's me. It's the Lone Ranger coming up from the side cause his heart is pounding in that special way that means he likes me."

Emily and Bobbi looked at each other and laughed. "Oh, somebody slipped you something," Emily said nervously. She was thinking of her cousin's disorder. The first prickling fears that her cousin was slipping identity was creeping into her.

Yig smiled with her eyes as the Lone Ranger came up from the side just as she predicted and asked her to dance. Emily and Bobbi had to drag their jaws off the floor while Yig returned to the dance floor, curled around him.

While they danced, the Lone Ranger's hands started to travel. Not where she didn't want him to go. She liked that. But his hands were starting to wander where she really didn't want them to go: her scarf. His finger tugged at it. She turned into his tug and said, "No."

"Oh, c'mon. I want to see if your lips are as pretty as your eyes."

But all she could think about was her teeth falling out all over this incredible-looking guy and scaring him off and ruining her evening.

And just like that, as if the thought piggy-backed an on-switch, Yig felt her front teeth loosening.

"Oh my God," she said. "Excuse me." She retreated from the dance floor immediately.

"Be right back," she told Emily and Bobbi as she hurdled the couch and made for the bathroom.

The bathroom was a typically dirty and disgusting club bathroom. Graffiti covered the walls and part of the mirror. The lighting flickered feverishly. The room smelled like a particularly wretched concoction of puke and sex and marijuana.

Yig kicked the bathroom door behind her shut and stumbled against the sink. She ripped off her scarf and screamed in pain. Teeth popped from their sockets. Long, triangular blades pushed up through her bleeding gums.

Her fingers flittered at her mouth. In the mirror, her mouth stretched and widened like a jack o'lantern's smile. With a sharp crack, her jaw broke. She fell to the floor on her hands and knees.

The nubs of the vertebra on her sweat-soaked back pushed against her skin. Her bones were breaking violently. Her skin was changing, thickening. From her back, a large dorsal fin rose up like a sail of flesh unfurling above her.

Yig arched her back in pain. Her eyes darkened into two black glass orbs that sucked all the light out of the universe.

She looked down at her hands and saw claws pushing her fingernails out of each of her fingers. Webbing grew from the skin between her fingers.

Then the air in her chest started to tighten, and she began to drown. Her claws reached for her swelling throat. Gills erupted in her skin. Imperceptibly, she felt her brain tighten from the pressure and lack of oxygen. She reached out, gasping desperately for air. Then, as quick as it had gone, she was suddenly breathing again. Air poured into her lungs like fresh water.

The bathroom was too small for her giant, sinewy body. Turning, she knocked over the cheap stall wall and found two girls in goth gear gripping each other tightly. They'd been smoking when they heard Yig's transformation and cowered down next to the toilet bowl, hoping Yig would ignore them.

Yig roared, then leaped over them and crashed through the old windows.

CHAPTER ELEVEN: RACE TO THE BAY

The wereshark flipped the dumpster on its side and took off down the empty alley. She had one goal on her mind: escaping to the bay. She could smell its sweet saltiness in her nostrils and feel its warmth on her scales. She jumped over a car and landed with a thud in the middle of the dormant street. The beast ran down the street under golden gas lamps and warm summer shadows.

On a nearby rooftop stood a dark-haired woman and a man. The man pulled out his pistol and aimed at the hunched monster charging down the street. The woman, who was carrying a giant silver-barbed pike, lowered the pike over his aim while telling him to put his gun down.

The man said, "Belén, we have to take the shot. It won't be better."

By the time Belén lowered her pike, the wereshark was gone.

"Dammit, sis," her brother said. His hair was slicked back. "Now we're chasing."

Her brother was built athletically, like a decathloner. He jumped over the side of the building and landed on a terrace balcony below. Belén followed her brother as he slid/shuffled down the side of the terrace to the sidewalk and ran off into the dark after the wereshark.

"Vara! Be careful!"

Belén and Vara ran down the old brick road and out onto a large, empty parking lot where people left their cars while they went away on cruises to Mexico and the Caribbean. A cruise liner was docked farther down the bayside. Up above, a silvery full moon watched them chase the wereshark.

Vara led the way. He was always fastest. Ahead of them, the beast dived into the water. By the time they caught up with the monster, it was nothing more than a sinister fin snaking its way out to deeper waters.

"She's huge," said Vara.

"And fast," Belén added. "We have to do something."

"What's this we stuff, sis? You let her go. You deal with her. We have other business on the island."

"I think I killed someone," Yig told Emily.

It was a Sunday morning, the one time when even CERBERUS took off. Yig and her cousin were sitting at an iron table in a coffee shop's outdoor patio. Along the seawall across the street, families were hurling themselves into the water. Kids rode boogie boards into the crashing surf. Sandcastles were being dug.

Emily put her coffee mug down and adjusted her sunglasses. "You started acting really strange last night."

Yig nodded but did not answer, so Emily kept prodding. "Did you leave before or after the toilet explosion in the bathroom? We heard it go off. I couldn't find anything except for two reaaally stoned Goth kids that were out of their Marilyn Manson minds."

"I don't know where I was. Don't tell Mom and Dad, but I don't remember anything after about ten o'clock."

"What's the last thing you remember?"

Yig hesitated. "The Strand. Ice cream?"

"Okay. I'm not going to say it is perfectly normal to black out at a party, but it's happened to people before. I wouldn't presume it's anything related to your, you know…"

"I know." Yig could feel the words snapping out of her mouth with way more spite than she wanted, but her identities was a raw nerve for her.

Emily leaned forward and took Yig's hand. "Your illness is what I was going to say, Yig. It is nothing to hide from or be ashamed of. It is as weird as getting a disease and should be treated that way, and you shouldn't be embarrassed."

"Thanks, Emily."

"Too many people think it is something to be shoved away to the back of the closet and forgotten like bad wardrobe choices, but those people are idiots. This is nothing like that."

"You're always the good one."

Emily smiled teasingly. "Only so much as I let you see. So tell me more about last night. What do you remember?"

Yig thought of a mouth that emptied into a black pit circled with terrible spiny teeth. It was an image that circled her dreams and her thoughts all the time now.

"I remember the art gallery with the print I wanted to buy. I remember standing in line, and then dancing with some guy in…a Lone Ranger mask?"

Emily raised her eyebrows questionably. "Who was that masked man?"

"I have no idea. I didn't even get to give him my number."

"You mean my number."

"Right."

"Good thing I got his number, then."

"You what?"

Emily sneered mischievously. "Oh, are we feeling better now, cuz?"

"Yes."

"I'll text it to you later. First tell me how you got home last night. "

"Honestly, I don't remember. Like, at all. That's part of the problem. This isn't the first time, either."

"What do you mean?"

Yig hesitated. Emily was one of her biggest supporters, but this would take it to a whole new level. She had to tell her. "The other night, I woke up and my floor was covered in blood and beach sand. And then I heard a report that some guy was killed on the beach."

Emily studied her cousin. She had grown up with Yig and known her all her life. Her goblin sister. Yig had always had problems fitting in with other people, more so than most. She had seen the ups and the downs and knew her and her identities probably better than anyone. Yig had never been the type of person to harm others. This was the only other member of CWAFOP, Cousins Who Are Friends of Pets. As childhood friends and members of CWAFOP, Emily and Yig took care of their dogs and fantasized about owning shelters and raising all kinds of animals. Emily decided that Yig wasn't a killer then, and she wasn't now.

"Yig, you remember when we were kids and you had the butterfly habitat, but somehow it got placed on the windowsill on a really hot day and pretty much baked the butterfly in its cocoon? You were so angry with yourself. You cried for like an hour until your Mom took us to the library and then out for ice cream. So no, I don't think you killed anyone, Yig."

"I don't think Yig did, either."

"What are you saying?"

"Maybe it was one of my other identities."

The question was who, though. Nadia was the closest to breaking the surface the night of the masquerade ball. But so far, only Petra Powerful had taken over as an identity.

Could Petra be the killer, or was there something else swimming around inside her mind, some leviathan of the deep taking over her body?

A night passed, and nothing happened. Yig didn't transform into a monster, and she didn't wake up covered in blood and sand. She went to work, ate an apple without losing any teeth (though she kept waiting for it to happen, like a dangerous game of chicken with her gum line).

Later, when she returned to her condo that night, she found a small, black tooth lying on the front porch of her condo.

CHAPTER TWELVE: INTRODUCING MAYHEM

Yig growled angrily at her hair. She might as well be wearing her box of cables, her hair was such a mess.

"Yig, calm down," her mother said, petting Yig's arm.

"This isn't working."

"Your tone isn't helping, dear."

Yig sighed. She put down the straightener. It was clearly broken.

"I can get another one from the store," her mother said.

"No, I have another one in my room." Yig dived into her hair with a set of combs. "Can you bring it to me while I try to attack this?"

Her mother nodded and went to Yig's room.

Two weeks had passed, and with each new day, Yig had felt stronger and stronger. She hadn't felt a twinge of pain in her leg since the day of the bite. In fact, she took up jogging, something she'd never been able to do all her life.

At work, she had a surge of confidence that Petra did not approve of, but Yig didn't care. Her team was compliant, and her supervisors were happy with the progress. Soon, the drone delivery system would be airborne, and Yig would be in line for an end-of-year sales bonus check.

Petra met once with a reporter from the New York Times who was doing a story on an increased number of shark bites in the Gulf (six so far in the summer). As Petra, Yig described the boating accident, careful to leave out anything about a wereshark. She also met with a biologist from Texas A&M at Galveston. The man identified her wound as a bull shark bite. It was healing slowly. The bruising had disappeared, and there was no sign of infection, but the wound itself still looked fresh, so the stitches hadn't been pulled yet. He told her a bit about the sharks, their aggression, and their ability to adapt to freshwater. She let him take a photo of the wound for his shark bite collection, and then he left. Nobody else asked to talk to her about the bite.

A few days after Yig was bitten, the LSU Rolex was identified as belonging to Jubal Finlay, a boater who had gone missing, along with his friend. What happened to Jubal and his friend Ed while they were out fishing was a mystery. No bodies were recovered. The Coast Guard assumed the two fishermen got lost and went out too far into the Gulf. The boat probably capsized in a large wave or took on water and sank, drowning them both. There was a better chance of snow in Galveston than there was that the bodies would turn up.

A ceremony was to be held in the cemetery for Jubal and his friend, Early. Since Yig was the one who found the Rolex, the family invited her to the funeral. She didn't know if she should go, but ultimately decided to go out of respect for people, like her Granddad, who had been lost to the Gulf. If she could get her hair to stop acting like a den of snakes.

Where is Mom anyway? Yig wondered.

"Mom? Did you find it? I don't want to look like a bush at cemetery bush at the funeral."

"Just a minute."

"Mom!"

"Hang on."

The funeral was in two hours, and she still had to take care of her, get dressed, apply makeup, and get over to the cemetery. She got up and went to check on her mother.

Opening the door, Yig found her mom sitting on the edge of her bed, her tablet in her feeble hands, and a strange look on her face, like she was crying, but also there was anger, confusion, and a mother's worry.

"Mom, that's private!"

Her mother pulled a tissue and wiped her eye

"These files. These journal entries. Yig, what is going on?"

Mother looked up at daughter, her face full of those strange looks. Yig did not understand, but she reached for her tablet.

"You have no right, Mom. I'm not fifteen anymore. You can't just go through my belongings."

Yig's mother pulled up one of the files and gave it to Yig to read.

"I thought you were finished with this crap." Her mother's voice was pleading. "I knew the stress of losing your grandfather was too much. I told your father you should be seeing Dr. Carter, but your father believed you actually looked better since your grandfather disappeared. He told me about how you were walking unaided and you were pain-free. Damn it, Yig. I can't do this. I only have so much in me, and between your father and your grandfather…"

Yig had begun to tear up, and her mother's eyes were red. She never finished what she was going to say. She shook her head and walked out of the room. She didn't come back until Yig was deep into her tablet, reading about her sanity coming undone.

Yig took the tablet, sat down on her bed, and read.

June 18.docx

Life is good. I got to be a little bit Nadia today while at work. I know I'm usually more Petra, but there is nothing wrong with being a little flirtatious if it is fun. All sides of the same coin and all, right?

His name is Garrison. He's not an islander, but he lives close, up in League City. He has these cute dimples when he smiles, which he does a lot, and he has this way of piercing your soul when he looks at you. It feels like he is looking right through you.

June 24.docx

Bad, bad, bad, bad day.

Granddad is missing. I don't know what to say or what to do. I mean, it's Granddad. Jesus.

June 24_2.docx

Okay, so what I know is this:

Granddad went fishing yesterday morning. He went out on the Gulf on his old boat. Some people at the pier saw him leaving alone. He sometimes is out for the day, but is always back by nightfall. So when he didn't come back, Dad got worried. Granddad always checks in when he comes home. Dad went over to Granddad's house and didn't see his truck or any sign that he'd returned. The door wasn't open, either. He went to the pier, found Granddad's Ford Ranger still there, and called the police. The police called the Coast Guard, and they are now searching the Gulf for any sign of Granddad's boat.

I left home from work. I can't believe they gave me the rest of the evening off. There will be a press conference in the morning. Mom and Dad don't want me there. They say it's just 'cause they don't want to put too much stress on me, but the truth is they don't want me to relapse. I won't relapse. Reduce and Accept. RA, RA, RA. I will keep my center.

June 24_3.docx

(Okay, last entry, I swear)

It is past midnight. Does that make it tomorrow's journal entry, or is it still today? I can't sleep. I did some work from the lair, sent out a few e-mails. Now all I'm doing is staring at the ceiling. I stare at the ceiling, and I think of Granddad. I think of playing games with him. When I was little, he loved Connect Four and Battleship.

I think of walking with him through the cemetery. I was older then, and Grandma had already passed away. I loved being in that cemetery, full of all of that history. I loved touching my fingers to the rough, weathered tombstones. I loved reading the etchings on the mausoleums and the pillars. My favorite was reading the poems, though I can't remember any now. I just remember feeling so comfortable there.

Granddad would lead me through the graveyard, and I learned to carefully tip-toe so as not to step on anyone's grave. Granddad said it was disrespectful. Granddad would sweep off Grandma's grave plate and sit down in one of the fold-up chairs he brought with him. I had one, too, and we would sit there in front of her grave. We listened to the sounds of cars passing by and the sound of the surf coming from far away. It was unbelievably romantic to me, to be buried in a graveyard next to the Gulf, and I remember often hoping that when I died, I would be buried near the Gulf like my Grandma.

Granddad would point out his grave marker, which was flat and smooth and blank. Grandma's plate had just her name, Evelyn Lee Waters Slaton. I liked to trace the letters with my fingers.

"Where's her years?" I asked Granddad.

"In here," he would say, and point to his heart. I remember one time I pressed him for her age, and all he said was "You never ask about a woman's age." They were always a strange couple. So are my parents, and so am I, too, I guess. I miss you, Granddad. Come home.

June 26.docx

Today, we went out to the docks again and waited for the Coast Guard helicopters to come back. I haven't been back to work since Granddad went missing. I hope I don't get grilled for it, but it's Granddad! It's not like I'm off on some Caribbean beach bungalow vacation (Alison).

June 27.docx

Mom and Dad mentioned to me again that I should go see Dr. Carter. Well, guess what? I saw him already. And he says I don't have to come in unless I feel I need to or I'm missing time. Well, I'm certainly not missing time because every fucking hour is accounted for while we wait for Granddad to be found. At this point, I'm not expecting him to be...I just want to know what happened. The police say they aren't looking into this as a criminal activity but as a missing persons' activity. I swear to you, I can hear something different in the liaison's voice. They think he drifted off course or maybe his electronics died on him and he got lost or he just decided to go away. They asked us about a family history of Alzheimer's or dementia. Of course, that's when I came up. Yig the Destroyer, every time!

June 29.docx

I don't even know where to begin. It's been the craziest 48 hours of my life. I was out searching for Granddad, and we came back late. The doctors say I was bitten by a shark when we hit a sandbar. The man I was with has not been found. The boat was smashed to pieces. Those are the facts. But I swear I've seen some things. Unimaginable things. And I know I'm not crazy. It took years of therapy to sort myself out. I'm not going back there. But the things I have seen…

I've pulled off my bandage and re-examined it three times. Every time I look, I think something terrible is happening to me. And it's not just another alter coming out. This isn't *that*. I swear, I think I've been bitten by a wereshark.

Does that even exist?

What the hell's wrong with me?

<photo>

June 30.docx

Bitch. Bitch. Bitch. Bitch. Bitch. Bitch! FUCK YOU

July 1.docx

Today, I went to work. The people there were great. I was AWESOME. I told that bitch Alison that I was going to cuntpunt her if she tried pulling any of that shit on me again. Ha!

July 2.docx

Hello, there.

July 3.docx

Peek-a-boo! I see you!

July 4.docx

Oh say can you see? By the dawn's early screams?

HAHAHAHAHAHA

I'm so funny.

July 5.docx

I've got the prettiest teeth in the world! All those beautiful babies, mewing for meat. I should feed them, shouldn't I? They just want to come out and play!

July 6.docx

I invented a new word today. "Landchum." Get it?

July 7.docx

I want to decorate the house with intestines. I will pin them up to the ceiling and hang them like streamers. Then I can stretch the folds of their skins over the lamps. Oh, how pretty they will be. Recycled art!

I will be like Martha Stewart. The Martha Stewart of Mayhem…

Yig stopped reading and threw the tablet onto the bed. Her hands were trembling. She didn't know what to say. Tears were running down her mother's eyes.

"Yig, the things I read in that book. That was dangerous. This new alter."

Yig started to protest, but her mother held up a finger. "Even if this is something different, baby, this looks like a new alter. Have you slipped time? Think hard."

Yig thought of the club and about a dozen other instances. She could not deny it. She nodded her head.

"You need to see Dr. Carter right away, Yig."

"Yes, Mom."

"This is the most violent alter you've ever manifested. It scares me. What if there are others? I knew your grandfather's loss would trigger the disorder again."

Yig's lip curled. She could feel the teeth pressing against her own. It was a sensation she hadn't felt in weeks. Yig wiggled a tooth and wasn't so sure this was a psychologically driven problem.

"Maybe it is something else, Mom."

"Don't talk like that. You know what this is. We all knew it was possible, and we knew that something as terrible as this tragedy could be a trigger. Yig, go see your therapist."

CHAPTER THIRTEEN: BAD CURRENTS

The Lanyon building where Dr. Carter held his practice looked completely different at night. During the day, the laughing faces carved into its exterior seemed to laugh at the elements. But at night, its angry gargoyles screamed against the lightning flashes. Another coastal storm was making landfall when Yig walked into the lobby. The half-moon peered out from behind the forecast. She took the elevator up to his office where she found Dr. Carter holding a stack of cases.

"Yig, thank you for meeting me so late."

"I've been having some scares."

"I want to hear all about it, but I need to put these files away. My secretary is on vacation, and I am absolutely flummoxed when it comes to her system. Please take a seat in my office. I will be right in."

Yig sat in Dr. Lynne Carter's office. The room was decorated to "open the mind and increase clarity." It looked like a coffee house designed by someone who dabbles in history as a hobby. All the furniture was made of dark-stained woods, mostly oak that looked old enough to have been brought over on Spanish Galleons. On one wall was a Texas Freedom map, the kind that was found at every Buckee's between Beaumont and San Antonio. This version of Texas was oversized compared to most Texas maps because a stretch of New Mexico and Colorado still dangled from the top of Texas.

The other wall was adorned with a map of Galveston from the thirties. Almost nothing existed on the island west of 61st Street, which was also the end of the Seawall. Certainly, there was no Jamaica Beach or Sea Isle or San Luis Road. There was Fort Crockett, however, and Fort San Jacinto (where the Coast Guard took over after World War II). She wondered if, when waiting for the Coast Guard to return after their daily searches for her father, she had stood on the same docks she saw depicted in the poster.

"It was a much smaller island back then," Dr. Carter said as he entered and closed the door behind him.

"I bet a bunch of the buildings haven't changed, though."

Dr. Carter avoided his desk. He sat down on a leather sofa opposite Yig. He had two coffees with him, which he placed on the oak table. "If you need sugar or half-and-half, I can get you some."

"No, thank you." She sipped the coffee.

"The Free State of Galveston," Dr. Carter said. From behind his horn-rimmed glasses, he looked at Yig for confirmation. When her lips did not part, he added, "Back then, the mafia was very influential in Galveston. History tends to think of the mafia as being something that only existed in New York, Las Vegas, and Chicago. But bootlegging was imported through Galveston, and in the forties and fifties, you could find any kind of vice you wanted on our island. But, if you will permit me, Galveston was like an island with a split personality. On the one side, drugs, prostitution, and gambling. On the other side, rotary clubs and civic causes. The two sides were so intertwined, it wouldn't be strange to see a mafia don entering the police department to say hello, and the mafia didn't allow city residents to gamble away all their money."

Yig smiled. "I like that. I guess it's time to talk about my identities now?"

"If you are ready."

"Okay." Yig turned to face him more directly. He sat comfortably in the sofa, sipping his coffee. "I feel like I should be confessing. Father, I have sinned. That kind of thing."

"Well, I'm not her to absolve you of anything, Yig. I'm just here to help you figure this out." He put his coffee down and leaned forward. "I want to remind you that I am not here to target any of your alters. The goal of the therapy is to help you embrace the alters and maintain control of your life."

"Reduce and Accept, right?"

"Exactly. How is your e-mail?"

"It's been a long time, but lately, I've been tempted."

"Interesting. And the techniques with the rainbow and the boat?"

"They work well."

"Good. Let's begin. Now, do you have any concerns?"

She nodded. "What if an alter is dangerous?"

"Why don't you tell me about this alter?"

She grimaced internally. Psychotherapy was never about the easy answers. She would have to go deep to find the answers.

"Well, I didn't think it was an alter at first. This is going to sound crazy to everyone but you, Doctor, but I had an experience out on a boat. You probably read about it. I think everybody read about it. I was out searching for my grandfather, and the boat I was in ran ashore and was destroyed, I was bitten by a shark. I don't think any of us expect to find him alive now. We just hope to recover him. But the part I want to tell you about, the part that I think sounds crazy, is that I wasn't just bitten by a shark, Dr. Carter. I was bitten by a creature that looked half shark and half human. I think it was a wereshark. It chased me out of the hospital, and it bit me on the streets of your little split personality city. Ever since then, I've been experiencing things."

Dr. Carter had leaned forward in his chair. "Sometimes an alter can materialize as a supernatural or mythological entity like a vampire, a ghost, or lycanthrope, perhaps even a wereshark. However, in regards to lycanthropy, there is a psychiatric syndrome called clinical lycanthropy. This syndrome covers all kinds of lycanthropy. People believe they transform into dogs, cats, foxes, cows, and even bees. Before I can diagnose you, I want to discuss this further. Have you had any hallucinations?"

"Yes. Auditory and visual. Tactile, too."

"I would appreciate it if you described these hallucinations me."

Yig paused.

Dr. Carter said, "You are here because of the image of the wereshark, and your interactions with it. They deeply trouble you. Remember that alters are a way for the mind to cope with traumatic memories. So if this is not lycanthropy, but rather a new alter, then your mind fabricated a fantasy alter to cope with a tragedy. The alter contains the memory so that the other identities are not traumatized. In that way, dissociative identity disorder is a function of memory, not personality. So it is important that we review all your experiences and that we discuss how they associate with your memories."

Yig nodded. Although she remembered his lessons from her therapy when she was a child, it was good to hear Dr. Carter reminding her of them, as if his voice gave shape and form to her problems and made it something concrete that she could conquer.

"I think I might have killed someone. Maybe more. To be honest, I'm not real sure, but I have these living nightmares where it is like I am this shark and I am killing people."

"What kind of shark?" His tone had not changed, but he was leaning in closer to her now.

"Does it matter?"

"Only you can answer that."

"Well, I'm not sure. I was bitten by a bull shark, so maybe my alter is a bull shark. What I do know is that the thing has lots of teeth, and sometimes I feel the teeth of the shark pushing through my teeth, and then my teeth fall out and my eyes go black and I can smell blood." The words came out of her in a fountain of misery, and as she finished, she discovered she'd teared up and started to cry.

Unaffected by her emotional state, Dr. Carter said, "Thank you. I know that this is difficult to talk about. I need to ask you something explicit now: do you remember killing people?"

She thought about it for a second, then said, "No."

He leaned back in contemplation and waited for Yig.

"There is something else. It is kind of hard to explain."

"Try."

"I…I can sense electricity. At first, I thought it was unrelated, but that made no sense, so did some research and found out that sharks can do the same. It is called electrical sensory perception. Kind of like birds being able to sense the earth's magnetosphere, I think, but instead sharks do it with electricity."

"Really? Can you do it now?"

She nodded.

"Please, show me." His voice was neither condemning nor sarcastic. Dr. Carter took Yig's words at face value.

She nodded again. She leaned back and forth a moment, then said, "Your phone is in your coat pocket."

"Which one?"

"Right side, lower inside pocket."

Dr. Carter reached into his jacket and pulled the phone out of his inner pocket. He placed the phone on the oak table.

"You may think that I saw you put it there, but your video recording will prove that I didn't."

"Can you give me another example?"

"Sure. The electricity is good in your office, but it is out in the office next door." Yig got up and walked to the side of the room. "It comes through these walls, but then something happens. It goes down into the basement. There is a bad current there." Yig closed her eyes, then told him something really crazy. As she spoke, lightning flashed through the windows, lighting her up like a black and white movie monster.

"Even though it is after hours, and so there is no reason for anyone to be in the building, there are two people in the room next door. One is standing to my left. He has a strong, steady heart. I think it is the man who was with you the last time I was here."

"Dr. Talbot? He is not here."

"I can hear the lie in your heart, Dr. Carter. It beats faster. The second person is a woman. Her heart is like a rave going on in my head. She is scared. I think she is scared of me because she is listening to the audio in her earbuds." Yig kneeled down against the wall and smiled. "No. She is scared because she's pregnant. I can sense the little heartbeat in her womb. Like a baby Energizer battery."

She opened her eyes and did not realize that her right hand was held outward like some kind of divining rod. Dr. Carter sat on the sofa, his face pale.

She said, "You believe me?"

Dr. Carter took a long sip of his coffee while Yig stood there in her black sundress and boots. He stood up, and walked outside. She followed him. He opened up the room next door, the room she'd been standing next to. Inside, Dr. Talbot stood listening to the audio next to a younger woman, maybe five years older than Yig.

"Yig, you know Dr. Talbot. This is Dr. Isabel Suarez." Dr. Talbot stood straight as starch. Dr. Suarez looked like she'd seen a ghost. "I did not want to tell you about them because I didn't want to upset you. They are colleagues of mine."

Yig knew she should be angry, and she felt like something illegal had just happened, but she couldn't help smiling. She was right! She was very impressed with her new skills. Scared to death, yes, but very impressed.

"I only found out yesterday," Dr. Suarez said.

"Is this enough data to confirm our belief, Dr. Carter?" Dr. Talbot asked. Dr. Carter brushed back his white hair evasively.

"Yig," Dr. Carter said. "There is a chance what you are experiencing could be comorbidity, which is another way of saying that it is not related to DID or clinical lycanthropy at all, but rather something else in your mind. I want to try a technique called Rapid Eye Movement Therapy. Think of it as a final test to determine whether you are experiencing a new alter, or you have become something new."

Yig stepped away. "You want to wake the demon? That could be dangerous. I could transform."

"I think I have an answer for that, but first, you must follow me."

Yig and the psychiatrists entered the elevator car. Like the rest of the building, the car was at least sixty or seventy years old. Once inside, Dr. Carter inserted an old brass key into the elevator's console. As he turned the key, the console popped open. Two more buttons appeared. They were unmarked.

"Where do those go?" Yig asked.

Dr. Carter said, "The Lanyon building was originally owned by the Sicilian Mafia. It was their headquarters. Upstairs, everything appeared normal. There were offices for their accountants, their liaisons, even the police had an office room. But down here, that's where the real money was made. There was a hidden casino, and a brothel, and so much more going on. The rooms are evacuated now, but we have some equipment to help make you feel more comfortable about the consequences of the treatment."

As the elevator car door opened, musky air entered the car. Yig held her hand to her nose.

"We are at sea level here, and these doors are not opened often for ventilation." He picked up a flashlight from a row of flashlights and lanterns.

"This is where the electricity in your office. Down here. It is weak."

"That's right. We use it as a headquarters for our research."

"What kind of research?"

Dr. Talbot said, "Dr. Carter, may I remind you of our credo?"

"I'm sorry," Yig said. Somewhere in the dark inside her, Petra scoffed. Others chastised her. Yig did her best to ignore them

"I'm sorry, but I am not at liberty to divulge that information just yet, Yig, but if our suspicions are correct, I will explain everything after the therapy."

As they moved down the hallway, the air dampened against Yig's skin, thick with humidity. The hallway was long but narrow. Beveled glass wall sconces, unlit, marked the way forward. The brass on the sconces rusted out sometime after World War II. Dr. Carter's beam of light showed her where doorways opened into small gambling parlors with vacant poker and blackjack tables. Dr. Carter continued his lecture, saying, "Steel doors were more for ambiance than anything else. There were few rival gangs in Galveston, and they all preferred to cooperate together. But the doors did have a sliding peephole so that the guards could look through and see who was coming in. Usually a senator or a famous actor or one of the many growing oil tycoons."

From one room, Yig smelled salt water. Its door was sandbagged.

"Don't open that door, Yig. They used that room to smuggle barrels of alcohol from a line of ships that was anchored a few miles off the coast. Smugglers would paddle into that room to deliver the barrels, which were then snuck upstairs and loaded onto trucks and shipped all over the country. That is a long way of saying that I don't know how much water would come pouring into the basement if you opened that door."

Dr. Carter opened a door on the far side of the smuggler's dock. Here, he flipped on low-level lighting. Yig felt the twinge in her arm as the electricity shot into the circuits. The room was square, with pipes running down one wall. A small raised platform stood in the center of the room. Yig's first thought was of an altar for worship. But the chains hanging from the ceiling suggested something else, something she did not understand.

"What was this room, Dr. Carter?"

"I wouldn't want to tell you because it is so scandalous."

"Okay, now I have to know."

Dr. Carter blushed. "Well, if you must know, this was a sex room. The raised platform had a bed, and voyeurs watched couples having sex."

"You make it sound so clinical," Dr. Suarez said.

Dr. Carter continued without missing a breath. "The chains were for the more extreme bondage scenarios. Like I said, Yig, you could find any kind of sin here. We have made some changes to fit your therapy."

The bed had been removed from the platform. Two chairs stood in its place, one a typical office chair and the other a large metal one. The larger chair was bolted to the ground and came with its own restraints. Yig couldn't help thinking of an old-time electric chair. She wouldn't have been surprised to see the name "Old Sparky" etched into the chair's backrest.

"Now for the weird part. Time to summon the monster," Dr. Talbot said.

Yig hesitated.

Dr. Carter said, "I know this is unconventional. My hope is that in the next half hour, we will have a much better idea of what we are dealing with, and perhaps a path forward."

Yig sat down. The three doctors began buckling her arms and legs into the restraints.

"They aren't too tight, are they?" Dr. Carter asked.

"Are you kidding? They aren't tight enough. Look, if something happens, do you have a way of protecting yourselves?"

"You mean like silver bullets?"

The idea had not dawned on her that the wereshark could be injured by silver, but as soon as the psychiatrist said the words, Yig knew it would be true. "Yes."

"I'm not worried about your transformation, but if it makes you feel better, Dr. Suarez is a skilled martial artist, Dr. Talbot is a concealed handgun owner, and I have a silver letter opener." He pulled the silver letter opener out of his pocket for her to see. "It's powerful."

"That won't be enough."

"Would you like to be chained to the ceiling?"

"You can do that? You should do that."

"Yig, I am unconventional, but I'm not a monster. We will be fine. We have taken other precautions, so stop worrying about us, Yig. Let's focus on you." While she tested her restraints (snug), Dr. Carter seated himself in the chair opposite her. The other stood and watched.

"Ignore them. Listen to me and me alone. They don't exist. Remember the rainbow technique."

Yig took a deep breath. As she exhaled, she said, "The rainbow is me. I am a many-colored thing with beautiful sides to who I am. I am one person made up of many personalities, but I am the sum of my parts, and I am stronger as one than I am apart. I am one person. One person."

"Good, Yig."

"It isn't easy. I can hear the electricity in your leg twitches. And in the recorder."

Dr. Carter had indeed just pushed record on the digital recorder he set up on the platform.

"Concentrate on my voice." He held up the letter opener in his hand for her to see. "I wasn't just kidding about this letter opener. I believe it can be your salvation. I want you to focus on it. Watch it as I wave it gently in front of you. It is like watching flowers dancing in the wind. As you watch the letter opener, you will feel your mind begin to drift. This is because the movement of the letter opener is triggering the parts of your brain that are active during REM sleep. Like I said earlier, one theory of DID, and I am a fan of this theory, is that your brain is not effectively storing memories during REM sleep. Since the mind is not dealing with the memories, the fantasy is constructed to store the memory. We are trying to unlock that memory, so as you feel yourself drifting, tell me what you are thinking and what you are feeling."

As the letter opener waved in front of her face, Yig felt calmer almost instantly. Dr. Carter's voice drowned out, like she was suddenly hearing it from the other end of a long pipe. So, too, were the sounds of the surf and the electricity.

"I once caught two blacktip sharks in half an hour. Those are some of the most aggressive sharks next to bulls and tigers. Had to throw one back because of regulations, you see."

Yig's grandfather sat in Dr. Carter's chair. He was talking about the kinds of fish he'd caught before. Mostly flounder, drum, and tarpon in the Bay, and snappers and amberjacks out on the Gulf. He also caught black tip sharks, which were some of the most aggressive sharks next to bulls and tigers.

His skin was ghost-white as ever. "Will I turn as pale as him?" Yig once asked her mother. Her mother's skin, like Yig's, had a faint bronze sheen to it. "Aging affects everyone differently," her mother said, "But I don't think so. Remember the picture of your Granddad and Grandma after the hurricane? They were always very pale."

"Did I ever tell you about the time I got dragged fifty yards by a tarpon? Biggest damn tarpon I ever saw, Yig." While her grandfather talked, she only partly listened. Granddad was very old, and many of his stories were big fish stories. The tarpon got bigger, the flounder tasted sweeter, and the black-tips were all great whites. When this began to happen, or when he began to rant about politics, Yig pulled out her phone and started checking messages and opening her favorite apps. That's when she noticed something red dripping off of Granddad's chair.

"Is that blood?"

Granddad looked down at his chair. "Yes, Yig. I believe it is." His voice was as calm as it could be, like he was noticing that the channel on the TV needed to be changed from SD to HD.

Yig crouched down next to her grandfather and looked for the cut.

"Don't worry about me, Yig. I'm just an old man. If we cut ourselves, we bleed a lot. It's nothing to be worried about. Blood thinners."

But she was worried. The blood was pooling beneath his chair.

"Granddad, this looks serious. We need to stop the bleeding and get you to a hospital."

"No, Yig. Don't worry about it. I'll be fine."

Yig tried to lift her grandfather up out of the chair so she could find the cut. But he was refusing. He could be stubborn at times, and as her mother liked to say, "When that man decides he don't wanta go, he ain't goin' nowhere."

"Granddad, please." She grabbed paper towels from his kitchen. While she was gone, her old grandfather ran for the bathroom. When Yig returned, her eyes went wide and she felt sick in her stomach. The chair was soaked in bright red blood. The blood dripped off the edge and ran down its legs and formed a thick puddle on the floor. The chair looked like someone had been executed on it. Her grandfather's tiny feet left little red footprints on the linoleum where he ran for the bathroom.

"Granddad, I'm scared. You need to go to the hospital."

"I'm fine!" he yelled from behind the door.

"Granddad!" Yig banged on the bathroom door.

"Not yet," she heard a voice growl from behind her. The air had suddenly gone heavy with humidity. Yig turned, and the wereshark leaped at her, fast and strong.

Dr. Carter listened to Yig while he waved the letter opener in front of her face. She began crying as she recounted the story of her grandfather bleeding out on his chair. It sounded like just the kind of horrible memory that a person with DID would fail to process naturally. Dr. Carter was thinking about the ramifications of the memory when he realized Yig had stopped talking about her grandfather and was just sitting there, watching him.

"Doctor," one of the others said.

Yig was smiling wide and long, like a crack had opened in her skull. And her eyes were jet black.

"I can smell ya," the wereshark purred.

Dr. Carter jumped, then moved toward her. "Intense pupil dilation," he said for the record.

The Thing in The Chair chuckled.

"Got somethin' for ya." Her voice sounded wet, like she had spent the evening drinking. As she spoke, blood spilled from her mouth, leaving a long ribbon down her chin, then her neck, and then the front of her dress. Without hesitation, she regurgitated all her teeth in a giant belch of blood and bile. The teeth dropped into her lap.

The other psychiatrists rushed to the stage. "Mass dental expunction."

Dr. Carter reached for Yig's eyes to pull them open farther. She snapped at his hand with dark, pointed teeth, barely missing his fingers. He watched in horror as Yig's shark-like jaw slowly pulled back under her lips.

"Dark, triangular teeth," Dr. Talbot said.

"Carcharodon carcharias?" Dr. Carter asked.

"Carcharodon leucas. Bull shark," Dr. Talbot corrected.

"You are always the taxonomist, Dr. Talbot."

"A real live wereshark," Dr. Talbot said. He placed his briefcase on the ground in front of Yig and opened it. "The Carfax Society is back. Ex Monasteriense prognatus licentia quod Scientia en rememdium."

"Let's not count our monsters before they hatch," Dr. Carter said.

"Hurry, Doctor. We don't want to lose her," added Dr. Suarez.

"We won't." Dr. Talbot pulled a syringe out and checked the dosage. 25 mg of silver mixed with morphine.

Dr. Carter said, "Not too much, either. We don't want to kill her."

"We won't."

"An honest-to-God wereshark. They were always rumors, but I've here it is now in the flesh. Do you know what this means? The ramifications for medical science?"

Invisible to them, the storm loomed over Galveston. Its thunder rumbled even in the dark basement.

The wereshark said, "Dr. Carter, guess what? I saw a rainbow, and I ate it. Ha! Ha! Ha!"

Her neck began to stretch upward. The grisly sight of the elongated head made Dr. Suarez sick to her stomach.

The head wavered above them. "I will devour you all," the Thing in the Chair announced.

The teeth lashed out at Dr. Talbot as he tried to stick her with the needle.

The creature's arms and legs thickened, and her hands and feet ruptured into claws.

"Quickly, Doctor," Dr. Carter said. They had mere seconds before the creature burst out of its restraints.

"I will chomp you into bits, landchum. I will gorge on your flesh, your bones, your tender organs."

Dr. Talbot tried the arm again, and once more Yig bit at him. This time, her sharp teeth tore away his suit jacket.

"Try the legs! Hurry, damn it!" Dr. Carter yelled. He had latched on to an arm that was freed by the pectoral fin erupting from her forearm and bursting through the restraint.

Dr. Talbot shoved the needle into the wereshark's thigh and pushed down hard on the plunger. Yig yelled painfully. She pulled her other arm free and shoved Dr. Carter away.

She lowered her head toward Dr. Suarez. "I can taste your fear. It's…electric…." Slowly, she opened her mouth wide and her shark jaw pushed forward. She shut her jaw on his face, so close that he could feel her saliva drip on his skin. Dr. Suarez backed away from her and fell off the platform just as she swung one of the domination chains across her. She ran screaming from the dungeon.

As Dr. Suarez escaped into the hallway, she saw the door to the smuggling dock burst open, and a wave of water and sandbags rushed into the dungeon. She was a thin woman, not used to such tribulations. The wave of brown bay water knocked her body over as it surged forward. A second wave spilled into the dungeon.

Dr. Suarez pushed against the gritty water and tried to stand. The wave was more power than height. With so much sand and salt, it was a semi-solid wave that bit and scratched her as it flowed over.

Something dark in the corridor caught her eye. She thought it was a trick of the lights, which were now flickering in the dungeon. She looked closer. A broad shark's fin was coasting back and forth with the third wave. Dr. Suarez shrieked as the mouth lunged for her. She tried to jump out of the way, but there was nowhere to go. The bull shark's wide mouth shot out of the dark water. The mouth engulfed her head and thrashed back and forth, snapping the head from the body. As the shark turned, blood spurted from her neck and mixed with the bay water.

As he lay hunched in the corner where Yig threw him, Dr. Carter felt the warm bay water flooding the room. A thick brown fin zig-zagged into the room, and he yelled a one-word warning to Dr. Talbot. It was a warning so deeply entrenched in society, it would bring terror to anyone who heard it: "Shark!"

Dr. Talbot turned on the seven-foot shark as it closed in on him. He pulled a Colt .45 out of his jacket coolly, like he was a character in a Tarantino film. He rained bullets on the bull shark and hit it in the nose. The shark cornered and fled, blood gushing into the water.

"Always aim for the head," Dr. Talbot said for anyone who was listening.

Suddenly, the wall behind Dr. Talbot exploded. Cold stone and old wood blew past him. A giant wereshark, standing on two feet, appeared in the rubble. The wereshark snapped at Dr. Talbot, who shot at it. The wereshark bit down on his open hand, then pushed its jaws further up his forearm, biting down on his elbow.

"Oh, no, it's up to my elbow," the giant wereshark said.

Dr. Talbot screamed. His arm ended in a set of teeth. His hand had been slashed with the first bite. He was pretty sure he had lost two or three fingers. But he still had sensation in his index finger. He knew this for certain because as the shark mouth bit down on his elbow, he felt his finger touch the inside of its gills. They were fleshy and soft, like a handful of worms.

The monster took another bite. It now had him by the shoulder. The creature teased, saying, "Oh, heck, I'm up to his neck."

Then the monster shook him violently. Suddenly, Dr. Talbot felt his arm separate from his body. He flew across the room and slammed into the stone wall.

Dr. Carter watched the massacre unfolding in front of him while he regained his feet. Unbelievably, there was a bull shark in the room alongside two weresharks. The smaller lycanthrope, Yig, remained in a kind of half-transformative state. Her eyes were still solid black and her mouth was full of wicked shark teeth, but she did not have the full Carcharodon body of the other wereshark. The sedative was working. She was reverting to her old self.

Yig let go of the chain and fell back into the chair.

Dr. Carter pushed himself up off the floor. His old joints complained under the stress. He liked to think of himself as a fit man (and hated being told he was fit "for his age" – a term he considered the bane of all people who were not representative of the Hollywood demographic). He worked out at least once a week and ran every day. But as a doctor, he was also aware of his limitations. Right now, the little doctor in his head who was doubtful of everything in the world that looked dangerous and unsafe, told him his joints were too old for this scenario. The neurotic doctor in his head also reminded him of how many stitches are needed per tooth (five for a bull shark) and how quickly he could bleed out if the monster severed an artery (90 seconds). But Dr. Carter rarely conceded to the neurotic doctor in his head. He held the letter opener out, blade down, and ran at the wereshark while she was turned.

He stabbed her in the side with the silver letter opener, then jumped back as the wereshark barked with pain. The sound caught his attention because sharks have no vocal-producing organs. So any sound was a result of the human side of the lycanthrope. The wereshark reached to the open wound. When her hand pulled back, it was covered in blood.

Dr. Carter fell over something as he backed away from the wereshark. As he fell, he realized it was Yig, who was a mouth of hate away from being human.

"What is happening?" Yig asked through the effects of the sedative. Her body was fighting the drowsiness, but like even the biggest animals, it was a losing battle.

To Talbot, he pointed at the much larger shark and shouted, "It's the Mother!" Then he helped Yig stand. "We must escape, Yig."

Dr. Talbot groggily pulled himself up. He was bleeding out, but he was a warrior. He'd take that mother with him on the way out if nothing else. He fired his pistol at the wereshark. The creature, already weakened by the silver, raised her hand to shield her face against the bullets. It barked, but not at them.

The bull shark came swimming back into the room.

"Oh, shit," Dr. Carter said.

"Somebody else is here," Yig said. "I can hear their hearts. Two of them."

Seconds later, Belén and her brother ran into the room. Her brother fired at the shark just as it was about to slam into Dr. Carter. The gunfire hit the shark in the tail. It quickly turned and retreated out of the hole in the wall.

Belén held a large harpoon rifle in her hands. The tip of the harpoon glinted silver in the flickering light. Seeing the harpoon, the wereshark howled at Belén, then backed out the hole.

"Quickly," Belén said. "She will return with more. We have to leave now."

"Who are you?" Yig asked Belén, but her consciousness was already fading. The transformation had taken its toll. She could no longer resist the sleep.

"Tonight, I may just be your savior."

"That's debatable," Dr. Carter said. Dr. Talbot tried to raise his gun to Belén's brother while he slumped pale against the wall. Her brother raised his gun to Dr. Talbot. Yig passed out.

When Yig awoke, she was sitting across from the woman tasked with killing her.

CHAPTER FOURTEEN: TEETH

Dr. Lynne Carter sat at his desk, nursing his injuries. His elbow had been lacerated, not by a shark, but by landing on the floor. There was an irony in that, one he did not want to acknowledge when his colleague, Dr. Suarez, was gone from them. His nameplate was still bolted to the office next door. Dr. Carter tried to ignore his doubts and regrets – survivor's guilt, he knew all too well, but it was hard to ignore the loss of a comrade. Hell, a friend. He had known Isabel for twenty years.

Dr. Carter stared at the chair. It was the same chair that Yig had sat in the day before, when he recommended the REM treatment for her Dissociative Identity Disorder. DID. *Ha!,* he thought. That had been a brazen lie, of course. Yig had suffered from DID when she was younger, but this was something new. Something malevolent.

Eff it, Dr. Carter thought.

"There's nothing you could have done," the British voice on the phone said.

Dr. Carter disagreed vehemently. "I should've known better."

The person on the phone said, "We didn't know the girl had been bitten by the Mother or that the Mother would come for her."

"This is the worst day in the history of the Carfax Society."

"No, Dr. Carter. You and I know there have been far worse days. Much greater sacrifices have been made."

Dr. Carter wanted to shout his disagreement, but he knew better. It was true. He had been a member of Carfax for going on thirty years. He had heard the stories, had attended the funerals, and watched members go insane. Certain grotesque memories were so ingrained in his mind, they kept him up at night. Yes, sacrifices had been made. That didn't make this any easier to deal with.

"Damn it! Dr. Suarez is dead, and Dr. Talbot, a veteran of the War on Terror, is in the critical care unit at UTMB. *Got his arm chopped up by his own riding lawn mower.* Do you think he will ever recover from it? How is he going to feel knowing he can't type on a keyboard or hold a woman in both his arms? He'll always have trouble driving. He'll forever be watched wherever he goes for being different. How much of his life will he have that wasn't taken by the Carfax Society?"

"Talbot knew what he was buying into, Dr. Carter. Don't go off the deep end and mire away in guilt. Besides, there have been many advances in neurological resurrection. If the Colombian Chapter of the Carfax Society can make their breakthrough with the Hombre Caiman,

Dr. Talbot arm may grow back proper! I'm more concerned that the hospital won't believe that he chopped off his arm in a lawnmower accident. Once they examine the wound, they are bound to conclude that the injuries do not coincide with a lawnmower amputation."

"They will have to believe us. The alternative is that he was bitten by a shark, and no one wants to believe that shark bites happen here routinely."

"I've got something for you," the person on the phone said.

"Did New Orleans contact you?" Dr. Carter asked.

"No. There's been a development, though. You will need to see this. I'm sending you live satellite video now."

A new message blinked on the small computer behind him. Dr. Carter turned and opened the video file. The video showed a zoomed-in view of the Galveston downtown.

"Watch closely. I am going to zoom out so that you can see this."

On screen, Galveston's downtown dropped away. The video showed Broadway, then East Beach, then the murky depths of the Galveston coastline.

"My God," Dr. Carter said.

Just outside the beach, twenty large bull sharks swam at sea level. Their triangular fins jutted out of the salt water. The program zoomed in to within 100 feet of the water for a better view.

"Have you ever seen so many all at once in Texas, this close to the coast?" Dr. Talbot asked.

"It must be the Mother," Dr. Carter said. "She is calling them in."

"You haven't seen anything yet." The sharks grew smaller as the satellite view pulled out. Now the western end of Galveston was viewable. Dozens more schools of sharks appeared in the bay waters. The satellite video steered east. Everywhere along the coast that it zoomed into, more sharks appeared. Hundreds of bull sharks all circling the island. Their fins were like teeth from a giant jaw waiting to bite down on the island.

"What do you recommend?"

"What can we do, Dr. Stewart?" Dr. Carter said. "Call the police? Warn people and tell them to stay off the beach? Those might just be sharks. People would be killing them over and over."

"They might be weresharks, too. If they decide to attack, nobody is safe."

"What are they doing?" Dr. Stewart asked.

"Waiting. For the next full moon," Dr. Carter said. "I'd say we better get off the island before then. It's going to be a feeding frenzy the likes of which we've never known."

CHAPTER FIFTEEN: THE WITCH'S HAMMER

Yig woke from troubled sleep, greeted by the sound of wind streaming across flags and rolling the tide against the beach. She was laying on an Adirondack recliner on a porch balcony somewhere in West Beach. She knew it was West Beach in that natural way of people who have lived all their childhood and part of their adulthood in one geographical area. She knew it was afternoon by the way the heat prickled her skin, which meant the sun was west of her. No skyscrapers broke the western horizon, which meant Galveston lay to the east. There were additional clues, though. Like how the beach sand was coarser here than east beach or Bolivar, and the sand had a slightly cornflower yellow tincture. All this mental processing came to her naturally without really contemplating her position. If Yig had been asked how she knew where she was on the island, she would have shrugged. She just knew.

But there was another way Yig knew her location. A much less natural way. A way that scared her because she knew she was in West Beach by the electricity in the air. The current was different. All the car electricity was centralized in long rows along the beach, and the rental homes here crackled like electric volcanoes erupting with air conditioning demands.

And then there was the blood and the fish. The blood here was relaxed. Sugar-coated, yes, but relaxed. And the fish were putrid. She could smell a quarter mile away a redfish that had gotten caught ashore when the tide went out. Only a xylophone of its body was left. Its eyeballs had been plucked out by seagulls. She could smell the rot lining the orbit. Disgusting.

A strong easterly wind carried the squeals of unseen children playing at the beach that lay on the other side of grassy dunes that acted as a barrier between the houses and the fury of Gulf storms. On the beach house's lot below her were a set of vertical, rectangular flags. Half were red and half were black, and she saw strange symbols printed on them. A wooden bowl of fruit had been set out for her. The bowl was full of oranges and mangos and bananas. The smell offended Yig worse than the dead fish.

"How are you?" a woman asked. She was walking out through the sliding glass doors. From inside the house, Yig detected the electric burn of countless appliances. A window air conditioner whirred from the side of the beach house. Like the fruit and the fish, the air conditioner offended Yig. She did not like its abrasive electricity.

"I don't know," Yig said, though she could feel a headache starting. She couldn't remember what happened to her before she was in the house, but thinking about it made her feel horrible. "I feel weird. On edge."

The woman went back inside and turned off the air conditioner. Yig felt calmer. More together. Like a house that is surrounded by lawn crew operating mowers and blowers and cutters and edgers, and then suddenly all at once everybody stops and turns off their equipment and the silence is uplifting.

"That better?"

Yig nodded. A moment later, the young woman walked back outside and into Yig's view. She was even darker-skinned than Yig, the color of the Gulf when it is full of dark sand and the waters undulate. It is the only time that the Great Grey can be described as a Beautiful Brown.

The woman sat down in a chair across from Yig. She had long eyelashes and wavy hair the color of garden soil right after a storm. Yig thought she was beautiful, and envied her beauty.

"Thank you," Yig said. "Where am I?"

"My family's seaside cottage. We bought the land back in the 1920s as kind of a refuge from the rest of the island. Now, I don't think it is so much a refuge as an amendment."

Yig realized, *we are not far from where I was attacked.*

"What family is yours?" Yig asked.

"Spoken like a true island girl. We have our little alliances. Strange, isn't it? Sixty thousand people live here yet if I say a certain last name, you will know my family and my family's history instantly. There is no fame like the celebrity of small towns. And for such a large small town, our histories run deep. My name is Belén Treviño."

Yig gave her a puzzled look. "The Treviños on East End or Harborside?"

"See? Alliances. You wouldn't know us. We are very private."

Yig looked down at her clothes. She didn't remember dressing in a shawl and one-piece bathing suit.

"I hope you don't mind," Belén said. "We only have beachwear here."

"I'm trying to remember what happened last night. It is all so weird and fuzzy. All I have are images. Strange images."

While Yig sorted through the visions that drifted through her mind like seaweed in the tide, Belén put her hand on Yig's wrist and said, "I know that during the last full moon you were bitten by a wereshark. I know that you have been transforming into a beast since then, that you met with your psychiatrist because you have Dissociative Identity Disorder, that your psychiatrist, Dr. Lynne Carter then attempted REM Therapy. He said this was done to help you understand and interrelate with your memory problems, but really Dr. Carter used it to conjure the wereshark out of you, which is remarkable since it was not a full moon. Young were-creatures don't usually show that ability."

Yig buried her face in her knees.

"I know it's a lot to take in at once."

"No," Yig said. She sniffed back tears. "It's not that. It's that it's true, then. I am a monster."

Belén waited.

"I knew it was true. I remember some things. I shouldn't say this, but I don't care anymore who hears it. I think I've killed people." To Belén, she asked, "Are you here to kill me?"

"Yes."

"I deserve it."

"But I'm not going to. Not yet."

"Why not?"

"First, tell me about your encounter with the wereshark, the one that bit you. The one that came for you last night."

"I know nothing about her."

"But that's not true. You already know it is a woman."

Yig shrugged.

"Have you met any strange women on the island recently?"

"I work for an Internet sales company. Everybody there is strange."

"This would be somebody new. Somebody different."

Yig searched her memories, but she still felt like clutching at straws. "No, nothing."

"You were bitten by a very powerful wereshark, Yig. Perhaps the most powerful. In legend, she is known as the Mother of All Sharks. She rarely appears, but when she does, she brings disasters a thousand-fold."

"You've seen her?"

"No. I've just heard about her in legends and old stories. She is one of the most powerful, and most dangerous, monsters in the world."

"Most dangerous…? Who are you that you know all this?"

"Belén Treviño. Me and my brother, Vara de Moses, make up the Galveston area Malleus Maleficarum. The Witch's Hammer. At the height of the Inquisition, Pope Innocent VIII wrote a Papal Bull outlining the hunting of witches. Certain loyal families to the Pope were entrusted with the task of seeking out demons and witches throughout the Old World and the New. Since then, my family has been Inquisitors of the Wicked and Hunters of the Dark in a war against Hell. My ancestors came to Galveston hundreds of years ago and helped settle the first church in Texas. Our goal was to march to the Pacific, confronting western demons and sending them back to the pit. But in the late 1800s, we were forced to return to Galveston. We've been here ever since, doing God's work."

"Wait. So, your parents did this, too?"

"Every generation is recruited into the war against Hell, the only war that matters."

Yig stood up and walked behind the patio recliner.

"You cannot run from me, Yig. We've been watching you for a long time. There is no place we cannot find you. We know every inch of this island."

"Then why haven't you killed me yet?"

"If it were up to my brother, he'd have already shot you down with silver bullets. But I convinced him otherwise."

Belén selected a bright-colored orange from the wooden bowl and began to peel it. The peelings she let drop to the wooden floorboards, then kicked off the side of the patio. They fell into a clump that seagulls would scavenge later.

Yig shielded her nose and mouth with her hand. "Those smell horrible. Why?"

"Your tastes have changed, Yig. You've become a creature of the night that craves after flesh and blood. You can hunt people down by the electricity in their hearts. And after you follow that thin telegraph wire that is invisible to most humans, after you track them down and corner them, what will you do, Yig? Will you kill people?"

"I don't want to kill people."

"Do you deny that there's a side of you that lusts for feeding?"

A vision of a large black mouth full of teeth shaped like steak knives encompassed her mind. The vision nearly knocked her over.

"Please, tell me about what happened to your family."

"Over the centuries, our ties to Rome have dwindled. I think the Vatican would rather forget we ever existed. The Papal Bull creating the Malleus Maleficarum is now an Internet joke. The world would rather believe that the Pope never decreed such a thing and that monsters do not exist. But as you certainly know, monsters do exist, Yig. And in my experience, some of them are evil horrors that should be destroyed immediately." Belén bit into the orange. The juice dribbled down the sides of her mouth.

"Do I need to be, uh, destroyed immediately?" She could not settle the tremor in her voice.

"I don't know, Yig. But until I find out, I want to keep a close eye on you. I want to believe that you are a product of bad luck. I want to believe that you can control this thing inside you. I want to believe an old story I learned long ago."

"What story is that?"

"Weresharks have been coming to Galveston as long as people, so there is an old island saying. *When the silver of the moon touches the black o the water, the waters will run red with blood.*"

Yig felt a chill running up her spine, like the cold fingernail of a hag who haunted a hospital.

"You've heard this before?" Belén asked. Yig's pale skin and wide eyes confirmed Belén's suspicion. "You've met Madam Miteff? She died of yellow fever in the 1800s in the very same hospital where you were treated for your bite. Since then, she has wandered from building to building. You always know she is near when you hear dripping water. She died while being treated with hydrotherapy."

"So, you kill creatures like her?"

"Vara and I have come close to catching Madam Miteff several times, but she always finds a way to elude us. Sometimes we've sought her out for informational purposes. She is an old ghost and has witnessed much here. She told us the saying about the wereshark, but she gave us other information, some that I think will help you."

"What kind of information?"

Belén's phone buzzed. She pulled it out and looked at the message.

"What did Madam Miteff say?"

Belén put the phone away and said, "We need to leave. Quickly. Vara is coming. Vara does not share my tolerance for lycanthropes. Where I see a mistake that might be corrected, he only sees another sinner needing to be sent back to hell."

"But I didn't come from Hell."

"Try telling that to him when he's pointing a pistol loaded with silver bullets at your head. Hurry now."

They ran downstairs and across the sandy lot to a Jeep Wrangler with a lift kit and the doors removed. It was painted black with a red pentagram on the hood.

"Get in," Belén ordered.

But as Yig touched the side of the Jeep to climb into her seat, she felt a strange sensation. The Jeep felt cold and lifeless to her. Instantly, she knew something was wrong. "Somebody has disabled the engine."

Belén scowled.

"Run?" The words sounded strange and unfamiliar in her mouth. Other people ran. That's the way it always had been. Yig hadn't run 20 feet in her life.

The wind flung Belén's hair across her face. Belén tightened her eyes as she turned into the strong wind. "Today, the wind will save us. Come on."

Belén opened the first-floor utility closet that was the ballast of beach houses everywhere. She came out a moment later with two packs, harnesses, and two large-wheeled skateboards. Yig recognized the materials immediately as flyboarding equipment. She had done less than her fair share of flyboarding as a teenager on the island. Her leg always held her back.

Belén opened the pack and unfurled the parasail.

"I only did this once and it went really, really badly."

"You'll be surprised how quickly it comes back." She connected the harness to the sail and put a helmet on Yig's head. Her head felt loose in the helmet.

"Sorry. It's my brother's."

Belén tightened the harness around Yig's waist.

The wind was already opening up the parasail. "Remember to lean back. Stay too forward and you will be slammed into the ground. Use these grips to control direction. Other than that, it's just like flying a kite."

"Except that the kite can carry me..." Yig could not finish the sentence as the parasail launched upward and Yig rolled down the beach.

"I'll be right behind you!" Belén yelled.

Yig was a kid again, living in a time when motors and engines were for adults only, so she had to settle for vehicles that were powered by either people, wind, or water. Except for her, she was living a life she'd never lived. She'd always had special permission to sit out physical education, and when her friends wanted to go swimming or God forbid, parasailing, she always excused herself. So to be suddenly racing down the beach beside a blur of pop-ups, grills, sand castles felt nothing short of a miracle. It felt like she was in somebody else's Instagram life.

And she was. Above her, the kite soared. A naked woman with flowing blonde hair had been painted to the inside of the sail. The woman's nipples and Oh-My-Gods were covered with smiling sun faces. This wasn't just somebody else's Instagram feed, it was some frat boy's.

In front of Yig lay open space and the long road to...where? Belén never said where she wanted to go, but then again, maybe this was Yig's chance to escape. The wind was pulling her along at a fast enough clip that she feared what would happen if she lost control. Her legs still felt good, which was different from every other experience she'd ever had with an extreme sport.

If she could get to the next pocket park before Belén caught up with her, she could detach from the kite surfer and hide in a beach house in one of the nearby subdivisions. She could call someone from there. Maybe Emily or Bobbi could pick her up. Then she could get away from this weird cult and re-evaluate everything that had happened to her in the past 24 hours.

Belén raced up next to her. Her parasail was decorated with a handsome naked man with a smiling sun face covering his prick.

"Your family is a bunch of pervs." Yig tried to say to Belén, but Belén waved her off and pointed behind them. Her brother approached in a Jeep similar to the one Yig and Belén abandoned, except instead of black with a red pentagram, this one was red with a black pentagram.

Yig pulled down on her grips and steered the board toward the dunes. Belén flew towards the beachgoers. Now, her brother had to choose between the dunes and the beachgoers. He veered toward the dunes and the wereshark.

Yig was going fast, but the Jeep was faster. It roared up behind her, all grill and steel and sand. She let the parasail fly up. The Jeep bumped into her as she flew. Yig wavered on her board, then pushed off with the back of her heels to keep the board on her feet. She swerved to the left. The Jeep swerved with her. She stopped pulling on the grips and let the wind take her. The sail shot upward, and she flew up over the Jeep. Vara de Moses pulled a gun, but before he could get a shot off, Yig had cartwheeled over the Jeep and crashed into the sand behind him.

The brother Treviño hit the brakes.

"*Malditos monstruos,*" Vara growled.

Yig did not have time to catch her breath, as the parasail heaved her back up into the air. She was eight feet off the ground and continuing to go up. She wondered if anyone had ever been pulled up into the air and lost forever. *Second star on the right, and straight on till morning,* she thought, wondering if she might find herself in Neverland.

But then gravity got a hold of her, and she crashed into a cloud of sand in the dune.

The Jeep swerved so hard, its tires nudged off the beach. Vara aimed his pistols at Yig, but she was gone. Her parasail fluttered in the wind and rose into the land of the sun. Further down the beach, Vara's sister was racing on her board with Yig in tow. Belén had always been the best flyboarder in the family. Her brother gunned the Jeep.

Belén steered the boards into the crowds.

"Jump!" Belén yelled. Yig lifted her board to the best of her ability (holding onto Belén's halter, she had a very limited vision of what was happening in front of her). The board popped over a large man's whale-like gut. She heard him yowling out in pain, but she had no time to check on him. Belén was leading them to the beach. Two more jumps later (a sand castle and a cooler), and they were riding along the surf. A parade of people and cars was now between them and Vara de Moses.

Yig was amazed by Belén's skill with the flyboard. She was controlling the parasail with much more ease than Yig ever could. But something was happening. There was a weight in her stomach, like she wanted to throw up after eating fried Oreos at the county fair.

"Belén."

"Not now. I'm trying to save your ass."

"I don't feel well."

Belén swerved around a dog that danced and yipped at them. Her brother hadn't appeared yet, and the boat was in sight. It was the family speedboat, The Dark Star.

"If we make it to the speed boat, we'll be in the clear," Belén said. "He can't follow us onto the water."

"I can smell the people. I can smell their meat. God help me, I can taste their electricity, and it tastes so…gooooood." She retched out the word.

"Stop it, Yig! Control it!"

"I don't think I can!" The darkness in her stomach was expanding like a helium balloon.

"Yes, you can. This is something you get to choose, Yig. Get a grip. Now jump!"

This time, Yig didn't have it in her to jump. She collided with a giant sand sculpture—a shark no less—and rolled on the sand.

"What the hell?" the sculptor shouted.

Yig stood up and bared her shark teeth. "I smell dinner cooking."

The sculptor dropped his trowel and rag and ran.

Belén released the parasail and ran back to Yig.

"Yig, you've got this."

Yig grimaced and concentrated on reducing the size of the pit in her stomach.

"Yig, breathe slowly. Feel the air passing through your nostrils. It is hot air, and there is sand in it. You can smell the sunblock. You are human, Yig."

Yig nodded and opened her eyes, but not her mouth. She held up her hand to cover her mouth and said, "I'm better now."

Vara appeared then, roaring into the expanse of beach between them and the boat. But it wasn't Belén's brother that caught her attention. It was the dark fins cutting through the tide toward them. Belén smashed her knuckles together as she spoke in the language of the baptized dead. Yig felt the words more than heard them, like a fishhook through her soul. The words seemed to tug at the pit in her stomach where the darkness had been. She was freed from that abyss. All around her, palm trees burst into purple flames. The shadows were pulled toward Belén's fists. In the dark water, she saw the sharks' dorsal fins glowing like purple amethysts.

Belén grabbed Yig's hand and continued running toward the boat. Behind her, Vara angled his Wrangler toward the beach. He opened a compartment from the back of the Jeep and pulled out silver nets, like the kind for catching crabs. He twirled the nets as the weresharks approached the beach front. They were hammerheads, with wide faces. The weresharks stood up on their hind legs and bared their teeth, but they kept their distance from Vara.

Yig boarded the boat behind Belén. Belén took the key she'd been carrying and placed it in the ignition and started the engine. Yig came up behind Belén and grabbed the key.

"Tell me about my grandfather."

"Yig, this can wait."

"No. Earlier you said you knew something. I'm not leaving until you tell me what you know."

"Yig, I killed your grandfather."

The words did not make sense to her. As much as she had seen of ghosts and monsters, she felt like these were the impossible words. People didn't get killed anymore. Gangbangers and people who associated with criminals, sure. But regular people? They died of cancer and heart disease. They got lost in the ocean, but they didn't get killed.

Yig didn't have time to contemplate her world being turned upside down. A silver net fell around her, and the world turned black.

CHAPTER SIXTEEN: CHAINS

The dungeon cell was full of shadows. A thick, iron door with warding glyphs barred Yig's exit. High up close to the ceiling, a glass window revealed the dark night. Fog was settling onto the island.

Every inch of Yig was covered in thick, heavy manacles that chained her 100-pound body to the stone flooring. Even her neck was snapped into a thick manacle. She tried moving, but the manacles chafed like sand when it wedges between the toes. She slumped on the floor in her chains. She would have to be Cautious Clara, who formed when Yig went to college. After her treatment, Cautious Clara had found a corner spot in the back of Yig's mind. She was not as needed as Petra Powerful or even Nadia. Now, though, things were different.

Yig could not see Belén, but she could feel her heartbeat pulsating. From the dark, Belén said, "Did you ever wonder why your grandfather was so old? You must have thought about it. There is a family photo in your house of your grandmother and grandfather, a young couple rebuilding in the aftermath of the Galveston Hurricane. That would make them at least 18 years old in 1900, which would make your grandfather the oldest living person on the planet. Yet he had the body of a robust 60-year old man. He went fishing every day."

Yig had thought of it, had even asked her father about it once, but the question had been dismissed. "He's not as old as you think," her dad had said, "He's older."

"You let this happen," Yig said. Her voice was soft and accented, with a Southern lilt, more Alabama than East Texas. She spoke slowly and with deliberation, as if every word was chosen from a word bank floating above her head.

"I told you: I believe in you. And I believe that you have a condition that can be controlled. The same was not true for your grandfather. He preyed on the sick and the homeless and the insane."

"Don't say that."

"I am sorry, Yig. I know he meant a lot to you."

She paused. "I don't think there's an apology strong enough for 'I murdered your grandfather.'"

"I released his soul."

Yig wanted to protest. She grew up with this man a constant in her life. He was the family patriarch. The first time she went out on a boat was with him. When Tommy Counts broke up with her in eighth grade, her grandfather took her out for a shake. She knew this man as well as she knew anybody. His soul did not need releasing. "How did you kill him?"

"You don't want to know."

"You owe it to me."

Belén was silent for a long time, then she stepped into the moonlight and told Yig about her grandfather.

"Your grandparents arrived in Galveston in 1883 on the ship Persephone. They came from New York, and before that, Lancashire. Like many grindylow of the time, it was hard to detect them. There was less accounting for the lost and the dead. It is not like today, where databases track everything from fingerprints and DNA to unsolved cases and lists of missing persons."

"Wait, did you say that my grandparents are/were grindylow?"

"Yes."

"What does that mean?"

"By legend, it means that they are creatures who inhabit lakes, rivers, and bays and steal children who play too close to the water. But those are stories to keep children away from the water. In reality, they are a kind of creature like leeches. permalum bibit sanguinem. Blood drinkers."

"And they say I'm the one with a psychosis."

"No, you are a wereshark. Your parents and your grandparents are grindylows."

"Oh, so now my parents are these things, too."

Belén exhaled exasperation. "Islands attract monsters, especially water monsters. Mer folk, sea nymphs, kelpies, qalupaliks, morgawrs, grindylows. Even weresharks. It's what's kept my family busy here for the last hundred years, Yig."

"Don't call me Yig."

"I heard the change in accent. Who am I talking to?"

"Inside me, there are different names, but those are my names. I only give them out to the people I trust, and I don't trust you. So you can call me Mrs. Slaton."

"Alright, Mrs. Slaton. My family has been tracking your grandfather for over a hundred years. He was very cautious, so it was hard to build a case that he was, in fact, a grindylow. Your grandmother, however, we laid eyes on her feeding on a transient. So my father staked her with an iron rail spike blessed by Juan Diego. Your grandfather chased him off before he could cut off her head, so there is always the possibility that she could return, which is why your grandfather took you to visit her grave so often. We believe he was going to feed you to his wife if she woke up. But she hasn't woken up. Her grave is undisturbed to this day.

"Finally, me and Vara de Moses caught up to your grandfather on one of his fishing trips. When we came up on his boat, he was gone. I went onboard his boat while my brothers covered me. His rod and reel were just sitting there like he had walked away from it to go to the bathroom or get a beer. He kept a really big cooler, which made me nervous. I didn't know what to expect. A human body? His body? Had he seen us and now was hiding? I approached the cooler slowly. With my brother watching, their crossbows raised, I held the railroad spike in one hand and threw open the chest with the other. Redfish. Your grandfather was not on the boat."

"We did not hear your grandfather crawling out of the water. He was so good at what he did, we thought it was a wave. Your grandfather was vicious. He dropped a bloodless tarpon from his teeth as he attacked. We were lucky to escape with our lives. I stabbed your grandfather from behind. His eyes seemed more sad than angry in those last moments before death."

"The grindylow sat down in our boat, breathing heavily. *Tell my granddaughter Yig that I'm sorry*, he said. Then I cut off his head. It was swift, I promise. We chained his body in silver and blessed it before we tossed him overboard and sunk his boat. One of the reasons I won't let my brother kill you is because I have to know: what was he sorry about?"

Tears streamed down Yig's eyes and onto her chains. "I don't know. He was the best granddad I could want. He never had anything to be sorry about with me."

"My brother wants you killed. We have evidence of your lycanthropy, that you have appeared as a wereshark. The only reason you are still alive is because I am arguing that you can control this."

"You killed Granddad. Go to hell."

Belén walked out and shut the door behind her.

Yig's world swirled around in her head like a tilt-a-whirl. A few weeks ago, she was a hard-charging young woman with a chronically bad leg and a supportive family. The most interesting thing about her was the weird company she worked for. That seemed like a long-ago Yig, a different Yig's problems. The Yig of this moment was the granddaughter of murdered grindylows.

Her grandfather had been murdered. This alone was shocking enough. Murder was the most harrowing theft imaginable. Murder was shutting the door on a part of her life that she'd never have access to again. (Fuck them.) She had started to let go of the idea that her grandfather would be found alive. If he was found at all. She was beginning to think that he would be a life fading into the shadows of her world. A part of her life that she could never truly detach from because she didn't have that closure. There would have always been the chance he was out there somewhere. But now a new demon called Murder would inhabit those shadows. (Fuck them all, those bastards. I'm gonna murder them right back.)

Yig sniffed her nose. She had no Kleenex, and even if she did, she couldn't reach her nose from under the mountain of chains holding her down. She thought nobody in the world could relate to the pain she was going through. Maybe if someone discovered that their loved one was killed by the people they had worked for but never told anyone about— maybe that person could relate to Yig. But she didn't think there were many people in the world who could relate to that kind of betrayal and loss all at once. (When you're all alone in the world, Yiggy, you still have vengeance.)

Grindylow were no more real than werewolves or vampires, and to her vampires were glittery white knights that she'd fallen in love with when she was younger. Yes, she would admit that. Every girl her age went through that phase. They wouldn't admit it because they were too mature for glampires, but at home with the curtains drawn, Yig had been decidedly Team Edward. She read every book and went to the Premiere Cinema with Emily. She remembered they couldn't look at each other for a week without feeling guilty. So who did she take with her to see the rest of the films? Who could she trust to not judge her but to sit there, eat his popcorn, and then listen to her babble on about werewolf drama and vampire babies? Granddad. The irony that he is (was) a monster of the deep.

She wanted to deny it. Certainly, there had been no proof given. (Don't lie to yerself.) He didn't have fins for hands or gills on his neck, and he was a beer man, not a blood drinker! She couldn't remember seeing him swimming. He ate popcorn at movie theaters and ate turkey on Thanksgiving. (But think of the blood. All that blood.)

Yig shook her head. Something was seeping into her head, like water damage in the older houses downtown. Not just something. Martha. Martha was the monster inside her head. Martha was worse than any grindylow or water sprite in the outside world. Real monsters came from within.

(Snap, snap, snap goes the little necks of the Treviño family. You know you want vengeance. They killed your nana and they murdered, MURDERED your Granddad. They deserve to die.)

But I do not want to kill.

(Who else is gonna save you? The police? The Carfax Society? Don't make me laugh.)

You are evil.

(I'm an alter, remember? I'm another part of you.)

There is no part of me that wants to take the lives of other people.

(You're lying to yourself, Yiggy. Everybody has the capability for killing. How do you think humans climbed up the food chain? They're the sharks of the land. And these ass warts are dangerous little worms that'll eat you from the inside out if you don't kill them first. It's kill or be killed. Listen to them upstairs. You know you can. Their hearts ain't that far away. Listen to their fear. They're afraid of you and what you're capable of. Why do you think they have two hundred pounds of silver chains on a hundred-pound girl? Just listen.)

Yig listened. They were hard to pinpoint exactly. They were all upstairs, up on the second floor. Both of them. Their electricity was charged, like throttled engines. (Like fear, Yiggy.)

She could focus on them better once she concentrated. It was amazing what she could detect when she listened. It was like seeing people from the inside out, all their nerves spreading out like the branches of a tree. Yig could distinguish Vara de Moses and Belén. The electricity was different in males. Not stronger or faster, but maybe bluer than a female, which was more white, and more constant. More pulsating.

Vara stood to the side. (He's the one who wants to put your head on his mantle.) The electricity in his brain was weak. (Cancer, I bet, or a tumor.) But his heart was strong. Then there was Belén. She was easy to detect now. She was getting better at reading a person's electric current like a fingerprint. Belén had a signature to her current. Then she realized something. Vara and Belén were like blinking lights in a Christmas parade, always going off at the same predictable time. (They're twins.)

But there was something else in the room upstairs. If she could walk over to the side of the room closest to the others and wave her hands about, Yig was sure she could figure it out. These chains were holding her back in more ways than one.

(Concentrate. Focus.)

"There is somebody else up there."

(Give her a gold star.)

Another woman. This third woman was a total anomaly. Her current was so faint, it was almost undetectable. Even now that she had found it, Yig had a hard time focusing on it. It was different than Vara and Belén. Not a total stranger. Not family. (Or distant family, mebbe.)

But who is she, and why is her current so faint?

(You're so naïve. Let me take over, and I'll douse Miss Dim's electricity completely.)

No.

(I just wanna nibble on her skull a bit. Feel it bouncing around in my gullet.)

Why is her electricity so faint? Is she weak? Is she dying?

(Yiggy, she's the most dangerous person in that room. Sher Khan surrounded by little wolves. She may be the most dangerous woman in Galveston. You're sensing a master hunter of lycans who's learned to mask her electricity from us.)

So she is part of the Malleus Maleficarum?

(She is a specialist they've called in to hunt you down. The Lycan Hunter. She kills weres.)

Weres?

(Lycans. Were people. Wolves, tigers, sharks, bears, rats, pigs. Weres, you moron.)

Yig shivered, rattling her chains. The thought of a person who specialized in killing her was chilling.

(You gotta escape now, immediately, if you don't want them to kill you.)

There is no way I can get out of this. I'm a hundred-pound weakling. I don't do pullups, and I can't bench press thirty pounds.

(Let me take over. With me in control, I'll break these bonds and we'll escape together.)

Yig did not like the idea of Martha taking over. So she returned to the exercises Dr. Carter taught her when she was much younger and he was not a member of the Carfax Society. In her mind, she made an image of a rainbow.

"The rainbow is me. I am a many-colored thing with beautiful sides to who I am."

As she spoke, she exhaled slowly.

(What're you doing?)

Yig ignored the voice in her head and concentrated on the rainbow. In her mind, the rainbow came together, bleeding light that swirled like a kaleidoscope or colored clothes in a washing machine. As they spun, the colors bled into each other and became one. Black.

"I am one person made up of many personalities, but I am the sum of my parts, and I am stronger as one than I am apart. I am one person. One person."

(Are you fucking kidding me, kid? Do you really think that's gonna work on ME?) The voice was loud and growing louder.

Yig shook her head and concentrated on the blackness in front of her. It was like a black hole sucking all her personalities into one. It brought her to a black room with a black table and empty chairs. All around her inside her head, she heard laughter, and then silence. Yig emptied her mind of the image of the conference room. She opened her eyes and glanced around the room. She was alone.

(Still here…)

Yig jumped at the sound of the voice purring in her head. Her chains rattled.

(Oh, they must've heard that for sure. Let me out and let's have some play time.)

"I am one person. I am made up of many personalities, but I am the sum of my parts, and I am stronger as one than I am apart. I am one person. One person."

(Unless I'm stronger than the sum. Betcha they didn't teach that in Psychosis 101, did they?)

"Who are you?" she said aloud to the darkness.

(I am you.)

"If you were me, I would have more control over you. If you were really me, I wouldn't know of your existence. You'd be a fugue state I wasn't aware existed. It makes no sense."

(Of course it does. I'm the alter of the wereshark, remember? That's what Dr. Carter said.)

"This is different."

(Then what am I if I am not you?)

"Am I possessed? Are you a demon?"

Martha did not respond.

"Oh, God. I am possessed. Maybe the Malleus Maleficarum can help me. Maybe they know how to exorcise demons."

(Oh, they have a very good way to ensure I never come back. Problem is, you won't either.)

Yig heaved deep breaths.

(You're wondering how you can escape a monster that's inside your head. You can't. You know that better than anyone else in the world. You become the sum of your parts, isn't that what you said? I am a part of you, plain and simple. The only way to get rid of me is to take a pistol to your head, and you're not that kind of girl.)

Yig moaned.

(Hush now, or you'll get us both killed.)

Martha kept talking, describing in great detail how she would kill everyone in the Malleus Maleficarum. Yig tuned Martha's voice out by repeating over and over to herself, "Reduce and Accept, Reduce and Accept, Reduce and Accept…"

She slumped to the side and watched the fog rolling in past the moon. She might have finally drifted to sleep, or she was concentrating so hard on the moon, she didn't see the mist drifting into her dungeon cell.

"Wake up, my little pup."

Yig blinked her eyes. A figure stood in the darkness of the dungeon cell. Was it the one-armed were-specialist? Yig's ESP quickly told her that this was somebody different. She had a powerful electric signature. The woman was narrow at the hips, with a body that moved like a gently waving flag, or maybe more like a moray eel waiting for some small fish to pass close enough to her jaws. She was tall and bald. There was not a single hair on her head. She was completely naked except for all the leather necklaces full of shark teeth. With dread, Yig realized who was standing in front of her. This was the creature that Belén had warned Yig about. This was the Mother.

Yig felt the twinge in her stomach, the sign that Martha was trying to take over. She fought the urge as the creature stepped out of the shadows. She had olive skin and black eyes. She wore high heels that, on second inspection, seemed more like extensions of where her feet should be than heels. They were like the spiny projections from a fin, like thin membranes gripping to bone.

"You know who I am?"

"You're the Mother. Of All Sharks."

"Good. So the Malleus Maleficarum still maintains its records after all this time."

"All this time?"

"You know never to ask a woman her age, Yig. The rise and fall of religions are like the daily tide to me. The Empire of the Sea is the only true empire on this planet." Yig was astonished. The Mother appeared as a woman in her prime, at that perfect pinnacle between perky and powerful. Yet her eyes belied a creature as old as the sea. That kind of immortality scared the shit out of her.

"What do I call you?"

"You will call me what I am: your Mother, because the life you had before I bit you is no longer important. Only obedience to your Mother remains. I bore you out of death like all births, and I baptized you in the blood of your friend. You belong to me and will do as I command."

Yig wanted to argue against her, wanted to say that she was her own person and could do as she wished. But her mind was focused on pushing Martha down. She didn't have energy to contradict the Mother.

"Look at you, you poor soul," the Mother scoffed. "My child lies floundering on the floor like a baby seal. But you are no commoner. You are a Princess of the Open Sea, the Cold Shadow in the Water, and the

Terror of the Abyss. You are the Mouth That Appears from the Murk. A Devourer of the Deep. And you will rise up and break those chains."

"The chains outweigh me. They are made of silver."

The Mother made a sharp sound in the back of her throat, like a teacher being told that long division is impossible or that conjugations are beyond comprehension. "Do you really think that matters to *my* daughter? You're not a guppy. Now stand up. Stand up!"

Yig steeled herself. She placed first one foot on the ground, then she pushed herself up into a kneeling position, like she was waiting to be knighted. The chains felt heavy on her shoulders, and they scratched at her skin. Yig ignored the pain and stood up on both feet. The chains rattled and clanged against the dungeon floor.

"Yes! Now the hard part's over. All my little Ariel needs to do is break the chains. Get out of this prison. And when you do, we will find each other, and you will join your brothers and sisters, and we will ravage this island together."

Yig watched the Mother of All Sharks dissipate into a cloud of sea mist, which glided out of her barred window and disappeared into the night.

She looked to the iron door and listened with her ears and her heart for the sound of the Treviños approaching. She would welcome them. With the Mother's words still in her, she felt ready for anything.

She raised her arms and leaned into the chains, her hundred-pound body straining against the metal that outweighed her. Yig growled. That sinking feeling in her gut was pulling her down, but away from the fasteners. Yig did not know if she was accepting Martha Mayhem or feeling out for a better way to escape the chains.

In the moonlight, the chains had an eerie glow. Yig pushed farther. First one chain snapped behind her, then another. She dared not look back, but kept pushing against the chains, trying to force her way out. It was like ripping out threads. First one cord came loose, then another, and soon the cell was full of the sound of snapping metal and breaking chains.

As Yig ripped the last chain from her neck, the Belén and Vara de Moses opened the door. All of Yig's teeth were gone by then. The wereshark yelled at the family of Malleus Maleficarum, then tossed Belén across the room. As a rain of bullets hit her, she burst through the small upper window, exploding brick, and ran off into the night.

PART 3: HONORABLE YIG

There are many members, yet one body. And the eye cannot say to the hand, "I have no need of you"; nor again the head to the feet, "I have no need of you." No, much rather, those members of the body which seem to be weaker are necessary. And those members of the body which we think to be less honorable, on these we bestow greater honor.

-Corinthians 12

CHAPTER SEVENTEEN: ESP

Yig woke at five in the morning in her four-post bed. She checked around the house to make sure she was alone, then checked under her bed and in the closet, searching for clues as to what happened after Martha took over. There was no damage in her condo, and nothing was left behind. Not even shark teeth lying on the floor. The beast had been good and cleaned up after herself before retiring.

Assuming I'm not the beast, Yig wondered. A person with multiple identities bitten by a wereshark. She reminded herself that this was different. This was not an identity disorder, but a possession. Her body was being kidnapped. She needed to find out how to stop Martha from taking over.

Her phone rang. Malik. She picked up, the apology ready to leap from her lips.

"Why aren't you at work?" Malik started.

"I'll be right in."

"Good." He hung up. Martha would have to wait. Lycanthropy did not pay the bills.

She threw on a skirt, blouse, and pulled her hair back in a tight ponytail to hide the many clumps of her missing hair. Ever since she first turned, her hair had been slowly disappearing, like a chemo patient. One day, if she didn't fix her situation, her hair would vanish forever. It was an inevitability she was scared of, cause in her mind she thought, *what makes a woman more than her hair?* Her boobs, sure, but Yig had never had much in the boobs department. Nothing more than baseballs under her bra. Her hair, though, she could control. She could keep it clean and well combed, and she could use the right conditioners and pay for the hair stylists. She could keep it long like a model on the cover of Vogue. But once her hair started falling out, well, there was nothing to be done except buy a wig, and that thought made her shudder.

Walking into Cerberus's headquarters, Yig was thrown back into the day-to-day that she had seemingly forgone ever since she visited Dr. Carter's office during an evening thunderstorm. She presumed she'd been fired from the company. She had tested their leave policy when her grandfather went missing. (Was murdered.) She had been away without even a phone call for two days. Most companies would fire her for not calling in by the second day. She was shocked her badge worked on the badge reader.

The shock was nothing like what she would find upstairs.

Everything was different when viewed through electro-sensory perception. She could feel the electricity in the air, and it wasn't just the servers on the fifth floor. The place was abuzz with activity, an expression she had never fully realized until that day. She could literally see the difference between the people who were weak of spirit and the people who were strong. So when her team met her at her office cube, Keiko holding a paper that she started to read as Yig approached, Yig stopped her after her first sentence: "Yig Slaton, you are our supervisor, and we enjoy working on this project, but..."

"Stop," Yig said.

"But," Steve said.

"No." Yig held out her finger. "The world is full of sharks and minnows, as the old game goes." She perused their electricity. "And clearly, you are all minnows. I will not cater to the demands from the bottom of the food chain. You all had assignments when I last e-mailed you. Either you have finished your tasks, or you are behind. Every day was a chance to excel. Did you? The inaugural flight is only a few weeks away, so you better have. Otherwise, I will put you on a Performance Enhancement Plan. Or worse." She left them to consider what worse could be.

Her team scattered. On her desk was a prototype of the quadcopter that would be used for the first flight. She held it up and examined the model, making notes of questions for the engineers. She felt Malik's electricity long before he crossed to her desk.

"Riggs has requested you in her office," Malik said. He was acting differently. The two of them had always had a repertoire, a camaraderie. But now he was distant and cold. His electricity felt cold, too. No, different. So as they stood in the foyer waiting for the elevator, she pressed up close to him and tried to read him. Her body wavered in front of Malik, who was pressed against the wall trying to get away from her.

"Not so fast, landchum," she said. She jabbed her arm in his way so that he could not escape. Her other hand wandered from his neck toward his waist, stopping at the side of his stomach.

"Pancreatic cancer," she said ominously. "God, I'm sorry, Malik."

"How'd you know? Did you sneak into HR?"

"I guessed. You don't have long to live, either."

"The doctor gives me six months or more."

"He's giving you too much time. If your doctor could see what I can see, your doctor'd tell you it's time to take that dream vacation. Now."

The elevator dinged, and Yig climbed in while a gray-faced Malik asked her again where she got her information. She felt badly for him, but there was nothing she could do. She left him stunned and without any answers on the fourth floor while she went up to the top.

Yig looked into the elevator's mirrored walls and saw Martha staring back at her. Martha watched her with those dead eyes. Yig did not turn from her gaze, but met it straight on.

The elevator opened. Yig walked across the penthouse lobby. The same impeccably beautiful receptionist addressed Yig as she entered the foyer.

"Ms. Slaton, Riggs is in her office. She said to go on in when you arrived."

She liked how everybody called her CEO Riggs. It made her more approachable, and Riggs was always approachable, unless she didn't want you around. She was like a kennel master that way. As long as she wanted your attention, you were free to give it, but if she sent you outside, you had to wait at the back door until she was ready to let you back in.

The admin got the door for Yig. Walking inside, Yig was reminded that Riggs' office was larger than her first apartment. Riggs was facing the window. She turned around and smiled at Yig, who shrunk from her as soon as she saw her. The sanguine body movement, the dark eyes, the perfectly bald head.

"The Mother," Yig almost said. The Mother cut her off as she sent the admin away. He closed the door behind him, leaving the two alone.

"I should have guessed it was you."

"Careful, daughter. Watch your tone with Mother. After all, A is for Allison eaten by sharks. I'd hate to skip all the way to Y."

"So she is dead."

"Haven't you learned yet that death is as fluid as the ocean current? Or do you not remember that you are the granddaughter of a grindylow?"

"How did you know?"

"I hovered there in the water beneath your grandfather's boat when those second-class slayers did their foul deed. As I listened to them murder your grandfather, I felt a coldness growing in my stomach. I wanted vengeance for what they were doing to our kind. Do you know what we call them in our world? Skintoxins, because wherever they take their skins, they are a pollution. You can smell their sickness wherever they appear in the water. It is like sweat and disease and coral blight all combined together. I thought about ramming the boat and devouring them right then and there. It was stupid of them to be out in the open water. I could have killed them so easily. But I didn't. It wasn't just that their taste would have been so bad it would have been like slurping oil. I had another feast to attend, and a summons to answer. Later, when I came ashore, I saw you and your parents on television. I knew what you were before you had an inkling, child."

"You were weak, then. Like a baby bird that has fallen from the nest and broken her wing. I didn't need ESP to see the damage in your leg. The best thing to do would be to eat you, but my heart went out to you the same way your heart goes out to the baby bird. My little employee, the daughter of a grindylow. I knew I could do better than put a cast on your broken wing. I could heal you, and while I could not fix your family, I could offer you a new one. So I waited for you to come to me. That's the only way it works, you see. And came you did. You and that boy went out on the water. I knew better than to attack you when you were with the others. For my plan to work, I needed you alone. So I got rid of the skintoxin, and I nestled you like a child to my bosom. I lovingly bit you to make you my daughter, and you drank my blood, and then some fishermen found you. I could not finish what I started, so I had to locate you onshore. It wasn't very hard. You're never too far from water on an island. Had to get rid of that witch who wanted to kill you. You're welcome, by the way. You fled, and I had to catch you so that I could finish the ritual and make you…perfection."

Yig put her hand back on the table to hold herself upright. Suddenly, she remembered the bite, and she remembered dying in the murky Galveston Bay waters. With the full moon above her, she suckled at the Mother's breast and drank her blood. The blood that was in her now.

"God," Yig said as she backed away from the Mother.

"Better. And now that you've healed, I need to raise you. You must learn to hunt, and what better place for a pup to learn than in the cut-throat world of Cerberus?"

The Mother collected her narrow over-the-shoulder purse, then reached out to Yig. Her touch felt like coming home after a long trip abroad. Things that had been forgotten were new again and brought a warm smile to her lips: the honey cream nectar of nostalgia. But the nostalgia was for something she had never experienced before, because she had never known the Mother until a few weeks ago.

Riggs said, "A mother's comfort is never truly forgotten, no matter how dark the hour of conception."

Yig leaned back.

Riggs breathed into Yig's ear, "Martha. Wakey, wakey!"

CHAPTER EIGHTEEN: A GIRL NEVER ALONE GOES HOME

She walked with a swagger and a smirk back to her office. She opened up Outlook and typed an e-mail:

I am giving you all notice. You think you're here to win. That's the word. Win. You want to rise up in the company, make more money, get better perks, the company car, the million-dollar guarantee for surviving The Forge. But after eighteen long months here, I can tell you that winning looks a lot more like surviving. You undercut, you bicker, you try to prove why everybody else is wrong when you should be trying to prove why you are right. Our company has it backwards, and that goes all the way to the top. So I'm here to serve every damn one of you fleshlings notice: I'm going to set things right. I'm going to do better than you, and if you try to cross me, I will bite your fucking head off.

She sent it to Cerberus:All, then leaned back in her chair and grinned.

Malik was the first one to come up to her. He barged out of his office so fast, his door slammed against the wall. She'd never seen him move like that.

"What the hell, Yig?" He wasn't looking for a response.

"Not Yig. Something so much better."

"I don't care. You're so done here. I've seen mental breakdowns before. God knows we all thought you were having one of the most sensationalistic ones with everything that was going on with your grandfather, but this is outrageous. Put your things in a box. No, wait. Don't. I will get somebody to do that for you. Hand over your badge."

"No."

Malik's incredulous expression was worth it alone. By then, several other employees had gathered around her and Malik.

"You can't say no to me. I'm your supervisor. Now give me your badge." He reached for her ID badge, which hung from a lanyard around her neck. She slapped his hand hard enough to leave a red mark.

"I said no. The company doesn't work that way. You can't fire me on the spot."

"Like hell I can't."

"It's in my contract. There must be an HR review before any changes in job status, so no, you can't fire me. And one more thing: you even think of putting your hand on me again, and I'll break every bone in your fingers."

Malik thought about it.

With everybody watching, she reached out and grabbed his hand. She twisted it hard. Malik cried out as he was forced to the ground, his tie whirling around him as he crumpled.

"Yig, don't!"

It was Bobbi. She had a pile of papers in her hands. "Malik's a nice guy."

"Are you really a nice guy, Malik?"

"Go ahead," he said. "Break my fingers. Then I'll sue *your ass* for everything you got. You'll be broke. You'll never work again. So go ahead. Break my fingers and throw away your career."

She leaned in close. "You sound like a silly little guppy when you try to threaten me. And do you know what happens to little guppies who don't know the order of the food chain?"

"Go to Hell."

She twisted his hand.

Bones snapped.

Malik yelled out in pain.

"Oh, sorry! What was it you were saying?"

"I'm going to sue you for fucking everything. Look around you. See all those people? They're called witnesses, asshole."

She smiled and broke another finger. "You overestimate your position."

"Somebody call security!"

"Please do," she said, turning to the others. By then, most of her team was there, too. She looked at them and said, "Then we'll have us a grand time. Or you can walk away from this, and after I take Malik's position, I'll remember you all when it comes time for Christmas bonuses. How does F-150s sound to everyone?"

Slowly, the people started to turn back to their cubes. They walked away in ones and twos at first, then the rest of the group left. Only Malik, Bobbi, and she remained in the area.

"You want something better than an F-150?" she asked Bobbi.

"I want my friend back."

"No, you want something else. Go to Malik's office and wait for me. We'll talk later."

Bobbi went to Malik's office and closed the door behind her.

"Let go of my arm!" Malik shouted.

Another bone snapped. Malik howled. Martha spun him around and grabbed his other hand and began to twist.

"I'll leave you your pinky if you shut up, Malik. But say one thing more, and I'll take every last finger on both yer hands."

Malik cried quietly to himself.

Martha said, "The Forge Is Where Good Customer Relations Are Made, Malik. I've been changing, and today, I made a great mother fucking breakthrough. Revolutionary. It comes with some great perks, too. One of those perks is the ability to control my pheromones. It helps me control the people around me. People just can't help being convinced by my logic, even when it is as insane as 'ignore the man whose hand I'm breaking.'" Malik started to say something, but she cut him off with a withering look. She released him, and he slumped into a chair, cradling his broken hand. It looked corpse-like next to him, like bones splayed in every direction.

"Every Day Is A Chance To Excel, Malik. Now, you have no witnesses, and no play. So what you're gonna do is first, you're gonna go see a doctor and get those bones splinted. When the doctor asks, you'll tell them that you broke your fingers when you fell on some steps. Then you're going to schedule a visit with Riggs, where you'll convince her I should have your position."

"Why don't I just walk away and leave you to deal with this mess?"

"Because, Malik, I'm going to keep you along as my little Renfield. Every monster needs an Igor. You're going to help me take this place apart. That'll be your little middle finger to a world that's robbed you of everything you ever wanted. Cause deep down, I see a man who did everything he was supposed to do to get ahead, but still got fucked in the end. Sound good to you?"

Malik thought about her direction. "Okay. You and me."

"No, just me. I'll keep you as my Igor as long as it suits me. Now, fly away to the hospital."

Malik got up, holding his broken hand, the fingers clawed up next to his body. They were angled like buildings from a Lovecraft story, where the buildings all assume strange and asymmetrical positions and seem to be drawn into non-Euclidian directions.

Martha came up behind him. "One more thing, Malik. I warned you what would happen if you spoke." With two swift movements, she crunched the rest of Malik's fingers.

Bobbi waited in Malik's office, nervously picking at bits of dead skin around her cuticles. Malik had a curio on his desk. It was made to look like a sleeping black-and-white cat. It even had a little device that would push up and down to simulate breathing. Bobbi thought it was an odd little thing because it looked so lifelike. She began to pet the little robot cat. She went back to picking at her cuticles. Then Malik screamed, and she jerked, ripping out a cuticle from her index finger and drawing blood. She cursed, then grabbed a tissue from Malik's desk and held it to her finger.

"Oh, blood," Martha said. Bobbi hadn't heard her come in. Startled, she jumped.

"What are you doing, Yig?"

Martha smiled when she heard the other name mentioned out loud. She approached Bobbi and held her hand out. Bobbi put her bleeding finger in Martha's hand. Martha put her mouth around the finger and gingerly sucked the blood out.

"What is going on?"

"I've got a job for you."

"I don't want your job. I want you to act normal. You haven't acted normal since we went dancing."

"I'm more me than I've been in a long time. Stop hiding behind our friendship like it's some kind of emotional shield. You're here for the same reason as everybody else. You want to make your 18 months and get the million-dollar stock exchange plan. And since you worked in recruiting, and Malik was also the manager over your supervisor, that makes you technically one of my employees now, so I can assign you any task I want, and you have to take it."

"What do you want me to do?" she asked nervously.

"Recruiting. Cerberus needs to bring in a lot of employees. At least a hundred."

"What for? I haven't heard of any new hiring campaigns."

"I'm not looking for co-eds."

"What are you looking for, then?"

"Temporary workers. Homeless people, runaways, illegal immigrants. Discretely, I want you to run a campaign to attract these people from Houston, Beaumont, Port Aransas, everywhere. Tell them we have free housing and food, no questions asked."

"Why would we want to hire homeless people? Where will we house them? Here?"

"No, of course not. The warehouse where the drones are being built has more than enough room. And don't worry about what I need them for. Just tell them it is a mix of menial labor and office work."

"We've never done anything like this, Yig. I wouldn't know where to start."

"If Your Feet Aren't In the Fire, You Aren't Working Hard Enough."

"Right. Okay. But what's in it for me?"

"Not what, but who."

"I don't understand."

"There was a time when girls went to college to meet their future husbands. Get their MRS degree. We don't do that crap anymore, not really. We don't want to believe that we do that. We are woman, hear us fucking roar, right? So instead, we first get our degrees, and then we get positions where we can hopefully meet our future husbands because it's what's expected of us. How can we look each other in the eye if we aren't doing everything to be the best we can be while doing what we really want? Hold down a career, put our lures out online and at work, catch the right person, and nurture the relationship that'll feed our need for a lifetime."

"Well, that's a very appalling way of putting it."

"So cut the bullshit, Bobbi. You know where most people meet the man of their dreams? Through friends. You do this for me, I'll introduce you to people."

"You've never been a people person. You barely date as it is."

"That's the old me. The new me swims with a lot more people. I'm on the up and up, Bobbi. Are you riding with me? Or do you want to keep left-swiping every night?"

Bobbi waited a whole three seconds before she agreed.

By noon, Martha had lunched with a senior VP of International Development, who "liked her spirit" as well as the deep blackness of her eyes. He was tall and blond, and had a commanding personality. Just the sort of character that the always-affable Bobbi gravitated to. He was also married, but Martha knew ways to correct that problem.

By 2, Malik was back in the building with splints on his hands. He found that his office was no longer his office. Over lunch, admins had switched his belongings with Martha's. She now sat in his office. Behind her desk, she had placed a motivational poster. It showed a giant-mouthed shark about to snatch its jaws on a little fish. "Ambition" the poster read "If You Can't Swim With The Big Fish, Stay Out Of The Water."

By 4, Martha was meeting with Riggs' executive staff and showing off her shark bite. There were two men there whom she thought had potential for Bobbi. They were maybe a little more domineering than Bobbi preferred, but Martha liked them, so she asked them out for drinks. Even the married man said yes. She liked her pheromones.

She also pushed up the schedule on the drone flight test to three days away to coincide with the full moon.

Her bosses were very impressed.

By 6, she had given her team the new date on the flight test. They were beside themselves in frustration. She quoted The Forge to them. "If You Can't Stand The Heat, Get Out Of The Kitchen."

By 7, she was ready to head out for drinks with the senior executive staff. She finished her e-mail, logged off the computer, and walked out, only to find Belén in a red hoodie waiting for her outside her office door and carrying a silver knife. Belén shoved her back inside and closed the door behind her.

"How the fuck did you get in this building?"

"Check your records. I've been working here for months."

"Well, you're fired. In fact, consider your termination permanent." Martha's mouth split at the ends as she exposed her shark teeth. Belén raised her knife.

"I broke loose from your jacket of silver chains. What makes you think that little butter knife's going to do anything to me?"

"Cause silver still hurts like hell." She raked the knife across Martha's forearm. The wereshark inhaled sharply as she sneered at the hunter.

"I should kill you."

"I was sent to kill you."

"But you're not gonna kill me. Otherwise, you'd have brought something more deadly than your butter knife."

"I believe this is something you can control, Yig. You are more powerful than this thing."

Martha frowned.

"I'm not talking to Yig anymore, am I?"

Martha smiled. Shook her head slow and easy.

"Yig, you have to fight this thing inside you. You have to regain control. Lycanthropes are two sides to the same coin, something you can choose to give up on, or something you can fight to control."

"You say Yig one more time, and I'm going to shove that pretty little brown face of yours down my gullet."

"Fine. What do I call this monster in front of me?"

"Martha."

"Martha, you don't have to kill tonight."

"Who said I was going to kill anyone? I was going to have drinks with a few men, maybe do a little diddling with one of them, and then— oh, hell. You're right. Somebody's head was going to get eaten. There ain't nothing quite like the sensation of a head rolling around in your throat, especially when it's still screaming inside you. It tickles..." While she spoke, her shark-like jaws slid out of her lips and hung in the air.

"You don't scare me, Martha."

"Your electric scent tells a different story, little girl."

Belén reached into her hoodie and pulled out a crucifix on a long chain. "I want you to wear this tonight."

Martha laughed.

"It will keep you from killing again."

"I'm not a vampire, girlie."

"No, you're a thinking, rationalizing creature. So you know I'm speaking the truth when I say it will prevent you from killing tonight. Or do your extra sensory perceptions tell you I'm lying? Is my heart racing? Is the smell of lies on my tongue?"

Martha didn't respond. Belén reached toward the broken face with the soulless eyes and the hanging jaw. She had to tiptoe to reach over Martha's head. They were as close as lovers now, about to embrace in a deadly kiss. With her flesh just inches away from the shark's teeth, Belén placed the crucifix over Martha's head and around her neck.

Martha held up the metal crucifix. It shined in her black eyes.

"I don't feel no different, landchum."

"But the spell has been cast. You will not kill tonight."

Belén backed out of the office, hopeful and praying.

CHAPTER NINETEEN: CIRCLING THE WAGONS

The fire of the hearth flung the black silhouettes of Belén, Vara de Moses, and the lycan hunter on the stone walls, where they curved and distorted to fit the contours of crosses, skulls, and chrism jars: the many relics and trophies from the Treviño family's long history of hunting the unholy.

"Enough of this," the lycan hunter said. "I will take care of this wereshark."

Belén said, "But I gave her the crucifix. That will stop her, at least for tonight."

"And what of the full moon?" Vara de Moses demanded. "Days away, and the Mother is on the island. She's been here, in our house, Belén."

"Yes, but still…"

Vara made a clicking sound in his throat as he swiped his hand angrily over his sister. "I gave you a chance to fix what you started, and instead you put a Band-Aid where a tourniquet is needed?"

"This is what you get for relaxing your grip," the lycan hunter said.

"Katrina, this is our island. You are a guest here." Vara said.

"A guest? I was sent here by New York. I'm not a guest. I'm here to make sure your mess doesn't spread inland," the lycan hunter said. Katrina was a blond woman taller than everyone else in the room. She had fair skin and crystalline eyes. She wore a jacket and blue jeans over a scuba suit. The jacket was stitched together from the skins of the various werecreatures Katrina had killed. So while one patch might be the pure black of an alpha wolf from Wyoming, it would be stitched to the striped hide of a weretiger from India, which was itself stitched to the thick fur of an Alaskan werebear, and so on and so on. Looped to her belt was a machete and a Magnum.

"What do we do now?" Belén asked.

"Nothing. I have waited long enough," Katrina said. "I will kill the beast."

"But what if there is a chance to save her?" Belén interjected. "Doesn't the church preach redemption?"

"Redemption doesn't exist for devils, Belén," Katrina said.

Just then, a knock came at the Treviño's front door.

Vara de Moses checked the security camera on his phone.

"It's one of those commie scientists from the Carfax Society," Vara de Moses said.

"What are they doing here?" Belén said.

"Belén, get rid of them," Vara de Moses said. "Katrina and I will discuss our next step. Tell Dr. Carter nothing."

After Belén left the room, Katrina pulled out a map of Galveston and unfurled it on the grand family table. The large table was black and heavy, with claws for feet.

"We can still salvage this, Vara. You and your sister can help me with killing this new wereshark. We will use it as bait for the Mother."

Just then, Belén burst through the door with Dr. Carter and Dr. Talbot from the Carfax Society.

"What is the meaning of this?" Vara demanded. "*Mija*, I told you to get rid of them. What are they doing in here?"

"These men have important news from the Carfax Society."

Vara de Moses waved them in. "We have rarely allowed outsiders into our sanctum sanctorum, doctors, so this better be good."

Dr. Carter said, "Thank you, sir. We have long been wary of each other on this island, and we do our best to stay out of each other's way…"

"Though more often than not, you interfere with our duties to the Church," Vara said. "There is a lot of that going around."

Dr. Carter paused to absorb the insult, then said, "I will get to the point. My name is Dr. Lynne Carter. This is Dr. James Talbot."

"What happened to his arm?"

"He was bitten by a wereshark. The wereshark. We are all that is left of the Carfax Society on the island. The rest have either been killed or fled. Our members are leaving because a wave of destruction is about to hit Galveston."

Vara de Moses smiled like a father who has been approached by a child with a Chicken Little story. He nodded to Dr. Carter to continue.

"I know this seems unbelievable, but we have aerial footage of dozens and dozens of sharks swimming around the island. More are coming. We believe that these are all weres summoned by the Mother."

"Not summoned, Dr. Carter," Katrina said. "They follow her wherever she goes."

To Dr. Talbot, she raised her hand and removed a glove. Underneath, only her thumb and index finger remained. All the rest had been bitten off. "It's how handy we become after we've been kicked down," she said to him. "Werebear."

He stared at her, a pale, sweaty look on his face, but he nodded.

Belén recited, saying, *"When the silver of the moon touches the black of the water, the waters will run red with blood."*

"You must understand that something really bad is about to hit this island, and when it does, it will be like nothing you have ever seen."

Vara looked to the lycan hunter.

"If you kill the Mother, the others will leave," Katrina said. "I have done it before, and I have seen the results. They will retreat to the ocean once the Mother is dead."

"*If* you can kill the Mother," Dr. Carter said.

"I have been studying weres all my life, Dr. Carter. I have killed Mothers and Fathers, and I can kill this one, too."

"Dr. Carter, you say that if the Mother came ashore, it would be like nothing we have ever seen," Vara de Moses said. "This is because your Carfax Society has only been around since 1905. The Malleus Maleficarum is older by centuries, and we have all the wisdom and knowledge of the Catholic Church behind us. There is precedent for this, Dr. Carter. Over a hundred years ago, before your vampire problem in England, many monsters surrounded this island. My family did everything we could to stop them, but we had neither the technology nor the techniques that we have today. The monsters came ashore riding a hurricane, and they killed thousands. I lost many members of my family that night."

"You're saying the Galveston Hurricane of 1900 was caused by weresharks?"

"Something else, though still supernatural, caused the island's destruction in 1900. I am saying that we have seen this kind of behavior before, and we are better prepared for it. We can stop it."

"If you stop the Mother," Katrina said. "That's a pretty big if."

Belén said, "The Mother is not the key. Yig is."

"Yig?" Dr. Carter asked.

"She's been taken over by a wereshark. As a first generation descendent, Yig can challenge the Mother."

"There's something you need to understand about Yig," Dr. Carter said. "She has a complicated past. There's more to her than being a wereshark."

"She is part grindylow. We know."

"What? No. She is?"

"What is it you wanted to tell us?" Vara de Moses asked.

Dr. Carter looked at Dr. Talbot, who motioned his support with his hands.

"What I am about to tell you breaks client privilege, but this goes beyond the common laws of the world, I think. Yig suffers from Dissociative Identity Disorder, what used to be called Multiple Personality Disorder. Her disorder was triggered by a memory of her grandfather, which I think I am finally starting to understand much better than I ever did before. When a person like Yig, who was already prone to anxiety disorder, is put into extreme scenarios, her mind creates different identities, what we call alters, to absorb certain trauma-inducing memories. The goal of treatment is for the patient to confront and accept the memories, and also to assimilate their identities. This is harder than you can imagine. DID usually doesn't work alone. Schizophrenia, bipolar disorder, all these usually coincide in the mind of the afflicted."

Dr. Carter looked around the room. All eyes were on him, so he continued. "So it isn't as simple as making her accept the wereshark. For her, the wereshark will be much more amplified than it is in a normal person. She will see it as another identity."

"Martha," Belén said. "She said her name was Martha."

Dr. Carter's hand absently covered his mouth. "She is probably suffering from fugues, blackouts. She may think she is possessed."

"Did you say possessed? We can exorcise demons," Vara said with pride.

Dr. Carter believed him. "It must be done carefully. We must get her to accept the alter of the wereshark. Then she can confront the Mother."

"And if she does not?" Vara said.

"Then I will kill her," Katrina said.

CHAPTER TWENTY: FEEDING FRENZY

The *Aglaea* was an 80-foot fiberglass yacht with room for up to fifteen guests and thirty crew. Like the Internet tycoon who owned it, the yacht was both efficient and eccentric. It was a gas motor cruiser with a swimming pool, slide-out porch, and palm trees submerged into the hull. Normally used for entertaining guests for Cerberus (Riggs technically did not own the yacht), it was now being used to test Cerberus' newest innovation, the Naval Drone Delivery System. As such, the boat was anchored 1 mile offshore.

One hundred yards away from the Aglaea, Martha stood on the bridge of the *Hallelujah Goat*, a large dual-hull catamaran. The catamaran's steadiness was ideal for videotaping the delivery. Three video cameras would watch over the first-time naval delivery service system's flight. Two drones would record the service from the air.

The *Hallelujah Goat's* living quarters had been transformed into a secondary mission control from which Martha and her team could watch all cameras and diagnostics from the drone.

"Don't you think this is overkill?" Malik asked from his position beside Martha. Both his hands were in casts. One was stroking his little robot cat that he kept in his office, the one made to look like it was breathing while sleeping.

Martha smiled as she twirled the crucifix in her fingers. "We are pioneers of the Internet Age. We thrive on overkill."

Martha toggled through various cameras positioned on board the *Aglaea*. Devon and Emmett from her team were onboard the *Aglaea*. They would intervene if there were any problems with the drone's landing. They had volunteered to man the Aglaea because they were engaged and wanted to spend as much time together as possible.

"And going all out included filling your boss's boat with homeless people?"

"You got a feisty mouth today, Malik, especially considering how our last encounter went. The homeless people are paid actors. I dressed them to look like hardy sea types, which will give the video an authentic look." Malik wasn't so sure of Martha's intentions, but he kept his mouth shut.

"Three...two...one...the drone is away," Keiko announced from the Cerberus headquarters in downtown Galveston. Steve was piloting the drone, which had been dubbed the 'Cerberus 1.' The view from the drone showed Galveston falling beneath it while the drone rose up in the air.

"How's wind?" Martha asked her small crew on the *Hallelujah Goat*. From his console, the weather advisor (a local news channel meteorologist—Riggs loved that touch) said, "Winds at 5 miles per hour from the west. We should be good. This is a beautiful evening for a launch."

"Of course it is," Martha said. "It's the magic hour. Isn't that what cinematographers call it? This is gonna look great on YouTube, and perhaps in a television ad one day."

The drone, which had nine rotors, whooshed over Galveston, the iron-on-sandstone logo of Cerberus emblazoned on the side of the drone. Two drones followed it from the two o'clock and seven o'clock positions to capture Cerberus 1 in the best light.

Back at Cerberus headquarters, Keiko was surrounded by a crowded group of enthusiastic Cerberus employees gathered in a conference room that had been transformed into their mission control. Everyone wore newly purchased Cerberus team polo shirts. Steve worked off a desktop interfaced to the drone's joystick controls.

Several large screens showed the same camera angles that Martha saw from onboard the *Hallelujah Goat*. Cameras had been set up around the conference room to capture the drama and emotion from the crowd's point of view.

Keiko put her hand on Steve and said, "Whatever you do, don't crash the drone."

Steve wet his lips. His eyes never left his monitor, which showed the X, Y, and Z axis for the drone. For the first delivery demonstration, Steve was manually piloting the CERBERUS-1. Later, the intent was for computerized piloting systems to guide the drone delivery system.

On the catamaran, one of the screens showed Riggs, who was watching from her executive office. Riggs was in her chair sipping champagne. She leaned in close to the camera and said, "For what it's worth, Yig, I'm really excited about this. Some might say you are changing the future of the Internet here. I believe you're changing the world."

"Thank you," Martha said, though she maintained that sinister smile that crossed her face when somebody called her Yig. She brushed back what little remained of her hair as the drone flew out over the seawall and entered the big blue.

"Keep it steady," Martha said on her intercom to Steve.

"You got it, boss. ETA is two minutes."

"What is that in the water?" Malik asked. He pointed one of his club hands to the screen showing the entire width of the Aglaea. He poked at the screen console controller, saying, "I saw something near the boat. Can you go back to the camera that is flying behind the Cerberus 1?"

The screen console controller placed the requested camera angle on the main screen. The Cerberus 1 was slowing down before it began its descent onto the Aglaea. Both the yacht and the catamaran appeared on the lower end of the screen. The Gulf water scintillated like fish scales in the fading light. The boats mirrored themselves in the water, like two worlds coming together, the world of air and the world of water.

"There it is!" Malik pointed to an iconic black triangle emerging from the watery depths near the yacht. "Zoom in. I think there are sharks in the water."

"Who cares?" Martha responded dismissively. "We aren't swimming here."

"But there's more, I swear."

"I see three shark fins," the console operator said. "Should we be worried about that? Those sharks aren't far from us."

"Don't abort," Martha said. "And don't be overly concerned. I'm the only one here who's actually been bitten by a shark, and you don't see me dancing around like a 1950s housewife running from a mouse, do you? Keep yer eye on that drone."

On the deck of the *Aglaea*, Devon and Emmett stood hand-in-hand, watching the drone descend. Its bright red package container was like Rudolph's nose in a snowstorm. They hoped it would lead them to riches and fortune, and maybe a little Central Texas bungalow for them and their baby, when they finally decided to have one. As the Cerberus 1 began its descent, some of the "crew" strayed to the yacht's edge. They were pointing over the sides.

"Hey, guys, we need you over here," Emmett said to them.

He thought that they must not be able to hear him over the ocean spray because they didn't come away from the rails, so Emmett crossed the deck to remind them of what they were getting paid to do.

"What's going on?" he asked. "You all need to return to your positions. The Cerberus 1 is almost here." He grabbed the sleeve of a homeless man, who muttered "Tiburon," and pointed to the water.

Emmett looked into the water and gasped at what he saw. He knew nothing of sharks beyond Jaws, Sharknado, and a few minutes of Shark Week. The fact that they weren't all cold-blooded stalkers of humanity mattered little to him in that moment. An icy dread spread up and down his back. He counted six, each one as long as a sedan. He ran to the far side of the boat.

"What are you doing, Emmet?" Devon called out. "We need to be in our places."

Emmett saw ten sharks on the southern-facing side of the yacht.

"They're everywhere," he said.

"Fuck that," said the homeless man nearest Emmett. "They're circling for the kill."

Emmett pushed down on the panic rising up inside of him. That allowed him to concentrate and remember something he had learned from Shark Week.

He said, "Sometimes sharks are attracted to the electricity in the motors. Don't worry about too much about this. Get back in position. It is crucial that you guys are in this shot. Otherwise, it doesn't sell it."

But the men wouldn't move until he led them by the arm back to their positions.

The cameras from the drones showed the Cerberus 1 descending on a sleek vessel manned by salt-of-the-earth men. A giant board with "C1" painted on it marked the landing spot. The Cerberus 1 made a perfect touchdown, but instead of crewmen waving cheerily to the drone system like they were having a perfect Buy-the-World-A-Coke moment, the crew were dashing to the sides of the yacht and looking overboard. One man screamed. Another barfed.

The drone released the small box from its capture mechanism right on top of the C1 logo. A beautiful young, techy-looking woman in glasses (Devon) approached the package as the Cerberus 1 ascended like an angel back into the air with a perfect take-off. As it lifted up, its entry/descent/landing camera showed the large C1 logo on the yacht, and a seaman running across the pad and to the yacht's cabin.

"Guess we'll be editing that out," Martha grumbled.

While everyone else was getting ready for the shoot, one of the homeless crew members had snuck down to the lower level of the yacht. There, eating an apple, he found the yacht's majestic swimming pool. The yacht pool was like the stuff that makes Hollywood dreams. A clear blue, serene swimming pool ended with a ledge overlooking the Gulf of

Mexico. From certain angles, it appeared like the swimming pool emptied into the Gulf. He looked around to make sure nobody was watching, then stripped down to his birthday suit and jumped into the pool.

He'd never been good at swimming, but he liked how the warm water felt on his skin, and he liked how it weighted down the hair in his beard and made it less shaggy. He could practically feel the dirt dissolving off his body. It was a wholly cleansing experience unlike any he could remember. He washed the chlorine over his face and under his armpits, then over his balls.

While enjoying the bliss, he felt something he hadn't felt since the time he worked as a cowboy in the Rockies. He used to move cattle for a ranch, and he remembered how out West he could feel the presence of a mountain. A mountain wasn't like other pieces of land. With a mountain, the sun could start to go down, and you could feel its cold shadow absorb you. He hadn't felt anything like that since working the ranch, but he sure as shit felt it now. The cold embrace, the looming presence of something bigger and more powerful than yourself.

Slowly, the homeless man turned around. A mountain of a wereshark loomed over him like a Lovecraftian god, grinning at its dinner. The homeless man knew he was going to die. Had his long story led him all these years to this moment? Was he to be nothing more than shark meal?

A second shark jumped out of the water and crashed on top of the homeless man, snapping its mouth around his torso and cutting him in half. Chomp! Chomp! The torso of the man disappeared into the shark's wide mouth. Beneath the shark, two naked legs and a pair of balls cleaner than they'd been in years sank to the bottom of the pool beneath a cloud of blood.

The two weresharks climbed on board.

"Dammit, those homeless people are ruining the shots," Martha growled.

"This is what happens when you rush things," Malik shot out as he took over the lead console. "We should have taken our time to figure out the shots, and we definitely shouldn't have hired homeless people to act for us."

But Martha had other things on her mind. Even from here, Martha could smell the fresh release of blood from the homeless man in the swimming pool, and she could sense the critical mass of electricity churning in the water. These sharks had been waiting a long time to feed, and now there was blood. She needed to join the frenzy before it started.

Malik radioed the captain of the *Aglaea*. The microphone was awkward to manipulate with his hands in casts, so the console worker helped him. "Captain Winters, we are picking up a large school of sharks around the boats. The 'extras' in the video shoot are getting nervous. Could you have your men check on them and assure them everything's okay?"

"Copy that," Captain Winters said from the pilot room.

"Thank you," Malik replied. He looked to the console worker and exhaled. "This is going to be a rough day." Then, to Martha, he said, "We're going to have to re-attempt the landing when the extras have been calmed down. On the plus side, the drone made it. Congratulations, Yig, your delivery system works."

Riggs signaled Martha from her office.

"Congratulations, Yig, but we can redo the shot, right? Cause that looked like a mess absolutely so big and so deep and so tall."

"We'll do it right away."

"Good pup."

Martha told Keiko and Steve to redo the landing, and then she left the room.

"Where you going?" Malik asked. "You can't leave now."

"You'll handle this, and you'll report it directly to Riggs. That gives you pull you've always coveted but never had in your short life."

Malik drew back, like a snail's eyestalk when touched. Only Martha knew about his cancer. "And you?"

Martha removed the crucifix from around her neck and draped it over Malik's shoulders. "I think my time in this position is about to end."

"The problem is getting on and off this island," Belén said to Vara, Katrina, and the doctors of the Carfax Society. Dr. Carter and Talbot watched the show from a feed they'd pirated from one of the Cerberus 1's cameras. "Most people would think to take a speed boat, if they had one, and drive out to the yacht. Problem is, we would be driving through wereshark-infested waters."

"So how do we get out there?" Dr. Carter asked.

"*We* don't. You stay here," Vara de Moses said. "The Malleus Maleficarum has prepared for such events."

"What? Do you have your own helicopter or something?"

"Or something," Belén said.

Captain Winters was used to odd requests from Cerberus. He had made trips to the Bahamas and Cancun almost at the drop of a hat, once through inclement weather. Another time, he'd had to talk a Miami man out of calling the cops because he thought he'd seen a pound of cocaine in the crew quarters. He never told that story, but he did have several stories about picking up and dropping off boys at docks, which he was willing to tell when somebody bought him his beer. All this is to say that Captain Winters was used to odd requests, and 'calming down the homeless people onboard' was just another peculiarity of the job to him. It was the price he paid for being an overcompensated limousine driver.

Walking down the side of the boat, he was taken aback by the number of sharks circling the boat. He'd once been on a shark-hunting cruise with Riggs and seen as many as a hundred blacktips schooling around the boat, but most of them were five and seven footers. He was seeing ten and twelve footers here, and they looked like mean bulls. His instinct was to drive the yacht somewhere else, but he had an owner to answer to, and unless Riggs told him to move the boat, he knew he would have to sit there and deal with the situation.

Captain Winters stopped two of the crew and told them about the company's orders.

"What about the sharks?" they asked, looking overboard.

"Don't worry about the sharks. They stay in the water, we stay in the boat. Everybody's happy."

The two crewmen fanned out to search for the homeless people. Captain Winters headed to the back deck where most of the homeless were. He heard a knock from inside the cabins. He thought to draw his pistol, then reminded himself that he was being way too overly cautious. None of the homeless men they had brought on board seemed anything other than willing to do as they were told. They were harmless.

Inside the cabin, he passed the spacious living room and the luxury bedrooms. From down below, he heard a scream.

"Who's there?"

Nobody answered.

"Shit." The captain drew his pistol and ran down the stairs.

The powered paraglider soared over the brown Galveston beaches and banked to the west. The paraglider was a standard colored cage with logo-less chutes. Belén drove, with Vara de Moses and Katrina at her side. Katrina looked like a modern-day pirate in her skinsuit and wereskin jacket and her machete and Magnum strapped to her legs. In the fading light, the waters beneath them seemed to seethe with sharks.

"This isn't going to be easy," Vara said over the radio.

Belén saw the Cerberus 1 flying back toward the Aglaea on its second attempt. The powered paraglider cut the drone's flight path off. She was betting that the drone was worth too much to ram it into her paraglider or rip into its chute. She hoped she was right. Otherwise, it was a plunge into angry shark-infested water.

Once over the yacht, Vara de Moses and Katrina unhooked their rappel lines, which fell fifty feet to the deck of the yacht. They double-checked their hitches, then unstrapped themselves from the paraglider's safety cage. Katrina beat Vara de Moses to the deck, zipping down the line quicker than Belén thought possible. For a woman in her thirties, she was fast. Once the two were on the yacht, they yanked the cord to let Belén know they were down. She retracted the rappel lines and banked away from the yacht.

"So, get the girl, avoid the weresharks. That about sums it up, right?" Vara de Moses said.

"Don't kill anybody who isn't a shapeshifter," Katrina added. They ran toward the cabin, one going left (aft), and the other going right (starboard).

"Yig, get back here," Malik said as Martha turned away. When she did not respond, he reached out and grabbed her hair by the ends of his fingers, which were all that stuck out of casts. As he pulled, a wig came slowly off Martha's bald head.

"Oh. My. God." The hair hung like a whip between his hands. "I am so sorry. I didn't mean to. I didn't know you were getting treatments, too."

"I don't have cancer," Martha growled. Her mouth broke her skull like a scarecrow's grin, like a broken egg, but instead of yolk, blood dripped out of her face. Her eyes blackened, and gills cut into her neck.

Malik tried to run, but Martha grabbed his wrist with her webbed hand. He could hear the bones snapping as her hands lengthened and claws emerged from her dead-white claws. Malik screamed and pulled away, but he was not strong enough to escape the monster's grip.

Martha rose up, stretching her arms outward. As she grew, her clothes shredded around her. "Never touch my hair."

Captain Winters slowly entered the lower cabin. This was the dining room. Somewhere in the dark was a long oak table and chairs for twelve people. Working lights would reveal that the plates and glasses were put away in the cabinet and the silverware (actual silver) was kept in the dresser.

Narrow beams of twilight bled through the portholes and cut into the darkness.

He moved his pistol to his left hand and tried the light switch. He found the switch for Riggs' aquarium instead and turned it on. A shark face watched him with angular, slitted snake eyes, making him jump. Then the little epaulette shark turned around in its tank and swam back among the crevices of the aquarium's plastic reefs.

He heard a noise.

Something moved in the dark.

Captain Winters squinted his eyes while he searched blindly for the light switch again. In the dark, the light of the evening sun floated at the edge of the dark oak table. The tip of something human teased the edge of the light. It was flesh, yes, but what part of the body?

Into the spot of light, a hand slammed down. Bloodless digits quivered in the light, then reached into the dark and pulled itself forward. The hand landed into the neon blue square on the table where the light from the aquarium hit. Captain Winters recognized the square tattoo on the hand. It belonged to Frank, a crewman who did a stint in Huntsville but had turned his life around.

Captain Winters gasped.

In the dark, the beam of twilight continued to float up against the wall. Streaks of crimson blood were highlighted in the golden light.

"Frank."

Captain Winters holstered his pistol and reached for the middle-aged crewman. Frank's hands were cold and clammy in the dark. Captain Winters pulled Frank's body to him, dragging it across the table. As he reached around him, he discovered why Frank was only using the one arm to drag himself across the floor. The other arm was gone, savagely ripped out of the socket. Tattered flesh like torn sheets reached for bone and muscle that were gone forever.

Frank fell off the table, knocking over a chair somewhere in the dark.

"I'm here to help, Frank," Captain Winters assured him. "I'm going to get you off this boat."

"Don't." Frank garbled though his dying lips. "Ru."

"Don't talk, Frank. Save your energy."

"Fru."

Captain Winters pulled Frank to his feet. Frank's torso was cold with blood loss that seeped into the captain's white shirt.

"Sh."

Frank's eyes rolled back in his head. He lost all control of his leg muscles and dropped dead to the floor.

"Shit."

Captain Winters checked Frank's pulse. He was practically jamming his finger in the man's throat vein, but he felt nothing.

Drenched in his friend's blood, he stood up and scanned the room for the murderer.

"I'm gonna kill you," he said coldly, pulling his gun on the dark.

He wanted vengeance, but he was not a fool. He backed up to the stairs. In the blue light of the aquarium, the epaulette shark twirled. Epaulette sharks are spotted like a leopard, with two giant false eyes on their sides. It was the giant black eye that caught Captain Winter's attention. A shape moved behind the aquarium, faster than he could track. Something gray and silent shot at him. Only glimpses of the creature were visible as it cut through the beams of evening light.

A fin.

A tooth.

And then something monstrous leaped into the light of the staircase.

Captain Winters fired on the open mouth as it crashed down on him and dragged him thrashing into the pool of black. Out of the dark, a dozen webbed hands reached to him. The hands gripped him tightly. He couldn't move. They lifted him up and him down on the table.

In the dark, he saw their pale faces like ghosts in the shadows. Then they rushed to him, claws outstretched and mouths agape.

All around him he heard thrashing tails and gnashing teeth.

Captain Winters felt an intense pressure in his legs and arms as more mouths leaped on him. He fired his pistol three times before his hand was bitten off. He screamed at them, but by then, he was screaming at futility. He was already dead. His body was down there on the table, which was now eerily lit by a large light above him. There were six or eight creatures of such shape as to make men go mad. The monsters feasted on him. His right arm was gone. So was his leg. The creature chomping on his leg pulled Captain Winter's pelvis to his mouth.

The others pulled back, and then suddenly they were all on top of his body, writhing and slipping and thrashing their tails. He could barely see himself at the bottom of the feeding frenzy. As the light began pulling him away to hopefully a better place with calm seas and sharkless waters, he saw his body reach to him. A shoulder pushed its way out of the seething mess of shark skin. His head appeared, too. Captain Winters had the kind of face shadow and cleft chin that made movie stars. It was one of the reasons he was hired, even if Riggs never fully admitted it. His fingers reached out to his spirit, but by then, the light was pulling him away, leaving his body in darkness.

The clean ricochet of pistol shots crashed through the air. By the sound of the shot, Katrina knew it came from inside the *Aglaea*. So did

Vara, and so did the homeless people, who started running around, looking for places to hide.

"The lycans are on the boat. Don't go down there," Katrina said.

"People are down there."

"It would be suicide."

Vara pushed a button to extend his staff. The extensions had silver-coated bars. "Not suicide. Martyrdom." Then he charged down into the cabin.

"Shit."

Devon and Emmett approached the lycan hunter from behind. "Excuse me," Devon said, "but what the *fuck* is going on?"

Seeing the Cerberus company logo emblazoned on their clothes, Katrina said, "Your company is run by a lycan, and your yacht is being overrun by weresharks."

"What?"

"Weresharks. Lycanthropes who have the ability to transform into sharks. They've been circling your boat for hours. Now the feeding frenzy has begun. I need to find Yig Slaton. She is the cause of all this."

"Yig? Really?"

"She's not here," Emmett said. "Yig is on the command boat. It's the catamaran about 100 meters away from here."

"Which direction?"

"That way. North of us."

"Okay. Here's what you're going to do: you're going to find a place to hide. Do you know what a Faraday cage is?"

Devon and Emmett nodded. They were clutching onto each other so hard, Katrina thought they looked like they had practically melded into one body. She noticed the ring on Devon's hand. "You need to find one and hide there. If you can't find one, find electrical equipment and get as close to it as you can. It's the only thing that can save you. Weresharks can hear the electricity when you move, when you breathe, when your heart beats. Now go. Run!"

She watched them run back across the dock, hand-in-hand, and hoped it would be enough to save them. Then Katrina radioed Belén.

In the water, the sharks circled wildly, hoping for the kill. The people who had identified them were wrong. There weren't just bull sharks in the water. There were hammerheads, goblins, and even sand tigers. And the electricity in them had been building up throughout the evening. Before long, it would be night, and they would wander back out to deeper waters. But at that moment, in that golden hour, they were tensed up with the ecstasy of the feed. Fins broke into claws and then arms and legs. Once appendages had burst out of their bodies, they began reaching up to the yacht and searching for the grab holds, ladders, and little nooks and crannies for pulling themselves up.

One of the homeless men saw the sharks climbing up to the boat. Seeing his death coming for him in wide-open mouths, he jumped overboard. Like many prey animals who, when confronted with a predator, act without any plan beyond avoiding imminent death, the homeless man had not thought about swimming one mile to shore or the clothes that would bog him down in the hot water.

He also had not considered that there were still very many sharks in the water, and they were all voraciously hungry. Within seconds of entering the water, he was bumped by the first shark. The man cried out as he brushed salt water from his eyes. He was encircled by large triangular fins. They were like teeth themselves, like the open mouth of Charybdis ready to snap shut on him. He could not see well. He rubbed his eyes again. It was just in time to clearly see the open mouth rushing toward him and the teeth, all those pretty teeth. His head popped off. His arms flailed about as arterial blood spurted from his headless body. Then a second shark grabbed him by the legs and pulled him under. More sharks swam at his corpse. The fins cut like knives through the water, and then disappeared down into the Gulf where he disappeared.

Emmett and Devon ran up to the *Aglaea*'s bridge. They found two men who were arguing over whether or not to move the yacht, regardless of the shots fired.

"What is going on out there?" one of the men asked Emmett and Devon when they entered the bridge.

"It wouldn't make any sense if we tried to explain it to you," Devon said. "I'm looking for a Faraday cage. Do you know if there is any chance the boat has one?"

"A what? Listen, we heard shots. Do you know where the captain is?"

"It's a cage with mesh to keep electric currents in or out," Emmett added.

"Screw this. We should just drive it ashore," the other man said. He reached for the wheel, but the other man stepped in front of him.

"We could lose our jobs."

"Fuck that. I don't want to die."

Devon and Emmett shared a look. This was not going to help them. "We need to get to the engines," Devon said. Emmett nodded. They turned to walk out as the first wereshark came over the bow of the yacht and jumped onto the area in front of the bridge.

"Mother Mary of God," the one crewmember said, reaching for his gun. The shark was a vicious-looking goblin wereshark. A long horn jutted from over its black eyes, and its white jaws hung out of its face like the mouth of an alien parasite bulging from the skin of a shark.

The wereshark broke through the glass, its parasite jaws snapping at everyone in the bridge. It hit Devon with one of its arms, knocking her out of the bridge. The two crewmembers opened fire on the shark, but their bullets had no effect on the shark. They might as well have been firing BBs.

The shark bit the one crewmember on the neck. His blood splashed on Emmett's face. The other crewmember pulled his knife and tried stabbing the wereshark, but every time he stabbed the shark, the wound resealed the second he pulled his knife out. The shark bit his hand off and spit out the gun. The man hollered in pain. His legs kicked out, and he fell on the ground. At that moment, Emmett jumped out of the bridge. He landed next to Devon, who had fallen on her back and knocked her breath out. He looked over his shoulder to see if the shark had come for them, too, but by the screams in the bridge and the splashes of blood squirting on the windowpane, he assumed the shark had stopped to devour the crew first.

He picked Devon up and ran for the entrance to the crew quarters and, hopefully, the engine room. Emmett was too freaked out of his mind to see the large hammerhead watching them from the side of the boat. As they re-entered the yacht, the hammerhead followed them.

CHAPTER TWENTY-ONE: MAYHEM

Vara de Moses crossed the cabin, anticipating the attack of the monsters. All his life, he'd been raised to fight the creatures of the night, so he knew to check his corners, scan ahead, and keep a crucifix near him always. As he walked, he recited the prayer his mother taught him, the one in the language of the baptized dead that would force all monsters into the light. As he finished reciting the prayer, more screams came from downstairs. Most people would have run, but Vara was a soldier of God. To him, this moment was the reason the Malleus Maleficarum existed. Vara de Moses went down the stairs.

The scene was like something out of the Black Book. A ghostly green glow—the effects of his prayer—lit up the otherwise darkened room. The blood of the captain was streaked on the broken chairs and on the walls. On the floor lay the table, which had capsized under the weight of the feeding frenzy. The blood had been pushed around, as if someone had tried to soak it up with a mop. Though he saw no bucket, Vara was pretty sure he knew where all the blood had gone. He had seen lycan attacks before, and he had encountered some truly horrible monsters in his time, but never had he encountered any creature as rapacious as weresharks. There were no bones. Only the smallest specs of flesh and detritus from the feast remained. The captain had been devoured whole.

The members of the feast and the food itself may have been gone, but a palpable presence filled the room, as if the sin of the death was now inseparable from the room. From his experience with ghosts, Vara knew the presence would last lifetimes, perhaps even thousands of years. If he had brought a divining rod into the dining room now, it would tickle and shake when he held it out. If he poured holy water on the floor, it would boil. Vara had other duties to keep. He made the sign of the cross and looked for the exit. The sharks that were here had not stormed the deck. They had gone elsewhere, but where?

Vara checked the dining room. There were no adjacent rooms, just cabinets for keeping dinnerware and glasses. He walked behind the aquarium and found a hidden passage in the wall. This was where the crew exited and entered with food and drink for Riggs' guests. He remembered his training and entered the passage to the kitchen.

After seeing the feast, he was afraid of what he might find in the kitchen.

Devon and Emmett rushed inside to the kitchen. The chef, two stewards, and the chef's mate were huddled in the center of the room. While the stewards were trying to get a signal on their cellphones, the chef had pulled a large butcher's knife. Food was still cooking in a wok over an open flame.

"What's happening?" she asked Devon and Emmett. "We've heard gunshots and screaming."

"We are looking for a place to hide. Someplace with electricity."

"The engine room. Who is attacking us? Did one of the homeless people go crazy?"

"It's a lot worse than that," Devon said. "How do we get to the engine room?"

The chef pointed to an open portal and a metal gang-ladder leading downstairs. "Come with us," Devon said to the chef.

She pulled a filet knife out. "This is my kitchen. Nobody will take it from me."

As Devon and Emmett fled, the outer door opened, and a large finned leg stepped into the room. Everyone except the chef screamed. The hammerhead ducked to fit through the door. Its long head swept side-to-side.

The chef's crew escaped to the dining room, leaving the chef behind. With grim tenacity, she pushed back her sleeves, revealing her tattoos, and angled herself away from the hammerhead, careful to keep the stainless steel cabinets between her and the shark. Behind her, her crew was meeting their gruesome fate as they encountered the bull sharks from the dining room.

"I don't know who or what you are, but I want you out of my kitchen," the chef said, pointing her knife to the shark. Its tail flickered with delight.

"Landchum that fights back. Delightful," the wereshark said. It leaped at her, and she threw the filet knife at the shark. The knife cut a gash in the shark's skin, but as quickly as it opened, it closed back up.

"Ignorant landchum," the wereshark said as it landed on the kitchen counter and loomed over her with its wide, bow-shaped head and frowning mouth. But the chef wasn't going down without a fight. She grabbed the large wok that she had left cooking and dumped its contents on the hammerhead's shoulder. Boiling oil rolled down the monster's side, scarring its flesh. It kicked and screamed in pain.

Downstairs, Devon and Emmett heard the commotion. They were running down the center of the low-ceilinged, narrow engine room. In front of them stood the boat's engineer, a puzzled look on his face.

"Hide!" they both yelled at the engineer. Unlike the chef, the engineer had no desire to confront whatever was going on topside. He ducked between two pipes.

Emmett grabbed a blanket, and Devon squeezed herself in a hole between some pipes and circuit boards. Emmett handed Devon the blanket. "Put this over your head, and maybe he won't find you."

"Get in here."

"There's not enough room."

"I will make enough room, Goddamnit, now get in here."

Emmett kissed Devon on the forehead. "Physics is not on our side today, my love. I'm sorry."

"Don't leave."

"There's another spot over here. Just do me a favor, and whatever happens, don't come out. In fact, close your eyes. See me at your wedding. I'm already at the altar, and I'm waiting for you. I'm in a black tie suit with a Gryffindor tie-tack. You are walking down the aisle in those shoes with "Mischief Managed" written on the sides, and you are the most beautiful bride in the world."

She couldn't see Emmett anymore. He had moved down deeper into the engine room.

The room was full of the tedious sounds of steam and pipes and currents knocking. Tears flowed down Devon's cheeks. She started to go find Emmett when she heard some a new sound.

"Landchum," growled the hammerhead as it entered the engine room.

Outside, on the deck of the *Aglaea*, dozens of weresharks climbed over the gunwales and attacked crew and homeless alike. Once one person went down, two or three sharks leaped onto the body and began ripping it apart in a frenzy. Limbs were thrown everywhere. The weresharks were so seeped into the bloodlust, they would bite and snap at each other, too, fighting for every last morsel. One homeless man tried to escape by climbing up a palm tree, but a wereshark grabbed him by his foot and dragged him back down into the swarm of teeth and mouths.

"Remember, we aren't here to kill her," Belén said to Katrina as the cord whirled down to the catamaran's deck. "We need to capture her and exorcise her."

"Yes, but if I am attacked, I will defend myself. Lethally, if necessary." Katrina unhooked herself from the paraglider and shimmied herself down the rappel cord.

She landed at an angle and had to steady herself as the smaller catamaran crested over a wave. Behind her, a bloated moon bulged out of the Gulf like a parasite trying to escape its host. On the far side of the boat, a bull shark was feeding on a body. She didn't know if it was the captain of this smaller yacht or somebody else. What she did know was that in the fading light, the sharks had a hard time seeing. So she made sure to step lightly around the hull.

Suddenly, the shark stopped eating and waved its head around. The creature was trying to detect her. But Katrina had developed a way to camouflage herself. The lycan hunter's scuba suit was not a fashion choice. It had a Faraday cage sewn into the fabric, disrupting the flow of electricity beyond the suit and making her almost undetectable.

Almost.

She waited.

The wereshark got up, leaned around as she scanned the room with her ESP, then finally returned to the kill.

Slowly, Katrina stalked up behind the wereshark. Any sound would alert her immediately, and at this close a distance, that would be the end of Katrina, so each foot step was a deliberate choice. Would that square of flooring hold her up? She only truly knew once she'd put her weight on it.

Second by second, step by step, Katrina got around the wereshark. She raised her machete above her head, and then PHMF! chopped off the dorsal fin, bringing the machete down with both hands wrapped around the pummel for more power. The strike nearly sliced through the monster's entire fin.

The shark howled in pain and turned on her. By then, Katrina had struck it again with the silver machete, this time on the gills. Wanting no more of this, the wereshark plunged back into the water, its bloody fin dragging alongside its body.

Vara de Moses ducked around the corner of the kitchen passage and entered the massacre of crewmembers. The bull sharks were still gobbling up body parts of kitchen staff like starved wolves.

"Devourers of the Living," Vara said in the language of the baptized dead. "Return to Hell."

The largest wereshark, a sand tiger with so many teeth they seemed to sprout from the sides of his mouth, turned his cyst-like eyes on Vara as he gulped down an arm holding a bloody butcher's knife. "You speak in tongues, little man. I wonder how your tongue will taste."

The sand tiger charged him, claws outstretched. Its tail thrashed from side to side, knocking over bowls and spice jars on the countertops.

Vara took a defensive pose, holding square to his body his staff with the silver tips.

"You brought a stick to a knife fight, little boy."

The sand tiger was fast, but Vara was faster. He ducked to the side and blasted the sand tiger's head with his staff. The wereshark howled in pain as it crashed into the counter. Vara hit the were in the side of the chest and heard ribs crack. In both spots, the creature's skin reddened and puckered as if enduring a chemical burn.

The bulls left their meal to circled Vara de Moses. "I'm going to eat you, landchum," one bull said.

The other said, "I want to put you in my stomach. I want to feel you still wiggling around as I digest you."

Vara twirled his staff as the sand tiger stood back up and joined the shiver of sharks. Vara was completely surrounded.

"My name is Vara de Moses. Do you even know what that means?"

"It means you will taste like cilantro and onions."

"Staff of Moses. I am named for the power of God. I am the serpent. The plague. The storm. The creeping death. I was baptized in the blood of martyrs. I was trained in the ways of the light to entrap the creatures of the dark. I have sent over a hundred demons back to hell, so give me your best shot."

Three weresharks charged Vara all at once. Vara leaped over the first, thumped the second on the head, and ducked under the sand tiger's lunge. With the sand tiger's vicious face over him, Vara de Moses jabbed the monster in the eye so hard the creature's eye burst. While the weres and tiger howled, Vara twirled his staff around the other two weres at a dizzying speed. He knocked hands and mouths away from his body, then jumped up on the counter to escape being knocked over by a tail. Each strike left another reddened, broken patch of skin. The weresharks were starting to more closely resemble ghouls.

Vara jumped back down on the next row. He eschewed backwards, forcing the weres to come down the row one at a time. He used his staff to roll one off its legs, then countered the hit from another. He was almost all the way down the aisle when his back foot slipped in the grease from the chef's attack on the hammerhead. As he fell to the ground, all three sharks jumped on him at once.

On the *Hallelujah Goat*, the lycan hunter had fewer weresharks to dispose. With the focus of the feeding frenzy at the *Aglaea*, Katrina did not need to fight through a gauntlet of teeth. Katrina climbed down into the catamaran and searched for Yig. The lights were out, and the screens on the wall were broken.

She could hear Yig munching on bones. Katrina pulled her hood up over her head. She kept it tucked under the wereskin jacket. The hood was more of the same Faraday cage material that was used in her scuba suit.

"I can't see yer electricity," Martha said. "But I can smell you. You're the hunter. From Belén's home." Martha spat the word "hunter" out of her mouth. Katrina did not answer, but continued moving through the catamaran.

"Tell me, specialist: how long you been hunting monsters?"

When Katrina did not answer, the wereshark continued its meal. She sat under the flickering lights of the broken screens. Blood dripped from her mouth and down her neck, outlining her scaly breasts. A pile of dead bodies lay on the floor like a stack of meat on the table of a morbidly obese man with a strange eating disorder. In the pile were the remains of Malik, the weatherman, and everyone else who had been on the boat. Belén's crucifix still hung from Malik's neck. Martha had the weatherman's femur in her mouth and was sucking the last bits of meat from the bone.

"Would you like to join me, lycan hunter? I saved you a seat. I could turn you. A little nibble is all you'd need, and then you could join my feast. We could be ravagers together."

A shadow came up behind Martha. Martha grinned like Mrs. Hyde. "You think you've hidden yourself well, but I can still hear that little heartbeat." She turned and chomped down, only to find she'd bitten into Malik's little cat robot and broken its engine. It tasted like battery.

Katrina appeared at her side and plunged a syringe into Martha's bicep.

"Oh, how I love...the hunnt." The hammerhead's voice sounded like a pierced lung sucking for air, taking deep breaths that just couldn't fill its needs. Disgusting webbed feet slapped against the gangway floor, making a heavy, wet sound like seaweed being thrown around. The monster stopped and reared its large, bow-shaped head. It swung its head from side to side in an attempt to locate them.

"Sssomebody warned you...we hunt using...electric sense. I think youuu will be...sssurprised...how well we can hear your electricccity, landchummms."

The wereshark took three more steps and stopped at the alcove where the engineer had hidden himself. The wereshark fanned his head a second time while taking a deep breath. "Thump-thump, thump-thummp, my little heart beaaats." Then he charged the alcove. The engineer screamed as the shark ripped open his guts, then flung his innards onto the floor.

"That's not the ones I came in here after," the hammerhead, adrenaline reducing the number of deep breaths he needed. "There's at least...two more of you in this little roommm." Again, the hammerhead took a few steps and stopped to hunt for them. The wereshark waited. Devon thought maybe something had happened to the wereshark, it was so quiet. Then his grey, clawed hand reached over the pipes that Devon was hiding under.

Devon held her breath and pulled the blanket over her head. In her mind, she tried to pacify her heart and tell it to slow down.

The shadow of the hammerhead's arm passed over her. He sniffed the air, then jumped into the little alcove where she was hiding.

"Thump! Thump! Thump! Thump!" the hammerhead yelled as it snapped at Devon. He was too gigantic and too wide to get to her easily. Pipes and machinery blocked his way. Devon shrieked and squirmed deeper into the pipes, her head still under the blanket.

Determined, the hammerhead shoved its arm farther into the pipes. The tips of its fingertips could barely reach the ends of the blanket. Slowly, it fingered the blanket until it had a grip, then pulled the blanket away. The blanket slipped down her waist and off her feet.

While the blanket disappeared into shreds, Devon kicked her way even farther back among the pipes. She was bruising her skin against hot pipes and jagged pinch edges, but she had to go farther if she was going to survive. If she could just get a little deeper...

"I seeee you!" the hammerhead announced as its hand shot out at her and snatched up air. Devon wasn't sure how she could possibly get any farther from the wereshark. Maybe if she pushed hard enough, she could dislocate her shoulder and get another inch. She tried wedging her feet on either side and pushing hard, but she couldn't bring herself to dislocate her shoulder.

The hammerhead maneuvered its head sideways in between the pipes. The eye angled so that it was looking straight at Devon. "Oh, goodyyyy," the shark said salaciously.

Through teary eyes, Devon saw the wereshark reach back into the crevice after studying it for a moment. Softly, deliberately, the webbed hand pushed deeper into the crevice. Its claws raked against her shirt. The shark took a deep breath, then tried again. Devon removed her shirt and threw it at the shark's hand. The hammerhead smelled the shirt deeply and smiled. "So young. So freshhh." Then it reached out again, almost touching her pink flesh with its pale claws.

"Sssoft skinnn," the monster purred. "Tasssty human fleshhh." Its claws raked across Devon's side, cutting her skin. Blood spilled from her side and dribbled onto the wereshark.

"Ooooh. Blood." The hammerhead pulled back its claws and licked them clean.

"Go away," Devon whimpered.

The hammerhead laughed so sordidly, it almost purred. Its claws came back, reaching for her one more time. The tip of its scaly claws touched her belly. "Tickle, tickle."

Then the hand moved down. Devon screamed. She tried to mash her legs in closer, but her body was already in a lot of pain from shoving herself as tight against the wall and pipes as she could get. As the hand glided down her pants leg, its grip became more and more firm. She kicked at the terrible hand, and that was her end. As she kicked, the hammerhead grabbed her by the ankle.

"Gotcha."

It began dragging her out.

Devon reached out and grabbed onto pipes, but the wereshark was too strong for her.

Suddenly, the hammerhead howled and let go of her. Emmett had jammed a piece of rebar into its gills.

The hammerhead backhanded Emmett and sent him flying across the room, bouncing off pipes. He hit his head against a large metal cylinder and fell down, bleeding from the head. The hammerhead then returned to Devon. Legs kicking, she tried to keep out of the monster's grasp. He pulled her out of her crevice while pushing her legs apart.

With a loud yell, Vara jumped into the engine room and hit the hammerhead on the back of his knee. The silver was like a battering ram hitting a house of sticks when it made contact with the lycanthrope's knee. The knee popped. The hammerhead roared. It turned on Vara with murder in its eyes and snapped its jaws at the monster hunter.

"You...ruinnned...dinnner!"

Vara leaped onto the hammerhead's chest and knocked the giant monster down onto the grated gangway. He rammed his staff down the hammerhead's throat. Its eyes went wild, and its claws lashed at Vara. He pushed his weight into the silver-tipped staff, impaling the wereshark on the grate. The hammerhead choked on his own burning blood and died.

Dead, the creature's body returned to human form. In this case, it was a boy, not older than fifteen years old. He had blue eyes and blond hair, and he was skinny. He looked kind of harmless, really, like he was a Boy Scout. The body had no wounds except for the smoke coming from his mouth where Vara had impaled him.

Vara de Moses, covered in blood, pulled his staff out of the boy's mouth. The head gave a little twitch as he removed his staff. He wiped the silver ends. Emmett, who had come to, was staring at the smoke blooming from the boy's mouth.

Devon crawled out from between the pipes. Emmett reached out to her, concussion and confusion colored all over his face. She went to her fiancée. "You're bleeding," she said.

"Is it bad?"

"Just a cut, I think."

Vara de Moses took off his shirt, which had a Virgin de Guadalupe stitched on the front, and handed it to Devon. She put it on.

"You should stay here," Vara said. "Lock the engine room door and don't come out until you've seen me or the authorities. Make sure you see credentials. These monsters can look like anyone else when they want to. They'll hide in plain sight and make you think that everything is okay, then attack you when you least expect it. Understand?"

Devon nodded. She followed Vara to the front of the engine room.

"One day, if you survive this, you may want answers. Leave me a message under the first shell in St. Mary's Cathedral."

"How are you going to stop them all? There must be dozens out there."

"Dozens of weresharks, but only one Vara de Moses."

Devon closed the door behind Vara de Moses as he ran out.

CHAPTER TWENTY-TWO: DEVOURER OF THE DEEP

Katrina double-belted the human form of Yig into the tandem paraglider. Then she climbed on with her. The paraglider could barely stay above water. Thankfully, most of the weresharks were descending on the *Aglaea*. The paraglider slowly climbed up into the air, but not before a giant tiger shark decided to make a go at it, jumping twenty feet in the air to the paraglider. Only Katrina's machete kept the tiger shark from dragging them to their deaths.

"I want you to drop me off at the yacht."

"Are you crazy? There must be twenty or thirty weresharks on that yacht."

"And there may be people still alive down there, including your brother."

"My brother's kind of a badass."

"So am I."

Katrina jumped off the paraglider.

"That's one crazy *gringa*." Belén steered the paraglider back to the island. It was time for Yig's exorcism.

Mid-fall, Katrina pulled her machete. She landed right on top of a bull shark werecreature, stabbing it as she came down on top of it. The bull had been rushing a crew member clambering up a ladder to the roof of the yacht.

The bull thudded to the floor, bleeding all over the deck while Katrina thwacked it two more times for good measure. She turned on another attacking wereshark and severed its jaw from the rest of its body. The wereshark howled in pain as it fell backward, reaching for a jaw that was now a gaping hole. Out of the corner of her eyes, Katrina saw more sharks pooling around her. She had their attention and their frenzy. Then Vara de Moses ran through them, his staff twirling in the moonlight.

"Good to see you, Vara, but I think this may be too much for you."

"Yea, though I walk through the valley of the shadow of death," Vara said.

"Thy rod and thy staff, they comfort me," Katrina responded.

The deck of the *Aglaea* filled with weresharks surrounding Katrina and Vara. Vara moved behind Katrina to cover her back. The weresharks started taunting them with gory descriptions of how they were going to eat the two warriors.

Suddenly, Katrina felt a rush of wind.

The weresharks turned to look overboard. Another werecreature jumped out of the water. It was the biggest, meanest-looking wereshark Katrina had ever seen. Immediately, Katrina knew it was the Mother. She washed aboard the *Aglaea* on a wave of water and landed among her weres.

"I am the Devourer of the Deep. Who are you to oppose me, woman?"

"The greatest lycan hunter who ever lived. If you doubt me, count the number of pelts stitched into my jacket."

The Mother chuckled. "Those may be wolves, my dear, but they are not wolves of the sea," she said, flashing her shark teeth in the moonlight. "I wonder if your carcass would be worth anything to the Pack Alpha."

The Mother reached out for Katrina. Vara de Moses stepped forward and spoke to her in the language of the baptized dead.

The Mother cringed. She pointed out across the Gulf. "Come, my pups. We have no more use for feasting tonight. A bigger feast awaits us. Return to the rig." Then she rose up on a wave of water and dove into the sea. Her weight was enough to rock the yacht. The other sharks followed her, each diving into the Gulf water.

"I can't believe that worked," Vara said when they were alone.

"Neither can I. Do you think she got Martha?"

"You mean Yig? No, but why is she so important?"

Katrina said, "These other weresharks may be her pups, but Yig is her princess. They both carry the same mark on their left shoulder."

"Wait. What?"

PART 4: THE GOBLIN SISTERS

This was a fish built to feed on all the fishes in the sea, that were so fast and strong and well-armed that they had no other enemy.

-Ernest Hemingway, The Old Man and the Sea

CHAPTER TWENTY-THREE: ALTER OF THE WERESHARK

Like the dungeon in the basement of the Treviño's home, their sanctuary had stone floors. Candlelight flickered against the adobe walls. A large crucifix stood at one end, with the family's private tabernacle. The wicker chairs had all been pushed to the side of the room as if the brother and sister were holding a dance.

Yig slept on the floor. Dr. Carter stood with the Malleus Maleficarum in a circle in the middle of the room. Dr. Carter showed them his tablet.

"I want to show you something," Dr. Carter said to the Treviño family. "This is personal information from Yig's files. I could get sued and lose my license for showing this to you, so I'm tell you this so that you know I mean business." He pulled up a few slides on his tablet. Each one showed a rainbow-colored pattern, like a Rorschach test, encased in the shape of a human head.

"See the different brain patterns? They look like different people, but they are all Yig. Only this one is the alter called Petra, and this one is Clara, and this one is Nadia. If you look at her pulse and heart rates in the lower corner, you can see that each alter is slightly different.

"I'm showing you this for a reason. This is a delicate thing we are doing, exorcising demons from a woman who has no demons in her body. There has been a lot of harm against people with Dissociative Identity Disorder who were given exorcisms. What happens is that a person with DID cannot explain this other identity existing in her head. She thinks she is possessed, so she goes to an exorcist, who banishes the identity. This can be extremely dangerous and scarring for a person with DID. They start to have problems not only when the identity eventually comes back, but also because the identity existed in the first place to shield them from powerful memories. So today boils down to not wanting to make things worse."

Vara de Moses asked, "How do you hold an exorcism without exorcising a demon?"

"We need some ground rules. This is not an actual exorcism. Am I clear? Yig is not possessed; she just thinks she is. We are going to go through the process as if she were possessed, but the goal will be different. Yig needs to confront Martha. We are not going to try to remove any of her personalities. Those are Petra, Clara, Nadia, and Martha."

Vara countered, saying, "But at one point, we will ask her to reveal to us her demons. That is a crucial part of the ritual. What do we do when she starts giving us names?"

"Exorcise any names she gives you that aren't one of her personalities. At the end of this ordeal, Yig must accept Martha as one of her alters. That is the only way for her to gain control of her lycanthropy. Reduce and accept. Who is performing the exorcism?"

Vara nodded to his sister. "Belén."

Belén was shocked. "Why me?"

"Because God help them, the Church does not allow women exorcists. So if this ever comes back to us, we can say that it was not a real exorcism because you were performing the ritual." Then he smiled wily and said, "Besides, despite the doctrine of the Church, one day you may be forced into a position where you have to perform an actual exorcism. Should that day ever come, you need to practice. This sick woman is perfect."

Dr. Carter said, "If Belén performs the rites, will that tip off Yig?"

"The woman is not a practicing Catholic. I don't think so."

"Okay, then." Dr. Carter handed Belén an earpiece. "That's so I can communicate with you." He handed another to Vara. "I cannot be in the room. Otherwise, she will see through our ploy. But with these, I can guide you through the therapy session. Remember: do not attempt to exorcise Martha."

Dr. Carter walked into the viewing room with the one-way mirror. Katrina was already in the room, finishing up the impromptu Faraday cage being built into the room.

"Do you think this will fully protect us?" Dr. Carter asked. He flicked his middle finger against the metal poles. "It looks like a shark cage."

Katrina said, "It'll reduce the chances of her hearing your heartbeat. That's it. If Martha decides she wants in here, nothing can stop her. Surely not a chalk line on the stone."

In the sanctuary, Vara de Moses said a blessing for Belén, then draped the priest's stole over her heads. They wore white sleeveless albs, what children referred to as "priest ponchos." The stoles were bright green for ordinary time, with large golden crucifixes emblazoned at the ends. Along the trim of the stoles had been sewn a border made up of the names of all the saints called out in the exorcism ritual.

"I'm not sure I'm ready," Belén said when the blessing was finished.

Vara de Moses said, "Neither was I when Dad directed me to my first exorcism. But he was with me, and he gave me strength. Now it is my turn to be here for you. You will do fine."

"I miss Mom and Dad."

"They gave their lives for the good of the world."

"Yeah. I just wish it hadn't gone down like that."

"Let me tell you something that Dad told me. When you are performing the exorcism, remember who you serve." He pointed to the door to the sanctuary and said, "Keep in this room the three things that God gave you: faith, hope, and love. Leave everything else outside. You will not need them."

He kissed his sister on the cheek, then turned to the girl and the pentagram. Belén looked down at the chalk pentagram nervously.

"Don't worry, sis. The pentagram only works if Yig believes she's possessed."

"And if she doesn't believe?"

"Better make her believe."

When Yig awoke, she found herself back in the house of the Malleus Maleficarum family. She realized then that this was the second time she had been in the house, but she did not know what it looked like on the outside. For all she knew, she could be in one of the old Victorian mansions along Broadway. Or maybe their home was one of the low-cost houses along the southern side of the island, and the run-down house was a front for all the work the family did in the shadows. Maybe this was a hidden room. She simply did not know, and she could not sense anything with her powers. Her memory of this place did her no favors. The one time she escaped, she did not remember how she got home.

Unlike the last time she was captured by the Treviños, this time, she was not chained to the floor in silver. She was laying on the floor in the middle of a pentagram. Across from her stood Belén and Vara de Moses. Belén held a *Rituale Romanum*, the book of exorcism rites, in her hands. An angry Jesus glared down at them from his cross overlooking the altar. There was one door in and out of the room, and a mirror.

The Treviños prayed silently until Yig awoke. Yig glanced around the room, then examined her arms and legs. She began sobbing immediately.

Belén kneeled down in front of Yig, just outside of the circle. "Yig, do you know where you are?"

Yig rolled over and moaned.

"Yig?"

Belén waited. Yig continued to cry. Just as Belén was about to get up and return to her praying, Yig said, "I think I…ate…people."

"Yig, what is the last thing you remember?"

"I don't know."

"Try."

She remembered the executive suite, and Riggs touching her forearm. "I was at work. Have I lost time?"

Dr. Carter said into her earpiece, "This is good. She is acknowledging the psychosis. Ask her if she can remember what time it was when she was at work. Or what day."

Belén asked. Yig shrugged. Belén asked again, only this time she said, "What day is today? What is the date?"

"July 23."

Belén looked to the one-way mirror.

"Tell her it is July 27."

She did. Yig moaned again.

"Do you know where you are?"

Yig looked around, taking in the stonework. She nodded.

"Yig, we brought you here to help you."

"I want to be helped."

"Good. My family, the Malleus Maleficarum, we have special orders that were given to us many years ago when we first came to America. One of them is the power to exorcise demons."

"What?"

"Yig, tonight we are going to help you. But I need you to do something first."

"What is that?"

"I need you to pray with me."

"But I haven't prayed before."

"That's alright. Will you pray with me?"

Yig rolled over and wiped the tears from her eyes. She looked at the pentagram on the floor. She rubbed her wrists.

"Last time I was here, you had me in chains."

"We underestimated you. We won't do it again."

"But what if the wereshark gets out?"

"She will be contained in this pentagram."

"But she is really powerful. You have no idea. She will kill all of you." Yig's voice started to raise. The fear was welling up inside her.

Calmly, Belén called to her. "Nothing is more powerful than my God. Yig, pray with me. Do you know the Our Father? Our Father in heaven, blessed be Thy name? Can you say it with me?"

"I don't know. Will I be able to?"

"There is no reason for you to be stopped."

"What about the others?"

Belén's grip on her book tightened.

"You mean the demons inside you? They can't hurt you unless you allow it."

Dr. Carter interjected. "Don't say things like that. Alters can and sometimes do hurt an Otherwise Normal Personality, even at their own cost. Tell her the point of this exercise is to reveal her demons."

"The point of this exorcism," Belén said, "is for you to confront the demons inside you."

"You sound like Dr. Carter."

Belén did not wait for Dr. Carter's response in her headphone. "Maybe psychology and religion aren't so different. Now pray with me. Our Father," she started, and waited for Yig to continue. But Yig didn't. She sat there on the floor as if a bolt of lightning had been shot through her.

"Our," Yig forced out, but then began to choke. Her eyes went wide. "They won't let me."

"You have to try, Yig."

"But I feel like I'm going to throw up."

"Take a deep breath, slow down, and say the words one at a time. I'll start for you."

Yig took a deep breath, but cantered on her knees like a mother trying to give birth or a teen trying to stop dry heaving after their first binge.

"Our Father," Yig started.

Yig formed an oval shape with her mouth, a small pucker of her lips. "Wh-wh-whooooo…"

She vomited blood and human flesh into the pentagram. One of the pieces of flesh had beard hair.

"Oh, God," Yig moaned. Then she vomited again.

Belén rejected every impulse in her body to throw up, too. She had seen a lot, and she had seen some weird things in exorcisms, but never had she seen human flesh regurgitated. Vara held her by the shoulder. He whispered into her ear and said, "The rule is that you cannot break the seal, or the demons will be unleashed. Regurgitation is normal during exorcisms."

"Help me," Yig begged. "Get them out of me."

Belén stood up and made the sign of the cross. "Yig, I need you to go away now. I need you to step back and allow the other spirit in you to step forward."

Yig looked at Belén oddly, then scared. Suddenly, Yig's eyes rolled back, and she hunched forward. Her arms folded behind, palms up, like wings.

Belén made the sign of the cross and said, "I command you to identify yourself, unclean spirits!"

A gravelly voice growled the words from Yig's mouth. "We are many."

Vara stood behind Belén and raised his hand in a sign of blessing.

"Fuck you!" Yig spat out.

"I want your name."

She laughed.

"Azaboth. Carell. Neobus. Ezekmial. Mortiban. Calislaught. Ebkai. Shazak the Dumb. Martha Mayhem. The Dead Girl." Each name came out of Yig's mouth like blackened paste.

In the viewing room, Katrina checked the electrical equipment while Dr. Carter wrote down the names of the demons on his yellow pad.

"That's recording, right?" Dr. Carter asked.

"Everything is working as it should be."

"Good. I think we are going to make history tonight."

"Lord have mercy," Belén said.

"Lord have mercy," Vara repeated.

They continued the rite of exorcism on Yig, calling out each of the demons she named. Belén was careful to leave out Martha.

As each demon was named, Yig growled. Her voice sounded utterly unearthly and would have made lesser people run scared from the room, but the Treviños had performed many exorcisms and seen actual demons pulled from the bodies of God's children. They did not scare easily.

The ritual lasted long into the night, and many prayers were said for Yig. Dr. Carter watched the exorcism intently, jotting down notes in his yellow pad throughout the night while Katrina watched.

During one of the breaks when Yig seemed to fall into a period of inactivity and the Treviños stopped for water, Dr. Carter put down his pad and studied the lycan hunter.

"We've met, but I don't believe we've been properly introduced. I am Dr. Lynne Carter, head of the Galveston Charter of the Carfax Society. And you are the lycan hunter?"

"Katrina."

"What is your story, Katrina?"

"My story?"

"How does one get to be a lycan hunter?"

"Well, I wasn't a lycan hunter at first."

"What were you at first?"

She paused for a moment. "I was a young girl who fell in love."

"Tell me more."

"I fell for a boy with the most amazing voice. This made another of my suitors jealous. He made a pact with a monster that killed them both. I hunted the monster to its lair and I killed it. But by then, I'd left a trail of dead bodies and become something monstrous myself. So I abandoned civilization and became a hunter of the darkness."

"Your story sounds very similar to how the Carfax Society started. A couple fell in love, and then a monster kidnapped the woman. The men who hunted the monster into the deepest, darkest mountains of Europe became the foundation of the Society. Have you thought of joining? I don't know if there is an association of hunters, but we could use a hunter to help us locate our monsters."

"The Society. Has a nice ring to it. But I gave up societies and decorums long ago. Sorry. But maybe you can help me with something. I know that silver works on weres. Everybody knows that. But why?" She looked at Yig, who was moaning and kicking her feet because the rites had started again, and Belén had placed a communion wafer on her forehead. Yig's open frown was a giant gaping wound in her face.

Katrina said, "I know that religious emblems and prayers affect certain monsters. Not weres. They are more from this world than most people think. But silver burns them. Kills them. Why?"

"The Chicago charter has a theory. They say that if you review the history of silver, it has some antibacterial properties. It's called the oligodynamic effect, and was actually discovered in the 1890s. So the theory is that the trigger in the werecreature must be like a virus. It may be transmitted by saliva in bite wounds. It's hard to say, though, since weres revert to their humanoid form when killed. But yes, that is the theory. Silver is antibacterial. You know, if the theory holds true, that means other metals may affect weres. Not just silver. Copper, gold, mercury. Maybe even aluminum."

Belén turned the page of the *Rituale Romanum*. She studied the words on the page, then approached Yig, who was standing on her tip-toes, her lips pulled back tightly and her arms spread outward. She looked like a body caught in rigor mortis with all the muscles clenched. Her eyes were wide but still white as spider silk.

"Be careful, exorcist," Dr. Carter said into her ear. "Yig is very susceptible to suggestion. One wrong word, and you could undo years of treatment."

Belén said, "I command you, unclean spirit, along with all your minions now attacking this servant of God, by the mysteries of the incarnation, passion, resurrection, and ascension of our Lord Jesus Christ, by the descent of the Holy Spirit, by the coming of our Lord for judgment, that you tell me by some sign your name, and the day and hour of your departure. I command you, moreover, to obey me to the letter, I who am a minister of God despite my unworthiness; nor shall you be emboldened to harm in any way this creature of God, or the bystanders, or any of their possessions."

"What's in a name, stick-follower? Your name is Spanish for Bethlehem, but Bethlehem was once known as David. Does that make you a boy?"

"You know my name, but to whom do I speak?"

"Who's left? You already nabbed so many. Off they go. On Azaboth, on Carell. On Neobus and Ezekmial. On Mortiban and Calislaught. On Ebkai and Shazak the Dumb. To the top of the roof, to the top of the wall, now dash away, dash away, dash away all."

"Martha?"

A cold hand reached for Belén's arm. The hand was already breaking with elongated fingers. Her mouth began to bleed.

"You got that right, bitch."

CHAPTER TWENTY-FOUR: THE FELLOWSHIP OF YIG

Yig sat in her apartment room at Calhoun Lofts on the University of Houston campus. Twice a week, she drove down to the island to meet with her psychotherapist, Dr. Lynne Carter. They worked on memory exercises and discussed the trauma that had caused her to start losing time. Even now, it was hard to see she was slipping time until she saw the stitches in reality, the gaps where she had studied for hours when she thought she had only studied for a few minutes. Or when sometimes she went to read at the library and discovered she'd been reading one book all day instead of doing research through the ten books she had checked out. That was when she started seeing Dr. Carter, who diagnosed her with dissociative memory. But one day she came in to see him, and he told her about Dissociative Identify Disorder.

"What is that?"

"Dissociative Identity Disorder is when two or more unique personalities inhabit a person."

"You mean split personality?"

Instead of answering, Dr. Carter said, "Do you know Petra?"

And that was how Yig learned she had different people inside her. She didn't begin to accept it until she began talking to them on an Internet forum that Dr. Carter set up. Once a personality replied to her forum, she set up an e-mail for them: Yig.com. So she had TheOriginalYig@Yig.com. Then she had Petra@Yig.com. Then came Clara@Yig.com and Nadia@Yig.com. Through e-mailing, she learned that Petra Powerful made her existence known during the traumatic experience when her grandfather nearly bled to death. She shielded Yig from the experience so that she did not have to react to it. Clara often slipped in to deal with stresses related to schoolwork and new places. Nadia handled social experiences. They were all protective alters with unique memories and feelings.

Once the alters had been identified through the forum and e-mail, Yig worked with Dr. Carter to bring the alters together. She started to see them all as parts of herself. She called them her "goblin sisters." She also began to attribute things in her normal life to each, and this helped bring together and make her feel like a singular entity. She knew she was "being Petra Powerful" at work, but she was still Yig and not losing time. At least until Martha began to take over. (I always do.)

Yig sat at the conference table in the darkened room. She was alone with her laptop. She sent an e-mail out to the Yig distribution group:

To: Yig All

From: TheOriginalYig@Yig.com

Subject: Meeting to Discuss New Roles and Responsibilities

To all,

I know it has been a long time, my goblin sisters, but we need to talk. There have been some drastic changes. I've been bitten, and I think the changes that have been happening to us are starting to take control over me. You know where I am. Attendance is mandatory.

Immediately, her e-mail chimed. A new message popped up from Petra. Her avatar was of a wolf: wise, strong, and powerful. The message read: I'm on my way.

Petra always responded to Yig's e-mail quickly, which made sense. Responding quickly to e-mail was good business.

The door to the conference room opened, and in walked a tall woman with long, thick black curls and a trim navy blouse. She had a way of taking up the presence of a room and a face that could have been twenty-five or forty. The woman sat down across from Yig at the far end of the table—an equal, if not her superior—and opened up her purse. She pulled out a laptop and powered it on, which made no sense down here. She placed down her coffee and a pad of paper.

"Hello," Petra said.

"Thank you for coming,"

"If you don't mind, I have some e-mail to take care of while we wait for the others."

"Cool."

Petra turned her attention to her keyboard, and her fingers began to attack the keys with the ferocity of a Bengal tiger. Yig wondered who she was e-mailing, and why? Was she e-mailing because she was the surface alter at the moment, and this room was just an interpretation of the sub-surface waters where her alters stayed until coming out?

This made her think of the sanctuary and the pentagram, and she didn't like thinking about it, so she shook her head.

Then Nadia came in. Nadia was perpetually twenty-one and an island girl. She wore bracelets and bangles on her wrist and nothing else except a smile on her face, which was how she faced all the problems in the world. She absorbed them with her positivity the way a boxer can take a punch and keep on fighting. Troubles didn't worry her because she was trouble-free.

"Hello," Nadia sang out as she entered the room. "Naked Nadia's in the House!" She walked over and kissed Yig on the lips, then went over to do the same to Petra, but Petra held out a hand to her.

"You know I don't like that."

Nadia shrugged and sat down. "Ooh, that's cold." She went to another chair. Liking it better, she leaned back and rested her arms on the chairs beside her, exposing her large, supple breasts. "What's the good word, Yig?"

Yig tried not to look at her amazing breasts. She went back to her computer.

For a person summoned to a meeting because of an attack on their world, Nadia didn't seem worried. "Did you know it's a Thursday? The weekend's almost here."

Nadia moved again, this time taking a seat next to Yig. "It's always a little weird seeing you 'cause you look like me," Nadia said.

"Yeah, I guess that's right."

"But you know what? It's always cool because you are so beautiful, and that means I am so beautiful. Isn't that great?"

"Yea," Yig mock-squealed.

Clara came in next, several books tucked under her arm. The DSM-V and The Life of Pi. She chose the chair in the middle of the conference table between Yig and Petra, opposite of Nadia. Of all her alters, Clara looked the least like Yig, even though she was closest to her in age. She had corn-yellow blonde, blue eyes, and dimples. While looking at Petra and Nadia was like looking at versions of herself, it was hard to see the gene pool relevance of Clara. Perhaps that was the point. Yig hated studying and abhorred schoolwork. She was also the reason Yig went to see Dr. Carter in the first place, though that was only later discovered, after Petra.

"Look at us," Petra said. "We are complete."

Yig was terrified of these encounters. Not only because they forced her to confront her mental illness, but because these personalities were so dominant. They all existed to protect her from parts of her life she feared. How do you tell your bodyguards to do something when you don't pay them?

"No, we are not complete," Yig said.

Suddenly, the room quivered, as if hit by a small earthquake not strong enough to rattle the laptops.

Yig said, "Something really bad is happening. You know I was bitten by a wereshark?"

The others nodded.

"The wereshark calls herself Martha. Martha Mayhem. She kills people. I also think she is a demon who has possessed this body."

"Can we exist in a possessed body?" Nadia asked. They all looked to Clara.

"Most possessions are actually sexual trauma," Clara said in her melodic southern accent. "That's why exorcisms seem to work for a while, but usually do not. Eventually, the memory comes back."

Nadia grimaced and folded her arms. "Were we?"

"No," Petra said flatly. "I would know. I would have been there."

Clara said, "Just because you are Powerful doesn't make you the bearer of the heaviest burdens, Petra. If Yig was abused, she would have likely created a new alter to deal specifically with that memory. Besides, she could have been abused much earlier than any of us," Clara said. "If the body was sexually abused, statistically, it likely would have happened before the age of twelve. That predates you, Petra."

"But not you, Clara," Yig said.

"Is it possible?" Nadia asked.

"Look, I'm not going to lie to you. It is possible you were sexually abused by a relative or a friend, and you repressed those memories. There may be another alter out there we are unaware of. I may have an alter that I am unaware of. There is always the chance."

"Wait. You have an alter?" Nadia asked.

"I *might* have an alter," Clara reiterated. "You might have an alter. Petra might have an alter. We don't know for sure until we find them. It is all very complex, so I doubt you'd understand, Nadia. It's not your specialty."

"I don't have an alter," Petra said.

The room rumbled again.

"What are they doing up there?" Clara asked. "Which one of us is the surface alter?"

Yig said, "I think it is me, but I'm really not there right now. Is it you, Petra?"

Petra shook her head. It was not her.

"Maybe that is the other alter," Nadia suggested. "Martha."

"The demon who possessed me," Yig said.

"We need to confront her," Petra said. "Upstairs, a group called the Malleus Maleficarum is trying to exorcise her, but only we can really do it. The power of us, of all of us, united against the demon. We can expel the beast." Petra looked to the others for alliance.

"I'm in," Clara said.

"Me, too," Nadia said.

Yig's psychic bodyguards were all in agreement, but Yig was still doubtful.

"You are wondering how we bring the demon to us," Petra said. "How do you summon a monster from the beyond?"

"A séance." Clara pulled out from under the stack of books a small, dusty tome on the occult.

The conference table was circular now with four chairs.

"Everybody, take hands," Clara said. She opened the book in front of her.

"I should be the one to read," Petra said.

"My book, my séance. Everyone, close your eyes. Let the spirits take over." Then she said, "I speak to the ghosts that exist between here and the afterlife. Dear spirits, bring to us the wereshark. Place the demon, Martha Mayhem, here before us."

After a moment, Nadia asked if it was working. Clara opened her eyes. They had gone white, cyst-like.

Before she could break the pentagram, Martha suddenly released her grip on Belén's arm and collapsed on the floor.

"What happened?" Belén asked out loud.

"I don't know," Vara said, pulling Belén away from the pentagram. Belén dropped the *Rituale Romanum* on the floor. It lay just on the other side of the pentagram's chalk line.

In the viewing room, Dr. Carter was on his feet and Katrina was at the door to the sanctuary.

Martha's now black eyes focused on the book laying inches away from her on the other side of the pentagram. Her webbed hand raised from her side. She crawled up to the edge of the pentagram and extended her hand to the lines.

Belén's arms broke out in gooseflesh.

Martha reached for the book.

Katrina drew her silver machete. Vara pulled Belén back to the sanctuary door.

They all watched the wereshark warily.

The fingers pressed forward, inching to the book. But at the pentagram, they met an invisible barrier that they could not penetrate. Martha growled angrily. She probed the air for an exit. Finding none, she furiously jammed her hand through the barrier, but it was like punching a wall. She jerked her hand back painfully.

Dr. Carter exhaled relief. "Well, glad to know that psychology works."

Belén crossed the room and picked up the *Rituale Romanum* while Martha watched from her prison, inches away. Martha was a battery of potential energy, like a nuclear bomb waiting to explode. She wanted to rip Belén's throat out, but was trapped in the pentagram.

Katrina lowered her machete while Dr. Carter said into the microphone, "Remember, this is an alter. Do not exorcise Martha."

"I do not want to speak to Martha," Belén said. "I want the other demon."

"There ain't no other demons, girlie."

Belén glanced at the one-way mirror. Dr. Carter was flipping through his notes.

"The Dead Girl," Dr. Carter said into the microphone. "That was the last one listed."

"Give me the Dead Girl," Belén ordered Martha. "Bring her to me."

"Fuck off," Martha said. "You can't have her."

"Wait," Dr. Carter said into the microphone.

Belén waited.

"What is it?" Katrina asked.

"I don't know. We need more time to think this through."

"We don't have time. We're in the middle of an exorcism," Vara whispered. Like Belén, he was hearing everything through his ear piece.

"Exactly."

"What're you two up to?" Martha asked, following Belén's side glances to the mirror. She raised her head like she was sniffing the air.

"I sense something. There's electricity in your right ear."

Belén knew she had to act quickly. If Martha figured out this wasn't a real exorcism, she would kill them all or be killed. And Belén still believed that this was something Yig could control. So she reacted without thinking and stepped into the pentagram. Placed her hand on top of Martha's face.

"No," Vara protested. He took a step toward his sister. In the viewing room, Katrina was running for the door. But Martha did not bite Belén. Her face contorted painfully under the pressure of Belén's blessed hands.

"I command you, unclean spirit, that you tell me by some sign your name and the hour of your departure."

Martha's eyes went white as spider's egg sacks, and she said, "I am Death."

The conference room rocked. The table shook. Clara's head bent backward until her head was almost gone from her neck. Then it snapped forward, and a concussive blast knocked the women from their chairs.

The table flew up in the air, and Yig was afraid for herself. On the far side of the room, Clara scrambled toward Yig, eyes as white as the moon. She clutched at Yig's neck like a harpy. Then Petra clotheslined her.

As Clara fell back, the table fell to the floor and the door burst from its hinges. Martha ran into the room, all teeth and kill, and lunged at the closest alter, which was now Petra. Petra was strong, but not very agile. She took the hit straight into the chest and was thrown to the side of the room.

Martha grabbed Yig by the throat and hefted her off the ground.

"I've wanted to eat you for a very long time."

"You eat her and you will only be killing yourself," Petra said. She was bleeding from her head, but she was back on her feet.

"I eat her, and I take charge of this body. It is mine."

"It's true," Clara said, now back to her old self. "If she kills Yig, she gets the body."

"Well, she can't have it!" Nadia yelled as she jumped on Martha's back, pounding her sides and clawing at her fin. Martha flung Nadia to the ground, too.

"There ain't no way for you to destroy me. Bring me a hundred alters, and you're all just humans. I am the Devourer of the Deep."

Petra said, "You may very well be, but you're not in the Gulf anymore. You're in our waters." She pulled out a pulse rifle and unloaded it into Martha. The beast roared in the gun light and retreated out of the room.

Petra ran after Martha. Clara looked down and found a giant sword, five feet long and one foot wide, with a narrow handle on one end. It was light as air. To her side, Nadia held a gravity gun.

"But we need silver," Yig said. "Only silver kills the beast."

"This is all happening inside our mind," Clara said. "It makes sense that things that aren't silver will work on Martha. We control this place, not her."

Yig drew a katana out of thin air and followed her alters out of the room. As soon as she exited, though, her leg erupted with an old pain. It tingled and buzzed like bees in her shin. As she limped down the corridor, Martha's voice came from the dark, taunting her. "Oh, look. Someone's got their bad leg back. Want me to get rid of your problem? It'll only take one bite, Yiggy!"

The corridor opened up to a room full of arcades and challenge games, like a cross between a Dave & Buster's and the set of American Ninja Warrior. The silhouettes of black, three-headed dogs were displayed on the walls. On the far side of the room was a foam pit and a balance beam. Yig recognized this place immediately. Among many of Riggs' eccentricities was her obsession with downtime. She insisted everyone take it, but take it in the breakroom, where employees were encouraged to compete with each other "for fun." This was the Cerberus break room.

The wereshark was already standing on the beam, which was split to allow one beam for every alter.

"Come one, come all. I wanta eat your souls!" Martha roared.

"This place is not your domain. You have no power over us," Petra declared. Something about her reminded Yig of Sigourney Weaver. Petra climbed up on the balance beam as another rumble shook the building. This time, the whole room shook.

"Somebody's in control," Martha said. "I'm not sure it's you."

Clara held her sword out in front of her as she stepped onto her beam. Then Nadia jumped up on hers. Yig came last. She was dressed in a yellow Bruce Lee jumpsuit like The Bride from Kill Bill, one of her favorite movies. She wished her leg gave her as much confidence as her katana.

"It's time to reduce and accept, landchummies. One by one until you're all gone."

Yig looked over into the foam pit. A water pit lay below them with tin caricature cutouts of sharks lined up in horizontal lines across the pit. Each shark cutout was a laughable shade of blue with white eyes and whiter teeth. They were attached to rods that sawed back and forth across the water. The whole thing seemed oddly like a Tim Burton creation. But despite the cartoonish quality of the danger, Yig knew the teeth were as sharp as razors, and her sanity was what would be cut up into a million pieces.

Petra shot first. But Martha had created a shield and held it up in front of her body. The bullets bounced off wildly. She then hit Petra with a padded staff. Petra started to fall, but Nadia caught her with the gravity gun. Instead of throwing Petra, she placed her back on the beam.

The four looked at each other knowingly, the plan suddenly apparent in each other's minds. Yig, Petra, and Clara went forward and attacked Martha. Nadia stayed back and caught anybody hit by Martha who might fall into the pit. This angered Martha. Every time she knocked Yig down, Nadia snatched her up from the jaws of tiny tin sharks and put her back into the fight.

Martha growled her discontent. Every time she hit someone, they got back up. Slowly, because Martha still had a lot of power behind her punch, even if they were only mental projections, but they stood back up.

In a flurry, Martha bull-rushed all three, swinging her head from side to side. One at a time, Nadia could handle, but all three at once? She couldn't save them from the jaws of death below. Martha struck Yig, and Yig dropped down into the watery pit.

On either side, she saw Clara and Petra falling with her. Clara's back was to the sharks, but Petra had her gun raised. She would die firing all her rounds until the very last breath.

The little sharks came up to meet them, closer and closer. They were snapping now, begging to rip apart soft flesh with their metal jaws. Yig wondered if she would die in her own body, or if she would merely lose this identity for the rest of her life, and become one with Martha. Regardless of the outcome, only Nadia and Martha would remain. *What a strange combination*, she thought, and for a second she wondered how the two identities would present themselves to the world.

All around her, the world shook violently. Above her, she heard Martha slipping on the balance beam herself, and falling down with them. (I grabbed that slut Nadia, too. Don't forget that.)

But the sharks stopped moving. It was like something jammed the sawing mechanism. The alters and the wereshark plummeted past the tin monsters and splashed into the watery pool.

Yig's feet rocked with pain. Thick and bulbous and Fat. Not just Radiating, but Growing. Petra and Clara helped her to her feet.

"You okay?" Clara asked.

"As good as I can be. Let's cut this fucking tumor out of my psyche."

The metal bars had fallen down around them as the whole room shook violently. Stones and metalwork fell down into the shallow pool. Opening her eyes, she knew where she was. The Lanyon Building. This was the smuggler's room in the basement of the Lanyon Building. It opened up to the Galveston Bay for smugglers to bring in prohibition whiskey and rum.

Somewhere under the water of the room was an angry bull shark.

Yig held her sword out in front of her to ward off the wereshark.

"Stay together," Petra said. She had lost her pulse rifle.

"Stay behind us," Yig said. "You don't have any weapons."

"No. I don't do that. I'm the protector, and your leg…"

"For now, just get in the back," Yig said. A dissatisfied Petra stood behind Clara and Yig and Nadia. They watched the moving waters for any sign of the shark, but the water was deeper than the smugglers' room she remembered, and they were on the steps of the loading dock.

A ripple of water splashed against the wall. Clara chopped at it with her butcher's cleaver of a broadsword, but nothing was there.

"Was that it?" Yig asked, her voice breaking.

"I don't know," Clara said.

"Stay together," Petra shouted over them.

The warm, salty Gulf water rubbed up against their legs, stinging. A reminder of how dangerous the water was.

"Somebody get us the fuck out of here," Yig said.

The doorway was blocked by a fallen beam, so Nadia aimed the gravity gun at the beam and turned on its tractor beam. The beam shook but did not lift. She scanned the room quickly.

"If you can't go through the door, make a window," Nadia said.

She aimed the gravity gun at an overturned barrel of whiskey. The barrel lifted up out of the murky water and into the air until it hovered in front of them like an angel. Then she flung it against the stone wall. The barrel smashed, showering them in good whiskey, but it made no impact.

"Yum," Nadia said.

"I think you're going to need something weightier," Yig offered.

"You've all got the wrong idea. We need to attack. Expel her," Petra said. "Give me the gun, Nadia."

Nadia shrugged and handed the gravity gun to Petra, who aimed the physics engine at the water and pressed the trigger. The water began to rise up, droplets at first, and then in bucketfuls.

"You can't hide from me forever, you fish," Petra said. To the other alters, she said, "If you see it, stab it."

Clara and Yig stepped forward under the rising water and searched for Martha among the stones and sand. Slowly, they edged further and further out into the loading dock. The pain in her leg kept growing, but she did everything in her mind to bury it. The water from the room hung over them like a small, grey cloud. Already, the tide was beginning to flow back into the room.

"It is possible she ran. She may be waiting around the corner of the loading dock, just outside where we can't see her."

The two alters circled to the far end of the loading dock and walked outside. As they searched, they tried to take in everything so that Martha could not sneak up on them. They looked up, down, and around the corners all at once.

"Do you see her?" Yig asked.

"No."

"That's 'cause you're looking in the wrong place."

Martha was behind them. They spun around but did not see her until they looked up. She was hanging from the rafters in the dock. She shot out of the rafters at them. Clara and Yig both swiped at her as they retreated, neither sure if they really hit her. Martha dove out into the tide.

Clara and Yig ran up the steps of the dock while Petra shoved the water like a wave at Martha. Her fin cut straight through the water like a razor. Shark and monster leaped out of the water at the four. She grabbed Yig's katana by the blade and snapped it.

Petra hit her with the gravity gun and slammed her into the wall. Martha grunted, the air having been knocked out of her lungs.

"I guess she does have lungs," Clara said.

Martha caught her breath and said, "That was a ripe hit, you bastard. I'm going to eat you first."

Petra hit her again with the gun, but Martha resisted the tractor beam like an indomitable spirit. She pushed forward through it.

"You can't stop me. You're all just a piece of a puzzle, but I'm the image the puzzle forms when all the pieces come together."

Yig's mind reeled. She refused to believe that at the end of it all, she was a front for this monster.

"I'd rather die than let you take over my body."

"That's the intent, Yiggy."

"Clara, get her," Nadia said as she backed up behind the others.

Clara knew that the wereshark was all business on the front end, so she went around her to go for the back attack. Her goal was to lob off Martha's tail, but when she got there, she found the tail just as dangerous. It thrashed back and forth. She jumped over the tail, then swiped at it, but only hit air and water. The tail swiped again. She ducked and cut. She noticed a pattern. The tail swiped, she jumped. She cut, but the tail swiped again, knocking her against the wall, making her lose the broadsword.

Clara retreated back to the others, but was caught when the thrashing tail hit her again. Petra, Yig, and Nadia stood guard over her. The four huddled in the corner of the room by the doorway. Martha towered over them.

"I'm more powerful than all of you put together. I'm stronger than your mind will ever be. From now on, I own this body, and you're just a parasite I need to kill."

The room began to shake again. Stones fell around them.

"Hear that? Mayhem's taking over."

Then Martha grimaced. "Who are you?"

Yig followed Martha's line of vision and looked behind her. There was a six-year-old girl with sticks and weeds for fingers and a skull where her head should be. She wore a black hood.

"I am the Dead Girl. And I am more powerful than you."

Chapter Twenty-Five: The Dead Girl

"Wait!" Dr. Carter yelled. "Stop!"

Belén removed her hand from the face that looked less and less like Martha.

"Break the circle."

"But that would allow Martha…"

"Just do it. That's not Martha. That's a whole new alter."

"She isn't a tumor, Yig. She's a whole new alter," the Dead Girl said, staring at the wereshark that loomed over the other four alters. "She thinks she is a demon who has possessed this body, but she is wrong. She is an alter you created, Yig. She is the alter who protects you from the memories you have as a wereshark."

"Wait. She's me?" Yig said.

"The rainbow is you. You are made up of many personalities," the Dead Girl said.

"But I am the sum of my parts, and I am stronger as one than I am apart. I am one person."

Yig turned to Martha. "I am one person."

"No! I am the demon!"

The little dead girl chuckled, making her skull grin even more menacing. "None of us deal with true demons, Martha, but two of us handle monsters."

"Wait. Are you saying there's another monster inside me?"

The Dead Girl stepped out of the pentagram and walked to a window. It was night outside, and some street light came through the beveled glass, but it was not clear where it came from.

"It has been a long time since I have seen anything with my own eyes. Did you know that if you shine a light on an eyeball, all the veins light up, and the whole thing looks like a reddish green forest? A forest burning under a yellow halo. That is where I have lived for a long, long time. It is good to see with my own eyes."

Dr. Carter said into his microphone, "There is a memory she holds for Yig, a special trauma that has never been unlocked before. Ask her about how she came to exist."

Belén said, "Why did you come here? Why now?"

"I am here while we handle Martha."

"We?"

The Dead Girl giggled and pointed to her head. "She is just another alter, you know. She isn't a demon. You can't exorcise her."

The door opened and Dr. Carter walked into the room. "We had to convince Yig that Martha was something she could confront. The Treviño family specializes in exorcisms."

The Dead Girl giggled again. The sound was so childish that it was disturbing to hear coming out of a grown woman's mouth.

"How did you come to exist?" Dr. Carter asked. "What trauma do you hide for Yig?"

"A long ago memory. A once upon a time there was murder and betrayal kind of story. You want to hear it, don't you?"

"More than anything."

"Once upon a time on a faraway island that looked like Galveston but was really not, there lived a drowned princess. This princess of drowning was named Yig. She was a happy child with beautiful parents, and she lived a good life. She liked the color yellow more than anything else. It was the color of sunshine and sand and sunflowers. So she was called Yig the Yellow.

"One day, her parents, the king and queen, sent her to visit her grandfather by the sea. So Yig the Yellow put on her yellow hood and yellow dress and yellow boots, and she skipped away to her grandfather's house. He did not live far from Yig, and she knew the path well because she had been there many times. Yig's grandfather was a mighty fisherman now that he was no longer the king, and Yig liked to see all the fish he brought back from his time at sea.

"But like all fairy tales, there is a monster at the center of the story, and this fairy tale was no different. The monster had already visited Yig's grandfather's house. So when Yig arrived, she did not find her grandfather. She found a monster with long fingers who drank people's blood. The monster was drinking the blood of a woman when Yig the Yellow entered the house. The princess screamed and the monster cried out, "No, I'm so sorry!" but it was too late. The damage was done. The monster ran away from the house because the monster and the grandfather, as you know, were the same. "

Dr. Carter said, "People live double lives sometimes."

"Not sometimes. All the time. You are only the mask you show to me. To your patients, you show one person, to your colleagues another, and to your family, yet another. Right now, you are trying to be brave, but inside you are scared. You are afraid of what I mean for Yig, and you are afraid of Martha. But I know the truth. There is somebody inside all of us. Inside you, too, is probably a monster just as scary as the ones inside Yig, but I am not afraid of monsters. The princess was afraid.

Princesses need saving. I saved her. I have shielded that memory from her. I hold it in a little music box that I keep tucked next to me in my house under the water where I sleep and wait for the right time to come out."

"Like now."

"And now that I'm here, you can call me Hattie. Hattie the Half-Grindylow."

A terrible knock boomed from the shadows. The Malleus Maleficarum pulled the weapons they were hiding under their albs. Katrina came running, machete drawn. There was a permeable darkness in the corner of the room that had not been there minutes ago. The darkness spread along the floor like black ichor, like brackish water flooding the sanctuary. Shadows of long fingers like sticks reached along the walls.

Belén recited the prayer in the language of the baptized dead to bring the monster into the light. But she did not finish before a creature with bloodshot eyes ringed red from tears stepped out into the open room. He appeared taller than normal, with a black cloak wrapped around him, and his fingers were like the branches in the water that drown children.

"Daddy!" Hattie called out and ran to her father. He accepted her with open arms and hugged her tight.

"How did you get in here?" Vara demanded.

Hattie's father did not answer. He kissed his daughter on her cheeks and forehead. "I am so sorry," he told her.

"No, Daddy. It is not your fault."

"I am a terrible father. We should have raised you in the clan. We discussed it many times over for hours on end, for days on end when you were born. The whole family. We decided that since you did not need to feed on blood, we could raise you like a normal child, and maybe your life would be uncomplicated. But we were wrong. If we had told you about everything, maybe this wouldn't have happened. If you had known what your grandparents were, what I was, maybe you would not have had all these problems."

"It's okay, Daddy. You are a good daddy."

"Thank you, Hattie."

"Wait, you knew about Hattie but never told me?" Dr. Carter asked. Oscar Slaton frowned at the doctor.

"*Ex Monasteriense prognatus licentia quod Scientia en rememdium.* Isn't that what you say in the Carfax Society? *From monsters are born freedom and knowledge?* You may have been the best-qualified psychologist for seeing our only daughter, but we knew you were a member. If we revealed Hattie to you, we feared what you would have done. We didn't know that you had gotten our daughter involved with the Malleus Maleficarum. We were preoccupied with my father's disappearance."

Oscar studied his daughter's eyes. "Not long after she found her grandfather feeding, she told us she wanted to be called Hattie. We called her Hattie for many years, and then suddenly she stopped answering to Hattie. She wanted to be Clara. Clara was very different from Hattie, and we worried. We used Grindylow methods to deal with her identities, and they worked for a while. But when she was in college, Clara resurfaced. She was much older then. Thirty-five, though she barely looked twenty. That's the Grindylow in her. Her mother was right. We were raising Yig as a human. She needed a human doctor. That was when we reached out to you. And you helped her with Clara and Petra and Nadia, and you made her whole again, or at least as close to whole as we thought possible. We wondered if we were wrong about Hattie, maybe it was a phase she went through before she became a full-blown sufferer of DID. And then her mother found her journal, and we feared the worst. We came here and we watched. We only allowed this farce of a treatment to go on because we believed there might be some use to it, some benefit to the outcome."

Katrina and the Treviños spread out in a half-circle around Oscar and Hattie and Dr. Carter.

"Nobody invited you in here. How did you enter my house?" Vara asked again.

Oscar's eyes sheened bright green. "We've been living here on this island with the Malleus Maleficarum for over a hundred years. There is no darkness we cannot penetrate, no shadow we cannot walk."

Vara held up a pistol. "I swore an oath to destroy all monsters."

"You are so blinded by your mission that you do not see the world for what it is."

"Wait," Dr. Carter said.

"With you it is always wait," Vara said. "Not this time."

"But grindylows may hold the secret to immortality. Don't attack each other. Oscar, I just want to run some tests. Think of the good it could do."

"My body is not your lab experiment, Dr. Carter, and neither is my daughter's any longer." As Katrina and the twins charged him, Oscar pulled the dark wetness around him like a cape, and then he and Yig were gone.

CHAPTER TWENTY-SIX: BITES

Belén stood at the front gate of the Slaton family's home, her hands held up to indicate she was unarmed and alone. In the pre-dawn darkness, the old Victorian house appeared vacated.

She hoped they wouldn't attack her immediately. Grindylows were notoriously quick to anger. She wasn't supposed to be here, but she slipped out unseen while Vara, Katrina, and Dr. Carter planned how best to destroy the weresharks before they all came ashore. They knew they had only two nights left until the full moon was over. Katrina had reached out to other hunters in Texas and Louisiana, but there was no guarantee they would arrive before the storm, which would occur either tonight or the next night. There were only two full moons left. Belén insisted Yig was their best option. Now she was putting her life on the line to prove it.

The front door opened and shut. A figure stood in the shadows.

The porch light was off, so Belén had no way of knowing who was waiting in the shadows. She could cast the spell to bring them into the light, but she was here to arrange an agreement based on mutual trust. Forcing the grindylow's position simply would not do.

"So you are in the Malleus Maleficarum. My uncle told me about you."

Emily Slaton.

"You are a grindylow?" Belén asked.

"Why did you come here?"

"I'm unarmed. I have a plan to defeat the Mother, but I need to speak to Yig."

"No way that's happening, Witch's Hammer. My cousin was torn inside out because of you."

"Which she is she?"

"She is the same person she's always been."

"I know you don't think so, but I care about her. I think that this lycanthropy is something she can control. She doesn't have to be hunted."

Emily stepped off the porch and onto the path to the gate. Her face reminded Belén of cats when they're trying to decide whether to let their owner feed them or whether they should just eat them instead. As she spoke, fangs grew out of her teeth, and her fingers elongated. "You think she can't be cured?"

"I didn't say that. I said I don't think this is something to cure."

"What is your plan then? Tell me, and I will take it to the clan, and we will tell you our decision."

Belén knew that in order for her plan to work, she needed to speak to Yig first.

"I will only tell Yig."

Emily crossed the front of the lot with the speed of a flooding river and stood on the other side of the gate. Belén suppressed the urge to run. "Well then you are in luck," Emily said. "Yig is available. Please, enter." Emily opened the gate and Belén walked through.

Emily followed her up the front porch. As if it had a mind of its own, the front door opened. Belén entered the grindylows' lair.

"Wait here," Emily said, pointing to an antique leather chair with studs. "I'll get her. Don't leave this chair."

Emily did not need to mandate a consequence, and Belén did not want to find out. In the dark, she heard movement. Her family's research into the Slatons told her there were potentially five grindylows in the clan, minus the grandfather. She had now met perhaps three of them. She reasoned that the creature in the shadows was either Oscar Slaton or one of Emily's parents and would easily rip out her jugular if given a reason.

A normal person would have run screaming from the house, but Belén had been hunting monsters since puberty. She had raided haunted houses, slain ghosts, and fought hand-to-hand with homunculi. So walking into a grindylow's lair was not completely unsettling to her. She remained calm and thought about what she would say to Yig.

Emily walked back downstairs, a candle in one hand, her cousin's hand in the other. Yig looked like a soul hollowed out, a ghost of the woman she had hunted through Galveston.

Belén stood up and followed the cousins into the dark internal organs of the house. Emily took them to the kitchen, which was tiled black and white. It should have given off a 1950s vibe, but instead made the whole kitchen feel twisted and sinister like carnival pinwheels at the horror house. She tried not to imagine what the kitchen was used for when it wasn't pretending to be a kitchen.

Yig took her seat in the kitchen. Her pupils floated in her eyes like black phantoms in a milk-colored fog. Belén's heart ached for the woman. Her exorcism wasn't a day old. *What's going through her head?* Belén wondered. *Who is she?*

Sitting next to her, Emily's face stretched as lean as uncooked fat, as dangerous and wicked as any creature of the night when it is finished pretending to be human. She looked almost nothing like the person who took Nadia dancing.

"I have an idea," Belén said as they sat down.

"I thought you said you had a plan."

Belén took Yig's hands in her own. "Remember what I said to you on the beach, about the saying?"

"You said it was just an old island story," Belén said.

"Yes. And I also said that I had new information from Madam Miteff, the ghost hag you met at the hospital."

Yig yawned. Belén could not help sneaking a peek at her teeth. They were square and white as tombstones.

"Could you get me a cup of coffee?" Yig asked Emily. Emily nodded and stepped out of the candlelight.

Belén recited: "*When the silver of the moon touches the black of the water, the waters will run red with blood. Silver can stop, teeth can end, but nothing keeps the shark away.*' Madam Miteff told me there is a way to control the transformations. Do you remember seeing the Mother of All Sharks?"

Yig remembered her encounters with the Mother all too well. She wished she could forget them.

"Madam Miteff told me the meaning of the second line. She said that 'silver can stop' means silver can hurt a wereshark and make it go away. It can even kill."

"Silver affects weresharks differently," Yig said. "I was able to break out of my chains."

"Yes. You are closer in lineage to the Mother than most weresharks. Think of it like being a copy of a copy. The first copy looks just like the first, but by the time you make the fiftieth, it hardly looks like the original at all. You, being bitten by the Mother, are a very powerful wereshark, much stronger than the others. That you are a grindylow makes you extra powerful. But that won't help you."

"What will?" Emily said as she walked back into the candlelight. The aroma of coffee filled the kitchen.

"Getting your tooth. Madam Miteff told me that the Mother carries shark teeth with her all the time, usually as a necklace. Each tooth on the necklace represents a person she has bitten. If you steal your tooth from her, then you will be able to control your transformations all the time."

"The first time I saw her, she was wearing necklaces with shark's teeth. Then when I saw her at Cerberus, she was wearing a shirt with a shark's tooth design."

"That's her collection, Yig. Steal your tooth, and get your life back."

"And if we get the tooth, will the Witch's Hammer and the Carfax Society leave my daughter alone?" Oscar asked from the shadows. When he stepped out, his face was drawn long and gaunt. On either side of him stood Yig's human mother and Emily's grindylow parents. The whole clan was there.

"Yig would still be a wereshark, and she would still be half-grindylow. The Maleficarum and the Society would not stop chasing her. This is not about stopping anything. This is about coping with lycanthropy."

"Hmph," Yig's Uncle Jeremy said. "You sound like a brochure."

"I want to do it," Yig said.

"But you don't know if it will work," her mother said. "All you have is the word of a ghost."

Yig said, "Word of a ghost, word of a grindylow, none of it makes sense. Is any of it worth anything?"

Her family fell silent. Yig pointed at Belén. "All she has ever done is try to help me. She risked her life coming here to convince you to do something that will improve my life. Hasn't every decision you've ever made, for better or worse, had the same goal? You didn't tell me growing up I was half-grindylow because you wanted me to have a normal life. You sent me to a psychologist you knew to be a member of the Carfax Society because you believed it would help me deal with my psychoses. If you really want to do what is best for me, trust her."

Oscar swooped in from the edge of the candlelight and took his daughter's hands in his own. "I was wrong, Yig, and I am willing to make it right. If this is what you want, we support you."

"I'm tired of living in a world of sorry. I'm tired of you being sorry for me, and I'm tired of everyone else being sorry for you. I'm tired of that weird sympathy of 'you are awesome because you are mentally fucking handicapped, but don't touch me because I don't want to catch your mental-fucking-handicapped-ness. Stay in your cage like a broken tiger because I am sad that the tiger is broken and my heart goes out to the tiger, but I don't want it any closer to me.' I'm tired of it all. I'm just me, and I know that's a lot more complicated than anyone else, but it's who I am."

Oscar hugged his daughter. To Yig, her father then looked less like the grindylow and more like the good-natured man she grew up knowing, the father who helped tie her shoelaces, encouraged her to play sports, and filled her room with balloons on her tenth birthday.

"So we're going for the tooth," Emily said. "But how, and when?"

Belén said, "The sharks are hiding out at Mitchell's Reef. It's a bunch of rigs dropped into the Gulf about twelve miles off the coast. They are waiting there for the Mother to tell them it's time to come ashore. I think they're waiting on you."

"But why would they wait on me?"

"It's a coming-out party for you. Most lycans center around a familial structure: packs, herds, prides. Weresharks are no different. For weresharks, it's the shiver. The Mother probably called to you last night, but you didn't hear her because of the exorcism. She will call to you again, and you'll feel a need to go to her. You'll feel this way down in your bones. We'll go with you, and we're going to surprise her and the other sharks. They won't expect us to be coming. That's when you grab your tooth, and we make our escape. The full moon will be over then, and the opportunity to run ashore will have ended, and the weresharks will go their separate ways."

"And the Mother? Won't she come for me?"

"She'll have the whole Water Clan to deal with," her father said, placing his gentle hand on her shoulder. "We're family." Yig smiled up at him.

Yig and her family gathered the supplies they needed. While the others walked outside, Yig's father kissed her mother.

"This is the right thing to do, isn't it?" she asked.

"It is the best option to bring a little peace to Yig." He sat her down in her armchair. She looked out the window the way she had when Yig's grandfather first went missing. Then she let out a gasp.

The house was surrounded by people whose shadows stretched across under the lamplight across the yard. It was Vara de Moses and Katrina and the Carfax Society.

Oscar swept outside as fast and cold as a mountain stream. He hissed, baring his fangs. "You are not welcome here," the patriarch warned the on comers. The blackest waters pooled out of the gutters and drained from the house roof.

Behind Oscar, the rest of the Water Clan and Belén appeared.

"You aren't going anywhere without us, Belén," Vara said.

"You won't like what I'm about to do."

"I don't like what you've done already," he said, nodding to the grindylows.

"It's the right thing to do, *hermano*. We don't need to kill the lycan. If she steals the tooth from the Mother, she can control her lycanthropy. Madam Miteff told me."

"Madam Miteff would lie to save her ghostly soul."

"You know that's not true. She is many things, but not a liar."

"And the grindylows?"

Emily said, "Would you believe we're pescatarians?"

CHAPTER TWENTY-SEVEN: THE GOBLIN SISTERS

Yig went back to bed. She'd had a very bad morning, and it was barely dawn yet. She stared at the ceiling and counted the dots in the ceiling paint. This had a strangely calming effect on her. Yig thought about her selves. She'd never known about Yig the Yellow, yet there was nobody closer to her. Who was she? She was having this existential crisis because she was discovering new identities she did not exist. The Dead Girl. Her first identity outside of her Otherwise Normal Identity. And now Martha Mayhem. In the ocean of her future, she saw only troubled waters, and they ran very deep.

Somehow she fell asleep. When she awoke, mid-morning light was streaming through her window. She was in her old bedroom, the one she grew up in.

The room was tidy. The room was painted yellow. Posters of Charlie's Angels, Farrah Fawcett, The Lost Boys, and The Cure adorned her wall. She also had The Crying Game, Taxi Driver, and Fight Club all on her walls. In one corner was a cardboard animal pen with "CWAFOP, Cousins Who Are Friends of Pets" scrawled in crayon across the cardboard pickets. Several stuffed animals were still waiting in the pen.

She took a deep breath, thinking to herself, *who is this*? Which one of the color wheel of personalities was upstairs? She exhaled, and she knew.

There was a knock at her door.

"Who is it?" Yig asked.

"It's me, Em. Your goblin sister."

Emily cracked the door open and peeked inside. "May I come in?"

Yig thought about this for a second. "And if I say no?"

"Well, that would be rude."

"But, I mean, can I say no? I mean, if I say no, can you not come in 'cause you're not allowed to?"

"I'm a grindylow, not a vampire."

The thought of her cousin being some monster sent a shrill up Yig's spine. The last 24 hours had been a confusing blur to her. She wasn't sure everything she remembered was real.

Emily opened the door and crossed the room. She sat on Yig's bed.

"You have a lot of questions."

"I wasn't sure any of it had happened."

"It's been a weird 24 hours. We should talk, shouldn't we?"

"I have an alter I didn't remember, I'm a wereshark, and I come from a family of grindylows. We should talk."

"Do you remember we used to call each other goblin sisters? Do you remember how we got that name?"

Yig shrugged. "I suppose you're going to tell me I'm part goblin, too."

Emily took Yig by the hand. "The story goes that you and I were very young. Maybe ten years old, but physically and mentally, four or five. We were out on the peninsula, at a birthday party on the beach. It was summertime, and the beach was really crowded. We were playing in the water when some fish went wiggling between us. I manifested. I reached down, grabbed a fish, and bit into it. You hadn't manifested, but you were going to join in, too. So you grabbed a fish and you bit into it. You spit it out, crying out *Yuck, that's gross*! But the kids around us were freaked out to say the least. These were all islanders. People Mom and Dad knew. If they lost their cool, it could blow their cover. So Dad, cool as a cucumber, dismisses everything in front of the other parents and says, *Oh, those girls. They think they're goblins. Come over here, goblin sisters!* And as soon as we were out of sight, he took me aside and checked my fangs. We left before presents or cake."

"I don't remember any of this. Was I me, or...?" And that was the conceit of DID. She didn't know if she couldn't remember something because she was too little to remember, or if it was because she was being shielded by an alter. The alters were both protectors and betrayers.

"Yig, I don't remember any of it. Our minds were like four year olds. But that's where the nickname came from. I wanted to tell you so that you knew this was always there."

"You were always a grindylow."

Emily nodded.

"What's a grindylow?"

"The short answer? We're water spirits from England, specifically rivers and lakes, but any body of water will do. They say when a child goes missing at the banks of a lake, a grindylow took them."

Yig's eyes widened. "Do you kill children?"

"No. But we are blood suckers. Fish, mostly."

"Pescatarians."

Emily smiled. "Exactly."

"Special powers?"

"I can breathe underwater."

"So much for Faith, Football, and Freedom."

Emily raised an eyebrow.

"You are my Rory Gilmore, remember? But now you're not."

"I'm still me."

Yig deflected. "And breathing underwater, it's helpful, but for a super power, that's not very exciting."

Emily held out her hand. Little black dots appeared on her palm, the sprouted into branches.

Yig slapped Emily's hand and kicked away.

"Yig, don't be scared. This is normal."

"It's really weird to me, though! I mean, here I am struggling with my identity, trying to figure out who I am, and my cousin, my family, are all living double lives. They appear human, but they're really monsters."

"I'm really sorry, but I wanted to be the first to tell you so that it always came from a place of love."

"Great. So you lie, but that's okay because it came from a place of love. I am fucking losing my mind and seeing a therapist, and my family is lying behind my back, but hold everything. It came from love? Fuck you."

Yig stomped out of her bedroom, Emily tailing behind. Both were in tears.

Her mother, father, aunt, and uncle were waiting for her at the bottom of the stairs.

Yig made the sign of the cross with her fingers as she hurried down the stairs. "Back away, foul demons. In the name of the Father, Son, and Holy Spirit, I condemn you."

Oscar grabbed his daughter's crossed fingers and separated them. "It doesn't work like that."

"One more thing you kept from me," she grumbled, and pushed through them.

Yig slammed the front door open and walked out onto the porch. "How the hell would I know what is true in this family anymore?"

Yig's mother pushed through her family. "Look at me, Yig."

Her mother had deep wrinkles and faded skin that wasn't quite the texture of old paper yet. As long as Yig could remember, her mother had looked twenty years older than her father. Yig realized that the opposite was true: her father was the older species, and her mother was aging faster than anyone in the family. She was the reason Yig was only half-grindylow.

"I'm sorry," Yig said to her mother, and they hugged tightly.

Yig went back into the house.

CHAPTER TWENTY-EIGHT: PERSONALITY INFLICTION

Dr. Carter drove the old Land Cruiser along Galveston's narrow streets. Dr. Talbot sat in the passenger side seat, his face set in quandary.

"Are you up for this?" Dr. Carter asked. "After everything you've been through. It is amazing that you recovered as quickly as you did."

"I don't have a choice in the matter. That monster took my arm, and I want payback. She'll be gone in days if we don't get her now."

"You really think so? With the company, she has set up deep roots in Galveston."

"She wouldn't be the first monster to set up appearances in a town and then relocate overnight. No, she is in this for her feast, for her parade of weresharks to come riding into town on a storm. And when they're finished, only after thousands of people have been killed, she will return to the ocean, one way or another, and we may not hear from her for a decade or two. I want to get her before she disappears, Lynne."

"Of course, James. But wanting something and capability to do something are two different things."

"I served my country on two tours. I've seen what monsters can do, and I've seen good men overcome injuries worse than this to fight again."

"Yes, sir," Dr. Carter said as he pulled up along the curb of the Slaton's two-story home. The Slatons and the Malleus Maleficarum were all sitting on antique chairs that had been brought outside. Only Belén and Yig were missing.

"Are you ready?" Vara de Moses asked as the two psychologists exited the Land Cruiser.

Dr. Carter gave them a thumbs up. "And you?"

Oscar said, "All but one. Yig is inside. We're waiting on her to change."

"If we go now, though, we'll have a better chance to surprise them," Katrina said.

"The girl needs to change into the wereshark," Dr. Carter said.

"Can't she do that on the way?" Vara asked.

"It isn't that easy," Dr. Carter said. "This isn't something Yig can just turn on and off."

"I've seen werewolves leap from man to beast in the middle of war," Katrina said.

•

"But they do not have a dissociative disorder. She isn't just switching between human and beast. She's switching between entire people."

Yig paced inside the kitchen in front of Belén. The kitchen appeared less foreboding in the daylight. Yig's hands thrummed nervously at her side.

"Do you want me to ask Dr. Carter to come in here? We can try that pen technique again if you like."

"No, thank you," Yig said with finality. "Just talk to me."

"About what?"

"You risked your life coming to my house last night. Why would you do that?"

"You're giving me too much credit. Apparently, my family was not far behind me."

Yig continued pacinge. Belén thought Yig looked like a pregnant woman trying to give birth, which in a way, she was. She said, "I was raised to fight monsters. And in a port city, there is a constant influx of monsters, ghosts, and demons from other countries. They come over like an invasive species hitchhiking a ride on a freighter, and they need to be eradicated."

"So you're pest control?"

"Pest control, border patrol, there are many metaphors for what my family does. What I do. But some time ago, I got this idea in my head that not all monsters fit into the definition of 'evil.' Not all of them needed to be treated so inhumanely. Some of them, in fact, were human. And this thing inside them that made them appear like a monster didn't make them a monster. It was more like a disability, if that's what you call it. And these people had learned to live with their disability. So I always argued that if they can learn to live with the disability, why can't we? Sometimes my family, the Malleus Maleficarum, would allow creatures like Madam Miteff to live because they helped us, but my family never saw it going any further than that. The monsters that help us kill other monsters, we leave alive. The ones who try to hurt the island, like the Mother, we show no mercy."

"You're a good person, Belén. A Hispanic Captain America," Yig said. She was leaning over the kitchen counter like she was working through contractions, or about to throw up.

"Do you need something? I feel like I should offer you a wet towel."

"No."

"Can I ask you something?"

Yig grunted.

"What's it like living with multiple personalities?"

"Have you ever walked into a room and not realized why you walked in there? It's like that, except so much worse. See, there is the side of us we show while at work, helpful and strong. There is the fun-loving person we pretend to be in front of our friends. There are the sides we show to our family, to our neighbors, and even the person we show ourselves in the mirror when we're alone. But then an outside force, what feels like a stranger, tries to set up shop in your personalities. It inflicts your world, and suddenly the problem is not that you can't remember why you walked into a room, but you can't figure out why it's now suddenly night time, and where you've been all day."

"What you describe sounds like a horror story."

Yig sat down in the chair opposite Belén. "It can be, but it's also refreshing in a weird way."

"What do you mean?"

"My alters deal with the hard parts in my life. School, work, interacting with complete strangers. Dealing with the fact that my parents are grindylows. I didn't have to deal with any of these things because of my alters. And as wrong as that may be, the truth is that they exist to protect me."

Yig took a deep breath and slumped into the chair. "It's time for them to care of me again."

Belén took a step back.

"And what happens after she changes?" Vara asked. The sun had reached its apex and was slowly beginning its fall into the horizon. "If the wereshark attacks me, I'm going to defend myself as violently as necessary. You haven't seen these monsters in action. They don't just kill. They ravage."

"Don't be so scared. Everything's going to be all right, Vara de Moses," Yig said from behind. Vara tensed, expecting the shark. He searched her eyes. Yig's eyes were sharp, but they weren't doll's eyes.

"You're not Martha," Katrina said.

"I'm better. I'm Petra. I will bring out Martha when the time is right. Until then, you'll need me."

CHAPTER TWENTY-NINE: VORTEX OF TEETH

Emily's parents stayed behind to watch over Yig's mother, who had neither the special abilities of the grindylows nor the training of the Malleus Maleficarum. The rest boarded the Carfax Society's research vessel, the *Westenra*, and motored out to Mitchell's Reef. The Malleus Maleficarum brought harpoon guns with silver-barbed harpoons.

Climbing onboard, Petra placed her hand on the gunwales. Her hand burned bright, and she pulled away.

"Careful," Dr. Talbot said. "They're silver-tipped."

"It's a shrimping boat?" Vara said disdainfully.

"What happened to the other lycan hunters?" Dr. Carter asked Katrina as she came onboard.

She shrugged. "Lycan hunters are a paranoid lot. We'll make do without them."

The three groups, temporarily joined, stayed mostly to themselves as the trawler headed out to the reef. The grindylows stayed indoors, and the Maleficarum stayed on the deck with the lycan hunter. The two Society doctors went inside with the grindylows.

"She's a forty-four-footer," Dr. Carter told Petra from behind the wheel of the shrimp boat. "I bought, well, I mean, The Carfax Society paid for it, but I did the research and found her. Then I used Society money to buy her off a Louisiana family. We spent three months renovating the kitchen and bunks so we had room to add a tracking station. The goal was two-fold: we wanted to search for a sea serpent that's been sighted in the islands from time to time. Second, we wanted to see what else was out there. Mermaids, weresharks, that sort of thing."

"Did you ever find the sea serpent?" Petra asked. While Dr. Carter lectured about sea monsters and research vessels, she had been organizing all three groups into her own org chart. There were three orgs as she saw it: Slatons, Treviños, and the Carfax Society. Or by function, monsters, monster slayers, and monster scholars. A side box for Katrina split from the monster slayers. A box for Petra (under monsters) was broken out into six boxes.

But all orgs, like Cerberus, eventually lead to one person. Every chain of command had a single commander on top. That was one of the truisms of org charts. And if you hadn't broken the org chart down to one person, you hadn't reached the top. So the question for her was which of the three: Vara de Moses, Dr. Carter, or her father?

Dr. Carter did not respond to Petra's question about the sea serpent. Petra could see the wheels spinning in his head. He pointed to the outriggers that were perpendicular to the boat. On the end of each outrigger was a little black box.

"That's sonar. By putting them on the ends of the outriggers, we can get a much wider, and deeper, view of what's going on underneath us by looking at this reader."

"But, Dr. Carter, did you meet your objective?"

"Yes and no. The bigger question is how you are doing, Petra. Are you meeting your goals and objectives?"

Petra smiled knowingly. "I see what you're trying to do, Dr. Carter. Lure me out with office talk. Do you think you can catch all my personalities in your nets?"

"I am first and foremost a doctor of psychology, Petra. There are no nets between us. So tell me how you are doing." And that's when she realized who was at the top of the org chart. She had made a mistake, and now needed to move one person from the bottom of the chart to the top.

"I am fine." Yig nodded to the laptop strapped to the console. "Do you have Wi-Fi?"

"Of course. And a booster to ensure the signal gets out."

Petra opened the laptop and turned it on.

Dr. Carter said, "The password to get in is…"

"I've got it," she said. The home screen came up. She connected to the internet, then to her e-mail.

"Are you e-mailing the rest of the identities?"

"No. Just one in particular. A co-worker I need to accept some tasks." She finished typing the e-mail, then shut the laptop.

"You have silver, Dr. Carter, but do you have any other defenses?"

He tapped a little red switch beneath the console.

"What's that do?"

"If lycanthropes take over the boat, I press this button and I make a lot of them go away."

"You sound like you plan on blowing up the boat," Oscar said as he came in from the kitchen and bunks.

"No. Well, maybe. I'm a scientist. I don't want to kill anything. I want to study it."

"A real pacifist."

"I didn't say that. I said I wanted to study it."

"For the betterment of mankind," Oscar said.

"That's right. We study creatures of the night, if you'll beg my pardon, in the hopes of curing diseases and making biological breakthroughs."

"Petra, go with your cousin."

"She's not *my* cousin," Petra said.

"Then go because I'm telling you to leave."

As Petra walked out, Oscar shut the door behind her.

Dr. Carter realized he was alone in a small room with a head grindylow. The leader of the Water Clan. His skin broke out in gooseflesh. He watched Oscar in the window's reflection and saw nothing of Yig's adoring father in the reflection.

Oscar placed a long-fingered hand on Dr. Carter's shoulder and looked at him with brackish eyes.

"Was it to the betterment of mankind when you bound my daughter to a chair and forced her to turn into a wereshark?"

"Please, Oscar. I was only acting in the name of science."

Oscar hissed as he spit out the last word. "I abhor your science."

Dr. Carter could feel the pressure of one of Oscar's nails tight against his skin.

"I want to make a deal with you," the grindylow said.

"What kind of a deal?"

"I am going to give you what you want. My blood." He showed the doctor a syringe he had been hiding in his other hand. He stuck the syringe into his arm and drew blood. "If I don't return, do with it what you want. On one condition. You get my daughter as far away from here as you can. Do we have a deal?" He placed the syringe in Dr. Carter's hand. The syringe felt strangely cold in his hands. There were little bits of flotsam and jetsam floating in the blood.

Dr. Carter nodded, and Oscar left behind a door that barely opened for his exit. Dr. Carter then exhaled excitedly (he hadn't realized he'd been holding his breath) and nearly dropped the syringe. He placed the syringe in an ammo box that he kept under the console.

Vara watched the people in the tight confines of the deck. They were nearly bumping into each other. The boat had come to a stop. In the distant water several buoys marked the artificial reef. And on the horizon, the sun was disappearing into the Gulf. Opposite the sun, Hecate's chariot was bringing forth the darkness.

Vara said, "Bow for the blessing."

The Water Clan and the Carfax Society emerged from the boat's quarters as Vara de Moses finished the blessing. The hunters were dressed in scuba suits like the one Katrina wore, with Faraday cages woven into the mesh.

Two fins broke the surface of the dark water.

"Should we be worried about that?" Belén asked.

"No. Those are just sharks," Katrina said.

Katrina said, "Now listen up and pay attention. We're about to go into a very dangerous situation, the likes of which I've never tried before. I've infiltrated packs, but never a shark shiver. The odds are worse than any I've ever attempted, but I've never worked with such a dangerous crew, either. If we use our talents and skills and put our differences aside, I think we have a chance, but only if we don't go off on our own little crusades."

"So we're going for Yig's tooth, then?" Emily said coldly. "That is why we came out here, right? Not to just slaughter lycans."

"Exactly," Katrina said. Looking directly at the scientists, Katrina added, "Or study them." To the Treviños she said, "Or banish demons. We have to set that aside for now. They're not expecting us, so if we move quickly, we can get to the Mother before the shiver knows we're here."

"You humans should stay up here," Oscar said. "Leave the wereshark problem to the monsters. We can move effortlessly through the water. Even in scuba suits and fins, you will be holding us up."

"No. We're coming, too."

"But they can't breathe underwater, and I don't think there's a dive suit made for this kind of dive, is there?"

"They now how we're getting down there," Vara de Moses said.

"Okay, so how?"

Katrina pulled her machete.

"Calm down, killer," Emily said. She took a knife to her hair and cut off a patch. She soaked it in the Gulf waters for a second or two, then handed the wet hair to Katrina. Katrina examined it for a moment, then put it in her mouth. It tasted as pleasant as eating briar patch, but more wormy. She made a disgusting face as she placed the hair in her mouth.

"Gillyweed," Emily said. "Harry Potter. Goblet of Fire. There is a little truth in every fiction. Gillyweed is based on grindylow hair."

"I don't like to read things that remind me about my real life," Katrina said.

"Grindylow hair separates water into hydrogen and oxygen. It helps us move up and down," Emily said to Petra. Emily cut off a clump for Vara de Moses, who put the hair into his mouth, saying, "It separates oxygen and hydrogen for about 40 minutes. That's more than enough time to get the tooth and get back unless you grindylows betray us down there."

"Who are you to talk about betrayal? You who've hunted people like us for centuries." Oscar stood up tall and loomed over the hunters.

"Damn right we've fought you, you blood suckers," Vara said. The two pushed into each other's faces.

"Do you know how easily I could slaughter you?" Emily asked.

Belén jumped between them, then looked up into the intense green-and-black eyes of the grindylow. "We'll be able to keep up with you," Belén said. "I brought holy Chrism. With the proper words, we'll be able to swim like the fish of the sea."

The grindylows scanned the people onboard and backed away. Oscar said, "Keep your holy oils away from us."

"Look," Vara de Moses said. He was looking over Katrina's shoulder to the open Gulf with the evil moon hanging in the sky. Shark fins cut back and forth in the dark water. *When the silver of the moon touches the black of the water, the waters will run red with blood. Silver can stop, teeth can end, but nothing keeps the shark away.*

The humans bathed in sacred Chrism while Belén spoke in the language of the baptized dead. Dr. Carter attached a small electronic device to the wench and trolleyed it out along the outrigger. The black box descended down the length of the outrigger and then into the saltwater.

"This device," Dr. Carter said, "will blink starting in twenty minutes. If you get lost there for whatever reason, look for the flashing light."

The others nodded. "Be careful," he added. "There are dangers besides weresharks at the reef. The Mitchell is a series of dropped oil rig derricks. It will be easy to get turned around down there."

"What about Petra?" Vara asked. "Doesn't this all hinge on her?"

"No, lunger, it does not," a voice said from behind them all. They looked back and stood aghast at the giant grey-skinned wereshark standing behind them.

"Hello, landchum. Martha's back." Everyone on the boat took a step away from her or readied their harpoons, not knowing what the powerful wereshark was going to do next.

"Don't worry about me, kiddies. I'm squared. I don't eat you, but you don't kill me. Keep that silver to yourself. Got it?"

Martha dove then into the Gulf, her tail slapping salt water on the people who had come there to save her. Emily and Oscar dove next. The two Treviños and Katrina put on goggles and dove into the water.

Belén jerked frightfully as soon as he entered the water. Martha was waiting, all mouth and black eyes, just under the surface. So too were the ghastly, long faces of the grindylows. Long branches jutted from their backs, hands, and feet. No wonder the sharks did not come near them.

"Don't jerk around like that," Martha cautioned. Belén was surprised that she could hear Martha as clear as if she was talking above water. She didn't know if it was the grindylow hair or the wereshark, or both.

Martha continued. "Sharks're guided by blood, sound, and electricity. Sometimes sight. You thrash around, they'll hear the fear in your movements and come to find out if you're worth eating."

As they moved to deeper waters, they each felt the descent in different ways. To Oscar, it felt like a bathing in calming black waters. To Emily, it was a return to a place she did not like to visit: that dark side of her where the light seemed as far away as a distant star. For the Malleus Maleficarum, covered in Chrism and bound by the words of the baptized dead, it was a descent into the open maw of a hellmouth. For Katrina, the darkness was a reminder of her worst nightmares and the black cloak of a ghost she knew too well. But for Martha, the deep black of the Gulf waters at night was a return to the conference room and the table and the Dead Girl.

She could feel the Dead Girl's cold hands on her back. She shuddered under their touch. She would have laughed at the thought of a giant wereshark trembling at the touch of a little six-year-old girl, except that she had seen the child in the labyrinth of her mind, and she had felt her cold touch on her heart, and she didn't want that ever again.

"What do you want?" Martha growled.

"I want you to remember to get the tooth and not harm the people who are here for you."

"I'm no idiot," the wereshark barked back.

"You are a protector, Martha. That is a big responsibility. Yig needs your help."

"I won't let nothing happen to her, Dead Girlie."

"You can call me Hattie."

"I prefer Dead Girl. You got X's over yer eyes. I'll do what I can. Now leave me to it."

From the periphery, sharks watched the uneasy truce of humans and monsters swim down to the derricks. Beneath the divers, shadows formed in the darkness. Slowly, the shadows took on shape, and a giant derrick emerged out of that darkness. They could see the top of its crown below them. It was like diving into the water and finding the skull of a body and the spinal column and rib cage below it, except this time it was the spine of American wealth.

The group felt the pressure increasing as they descended. The humans in the party worried about the damage to internal organs, but put their faith in the chrism and the grindylow hair. The encroaching darkness put the fear of death in all of them. The farther down they went, the farther they ventured away from the safety of the ship. Things began to move in their peripheral vision. Or was it just a trick of the eye motivated by a paranoid mind?

Suddenly, a white figure appeared out of the murk. Like a ghost levitating through the night, the sand tiger approached them. Vara, who had recently fought and killed weresharks, felt a cold chill crawl up his spine as the ancient predator with the chainsaw mouth floated toward them.

"If the sand tiger realizes who we are, he will warn the Mother," Oscar said. Vara de Moses realized then that the reason he heard voices so clearly was that he heard them in his mind.

"I can get her," Emily said.

Emily swam under the shark. She reached up to stroke the shark's pale underbelly with her elongated fingers. Her fingers cut through the sand tiger's belly like paper. The shark squirmed away from her, its intestines spilling out behind like untucked shirttails. As the shark began to disappear, it turned upside down and fell into the darkness and was gone.

Martha sensed the electricity of the sand tiger go out, and she also felt the electric field of a large predator, or many predators, down below. She could not pinpoint their location because there were so many. But the Mother had them all waiting down in the darkness below. She could feel the Mother's call coursing through her. It was more melody than words. The melody told Martha it was time to be a daughter of sharks. Time to join the shiver. Soon, the family would leave for Galveston as one identity, the shiver, and when they would swim to Galveston, they would stuff their bellies full of human nutrient.

"We're close," Martha said.

"I can't see anything in this water," Belén said.

"They're below us," Martha said.

"Is this a trap?" Belén asked her.

"I don't know. Maybe."

"Quiet," Oscar said. "If it is a trap, we will meet it head on."

From out of Martha's periphery, another ghostly shape appeared. It came from behind and above her, and it was not like anything she knew. It was a cold, white thing with little electricity and a silver harpoon through its head. The thing flashed like lights, first a shark, then a monster, then a woman. Martha thought it must be an angry, vengeful spirit because of the frightening look in its eyes. Goblin's eyes. She twitched as she fell, belly up, her blood leaking from the harpoon wound in her head, whirling ribbon-like around her.

Martha glanced up. Katrina waved grimly, then reloaded the harpoon gun.

The group moved on, swimming through the beams of the first derrick. Martha could feel the derrick better than she could see it. The derrick was like a black structure surrounded by blue electricity. Then they came to a second, lower derrick and a horrible sight that gave everyone reason to hesitate.

A funnel of sharks swarmed beneath them. The circling fins were a spiraling vortex of teeth and death, like looking down the inside of a giant monster's mouth. It was an utterly terrifying swarm of mouths and teeth and aggression. And in the center was the Mother.

The deadly call of the Mother was intoxicating to Martha. "Give up everything to me," the electric melody said. "Give up everything to me, and give in to the feast."

"It is a beautiful melody," Martha said.

Overhearing her, Oscar said, "You must fight the Mother's call, Yig."

Martha scowled. Oscar speaking that name pissed her off enough to shake off the Mother's call.

"New plan," Martha said, looking into the big black cloud that was the lower depths of the Gulf. "Anybody ain't human, swim like a motherfucker to the Mother. The rest of you, cover us. If it moves funny, fill it with silver."

"Watch your language," Oscar said.

"I wouldn't be on such a high horse, Pops. Ain't you the son of a bitch that caused all this to happen in the first place?" Martha said, then dove toward the lower derrick. Her father paused, caught off-guard by his daughter's hurtful words. What made them hurt worse was that he knew they were true. Ultimately, he was the grindylow, and he was the person who chose to not tell Yig about being half-grindylow.

As Martha dove, her arms and legs metamorphosed into powerful shark fins. The water slicked around her, quickening her dive. She was a driver racing the red light, one eye on the traffic light and another checking her sides for cops. Except in this case, she was gunning into darkness instead of across the intersection, and if she was busted, the cops would tear her fin to fin.

As the distance between her and the others increased, she felt an odd coldness in the water. More than just depth, the chill in the water was primordial. A rebuttal of progress and a turn to a much simpler epoch, a time of unmerciful killings. Of hunting and preying and gnashing and stomach filling until something much colder bit your life-force away. It was the cold of the shiver!

Martha detected movement to her right. A swish of tail, and then it was gone, returned to the fog-like darkness. Martha ignored it. She knew she had to dive deep to protect Yig, and by protecting Yig, save herself.

(Nothin can save me.)

More movement. She looked again to her right, and out of the cold darkness, a small eight-foot tiger shot like a torpedo at her. As soon as the tiger charged Martha, she felt something. (No. Not felt. I knew.) She knew the Mother knew. The Mother knew, and Martha knew.

"Fuck. We got a hive mind here, Pops," Martha roared to Oscar. "This close to her and the other lycans, she knows what I'm thinking as soon as I do. That means she knows what you're thinking, too."

All around Martha, the waters burned bright blue and green with electricity. Like lightning bolts were coursing through the murky depths. At the center of the vortex of teeth, the Mother called out to her army of sharks.

"Kill the dirt-born." The Mother's words cut through Martha like the ringing of a loud and clarion bell. She wanted to abort her mission for her Mother. She wanted to turn around and charge into her own family and bite down hard on their soft bodies. Martha had to shake off the command.

"What's the new plan?" Emily asked.

"Improvise," Martha shot back, and she lunged, all teeth, into the electric current of weresharks dashing at her side.

Five sharks swarmed around Martha, mouths reaching for her. She dove under and above and around them but only found a labyrinth of teeth and electricity wherever she turned. She twisted her body and narrowly missed being split in two by the largest great white she'd ever heard of. Easily 25 feet long, the giant female moved with surprising agility for a creature her size.

The great white rose like a volcano eruption out of the dark, her mouth opened wide enough to swallow a Fiat. Adrenaline pumping, Martha wiggled out of the way.

As she avoided one set of teeth, another reached like a hand for her. A long-snouted hammerhead grabbed her by the tail and used it as leverage to climb on top of her. It bit down on Martha's dorsal fin, and Martha screamed. Blood spilled into the water, inciting the tornado of teeth to greater amounts of intensity. Then, as suddenly as the hammerhead captured her, he released her. Glancing black, Martha saw a long silver-tipped harpoon impaled through the mouth of the hammerhead.

Katrina again.

"Thanks, again."

"I came here to hunt," Katrina responded matter-of-factly. "And hunting is good."

Emily and Oscar fared better than Martha. The sharks that came near them suddenly found themselves biting down on water as the grindylows dodged from shadow to shadow among the derrick beams. Finally, an ugly goblin wereshark trapped Emily in his arms. The wereshark held on to her and tried squeezing the life out of her. When that didn't work, it ejected its mouth in that way that only sharks can do, pushing its jaws out beyond its lips. White gums ringed with teeth reached for Emily's head, intent on biting it off.

As the goblin shark's jaw shot at her, Emily extended the branches out of her spine and legs. Black branches pierced the wereshark's skin and grew into the shark, invading its gills and cavities. The creature flung Emily back and forth and let go, but too late. He was caught in her trap like a fish on a line of hooks, and no matter how much he thrashed, he could not escape her. She bit down hard on the goblin wereshark's neck and ripped out its throat. The wereshark reached for its throat, but only found a hole where its gills once were. The wereshark gawked at her, more confused than angry. Then it flashed back into its human identity and died.

At the top of the vortex, the Malleus Maleficarum were more methodic in their attack, but they were running into a problem. They had weresharks and regular sharks in the area.

"I don't like how that shark's looking at me," Vara de Moses said. The bull shark was swimming back and forth twenty yards away from Vara.

"The sharks are having a hard time finding us," Belén said. "The Faraday cages seem to be working. If we're quiet, they won't bother

Belén knew this was only partly true. Although the bulls could not pinpoint their locations because of the Faraday cages, they could still detect the shot of the harpoon. Already, the sharks had turned to them when they shot their harpoons.

"It feels like a waste to hit them with the silver tips," Vara said.

"I read that when approached by a shark, the best thing to do is get out of the water," Belén suggested.

Her brother chuckled. At the same time, Belén snuck up beside a wereshark, this one a big blue tiger shark. She was close enough to reach out and touch the shark's mouth. She held the harpoon up to its skin, and the lycan paused in its path. She wondered if it saw her. Could it sense her? If not the movement of her legs, what about the movement of her gear?

The tiger turned toward her, and she reacted, pinching on the harpoon gun's trigger. This close, she was shooting the tiger execution-styled. The harpoon exploded through the shark's gills.

Surprised and hurt, the shark blasted away. Its flurry of flight knocked Belén to the side and rolled her in its wake. She cried out, which excited the bull sharks that were circling her and Vara.

"Belén! You okay?" Vara called out to her. He reached out and pulled her close by.

Belén needed to take a moment to reorient herself. This far down and at night, up and down were theories more than concrete facts.

"I'm okay. I don't think anything's broken. And that's a tiger that won't be killing anybody else." Down below, the tiger had transformed back into its human form. Its blood floated up to the bulls, exciting them even more. They began to make sudden movements.

"I think they know where we are," Vara said grimly. "Let's slowly back up to the derrick. That'll at least cut off some of their angles."

Belén folded her arms out and began another incantation in the language of the baptized dead. The water in front of her swirled. Vara felt it warming up, first like a gentle sauna, and then it grew slowly to a seething boil. Belén lashed at the sharks with the boiling cyclone, saying, "Saint Francis, forgive me," as sharks swam away from the overheated water.

"Hey, where'd Katrina go?" Vara asked.

Katrina swam away from the spiraling sharks. She plunged down and then cut across to the Mother. She hadn't lied when she told everyone they needed to work together. She meant it, but she also knew that killing the Mother got everyone what they wanted. The wereshark shiver would collapse, the sharks would return to the ocean depths, and Yig wouldn't need a tooth to control her transformations.

From her suit, Katrina pulled out a silver-coated karambit, a kind of knife with a curved blade. She approached the Mother from behind and anticipated carving a giant pumpkin smile into her neck.

The Mother stood, arms outstretched, admiring her vortex. A flurry of teeth and bubbles and blood floated above her while her weresharks fought with Martha and the invaders.

She had a mostly human form. Except for the fins on her naked, hairless body, she looked like a beautiful siren standing on the derrick's concrete blocks, sitting at the bottom of the Gulf of Mexico. A siren commanding all the sharks in the world, and wearing necklaces of shark teeth.

Katrina cleared her mind, then swam to the concrete block and the wereshark. The Mother would not hear her coming because of the Faraday cage. She would not sense her because Katrina's mind was cleared. She was invisible. She was a ghost.

The karambit felt cool and deadly in her hands. Her muscle memory would guide her hands how to use a knife under water. This would not be the last werecreature she slayed. But by killing the Mother, it would have repercussions through the entire lycan world. It would be a reminder that no lycan lived without consequence. Kill a human and be killed.

The knife reached out for the Mother. Her neck was so close. A few more inches, she could end all the pain and suffering. So close. Just another inch.

The blade curled like a bad finger around the Mother's neck.

The Mother turned, her black eyes full of fear. That was the difference between lycans and other monsters. They still had a foot in the natural world. But that meant they could be hurt, and they could be killed. Their connection to the natural world was their weakness.

The Mother snarled at Katrina and bit at the hand that stabbed her neck. Katrina felt intense pressure in her wrist. She dropped the karambit, the knife floating slowly to the sandy bottom. The Mother shook Katrina's hand back and forth wildly. In a spurt of blood, she ripped Katrina's hand from her wrist.

Katrina screamed through the grindylow hair in her mouth.

The Mother smiled wickedly, her body twisting and contorting as it morphed into a giant, ugly bull wereshark. Katrina's blood floated in the water around the Mother's mouth like misapplied lipstick. Katrina pulled back her arm, which was erupting in pain.

The Mother of all Sharks opened her mouth to show Katrina her hand, then gulped it down her gullet. Katrina pushed away, like a fleeing seal, and looked for a place to hide. There was a hole between two concrete blocks. It was really more of a wedge than a hole. Katrina pushed her body up into the wedge and pulled out another silver-tipped knife.

The Mother shot at her, mouth first. A ring of teeth and terror snapped down on Katrina, barely missing her where she was wedged.

"You are nothing more than an appetizer, lycan hunter. Curds and whey, and you taste just as bad. Like old, dry meat. Yack."

She changed shape again, this time becoming fully humanoid. Except for the many rings of teeth hanging from her neck, she was completely naked. But she also had much better reach. The Mother extended her slender arm deep into the wedge where Katrina had forced herself. Katrina tried to cut her with her knife, but the Mother pinned Katrina's only hand down. The Mother was not interested in the knife.

The Mother forced her free hand into Katrina's mouth and removed the grindylow hair.

"K is for Katrina, who was killed by her own karma. Let's see how long you can survive under water, lycan hunter."

Over the Mother's shoulder, the mass of sharks continued swarming. The Mother swam to them while Katrina reached for her throat.

From out of the depths of the ocean of teeth and blood, Martha burst out and launched herself at the Mother. Martha's sides and fins were cut up from the many battles she had fought on her way to the bottom of the vortex. Straggles of flesh hung from her sides where she had been bitten by dozens of weresharks. Martha surged at the Mother, mouth open. The Mother met her, mouth for mouth, and bit down on Martha's snout. Martha screamed. The pain was excruciating. Like nothing she had ever felt before. But while she was attacking the Mother, she reached out for her tooth. She knew it was there. Could feel it as easily as she felt a heartbeat with her ESP. She could not get to the necklace, though. The pain was too much, and she had to flee.

CHAPTER THIRTY: HEADACHES

"Martha Mayhem," the Mother said. "My daughter." The way she called her daughter, like a child talking to a little doll, unnerved Martha.

"I'm nobody's daughter."

"I created you when I bit you. You can call it possession, dissociation, use whatever fancy word you like. But I made you when I bit you. My blood runs through your blood. Blood and teeth and murder: these are the things little weresharks are made of. That mark on your shoulder makes means you are special, you are my close daughter. As close, if not closer, than anyone else's, so don't try to say otherwise."

The Mother approached Martha. She looked humanoid now except for her disastrous teeth and the black holes she had for eyes.

"I did all of this for you."

"Shut yer mouth and get out of my head, old lady."

"I told you tonight would be a celebration. A mad hatter's coming out party. Tonight will be a feast like no other. Tonight, my shiver will dine on human flesh by the thousands. We'll wash ashore in a wave of horrors, and we'll cut through the island like a fin through water. We will leave death and entrails in our wake. This is what a mother does for her children."

"I don't want it."

"You're a very unique and many-faceted quandary, Martha, but your pain is ultimately no different than any other's. It is the pain of loneliness. You long for connection with a family that betrayed you. I can see it in your thoughts. It is a connection your other personalities will not allow you to have. Do you really think that any of Yig's personalities will ever allow Martha out? If you kill me, if you get your tooth back, what do you think they will do with little Martha Mayhem? You will become nothing more than a shadow in her soul. Dine with me, or every year you will watch from afar while somebody else controls your body."

The black holes of the Mother's eyes drew Martha in, like the bioluminescent bait of an angler fish. They were so deep and penetrating, like she was seeing right to her soul. The next thing she knew, Martha was sitting back at the conference table. The others were there, too. Somebody was knocking at the door.

"Don't get that," Yig said to Martha. "Something's out there. It's been knocking since you left."

Martha looked from one alter to the other.

"Ain't nothing I can't handle," Martha said.

"Don't!"

"Don't think I haven't forgotten so quickly, Yiggy. The last time we met, you all tried to expel me."

Martha crossed the conference room and opened the door. The Mother stood there.

"Little pig, little pig, thank you for letting me in." To the others, she said, "Martha was always the key. The one who would let me in."

"You don't belong here," Petra stood up from her chair.

"Sit down," the Mother of All Sharks commanded. Petra did not sit, but she did not approach the Mother.

The Mother surveyed each one of the identities. "I like this. Is this like a horcrux thing?"

Clara said defiantly, "No."

The Mother perused Clara's long blond locks of hair. "I think I've met a few of you, but not all of you," she said. "You can call me Mother. I want to invite you all to a party. All your cousins and brothers and sisters will be there. It will be like Thanksgiving. A Thanksgiving where everyone is accepted and everyone is eaten. What do you say?"

"I say you're insane," Clara said.

The Mother laughed.

Yig said, "You call yourself the Mother, but you're selfish and puerile. You say you're throwing this big feast for your family, but it's really just about glorifying you. You're worse than some trashy celebreality mom. You don't know anything about motherhood or what it means to raise a child."

"What I know is identity. Unlike you, the identity of the shark is pure and unchanging. In all of human history, we have been the terror. Since man began paddling out into the ocean, our fins have been the shape of their fear. Our teeth have cut through their nightmares. We fed on stranded soldiers and attacked fisherman's boats and made them afraid of the water. Join me, and you will become a monster feared and reviled, and that will be your one, true identity."

To Petra, Yig said, "I don't want her here."

"Neither do I," said Nadia.

"Nor I," said Clara.

"Nor I," said Hattie.

"Nor I," said Petra.

The Mother looked to Martha. "And you, Martha? You want me here, don't you? You can't say no to Mother, can you?"

Martha looked over at the other alters.

The Mother said, "The difference between Martha and the rest of you is that she doesn't want to hitchhike in this head. She wants to be the sole owner and proprietor and eat when, where, and what she pleases."

Martha moved from face to face of each alter, who were all waiting on her response. She could have a mind all her own if she wanted.

"Let me show you how good it will be," the Mother said. She pressed the button for the giant monitor that sat at one end of the room. A video crystalized in HD. In the video, the Mother lay languid under the Gulf. Martha swam beside her. The Mother commanded the sharks, both weres and normals, and they cut through the remaining grindylows and humans. They lunged out of the water, a thousand fins, with the Mother of All Sharks chasing after them in her shark form. As she surpassed her children, she grew in size. She was a giant, vicious shark. At 100 feet long, she was bigger than a prehistoric Megalodon and larger than a Blue Whale. As she grew in size, she sped up. More sharks came to her side, but they were all like minnows beside her. They raced toward Galveston, a giant shiver of electric death. Her gargantuan torpedo-shaped head broke the water, and her pups coasted along her wake. She hit the Galveston Seawall with the impact of a nuclear bomb, cracking the concrete and throwing a surge of water over the island.

Sharks and weresharks coasted into the streets, biting at anything that moved. The weresharks tore tourists apart. The waves flooded the city with the power of a tsunami. The Mother walked ashore, now a giant bipedal shark, rampaging across the island. She pulled a screaming woman off the porch of her stilted house and bit her in half.

The Mother's children, children of the broken sea, bit and tore apart humanity until the waves were awash with human body parts: legs, arms, heads, anything that wasn't pushed down the throat immediately.

The Mother of All Sharks said to the identities, "A tisket, a tasket, Galveston in a casket. This is the only truth in the world. It is a truth as ancient as the first sea creatures. Devour or be devoured."

The film cut to black.

Martha licked her teeth. "I like yer thinking, Mother. And I love a feast. But it's like you said, devour or be devoured, and as you should know, at one point, every apex predator eventually becomes the devoured." Martha backhanded the Mother so hard the wereshark flew against the wall. The other alters showed their weapons, which they pointed at the Mother.

The Mother's body deformed and lengthened and changed into a giant bull wereshark that loomed over Martha. Martha jumped for her, and the two weresharks matched mouths, biting and raking at each other, locked into combat. The Mother pushed Martha back into the table, and then Martha shoved the Mother back against the wall.

"Somebody help her," Nadia implored her alters.

"Give me your katana," Petra said to Yig.

Yig said, "The only way this works is when I start owning my fears. You can't protect me forever, Petra."

The Mother tossed Martha aside. Martha's back snapped as it hit the edge of the overturned table.

Yig jumped painlessly over Martha. Seeing Yig, the Mother leaped at her, striking at her with her claws. Yig parried both sets of claws with her sword, then sliced through the wereshark's chest and torso as effortlessly as a filet knife through a fish's belly. The Mother fell to the floor, her entrails slopping underneath her.

Yig approached the Mother, her katana raised for a fatal blow.

"Go ahead. Cut my head off, Yig. Carve out my heart. Kill me a hundred times. But I'll always be here. One way or another, I'll always be in your head."

Yig severed the wereshark's head in one blow.

CHAPTER THIRTY-ONE: A TISKET, A TASKET

The shark fins had disappeared. Dr. Talbot and Dr. Carter went to their sonar equipment to try to track the battle, but there was too much noise beneath them to understand what they were seeing. Too many large beasts in too small an area.

Twenty minutes passed. The moon glared down at them from the night sky.

"I think I'll set the light out now," Dr. Carter said. Dr. Talbot nodded. Dr. Carter went outside and turned on the winch. The little black box crawled up the length of rope and down the outrigger to Dr. Carter. He turned it on, then sent it back out. The box disappeared in the water. Then they waited.

Ten minutes passed, and still no movement.

"They have ten more minutes," Dr. Talbot said. "And then the grindylow hair will stop working."

Dr. Carter just watched the Great Grey, now black as ink, for any signs.

"I'm sure they will be fine, Lynne," Dr. Talbot said.

Ten more minutes passed. Dr. Carter turned on his stopwatch. One minute passed. At 1:35, a face finally breached the water, gasping for air. It was Vara de Moses. Katrina was unconscious in his arms.

"Quickly! The Mother pulled out the grindylow hair in her mouth."

Dr. Carter pulled out a rescue hook and pulled them to the boat. Once onboard, he checked her windpipe, then listened for a heartbeat.

"She has a pulse," he said. He started mouth to mouth while Dr. Talbot pulled Vara aboard with his one hand. As they watched, Katrina's body convulsed, and then she vomited water and food. Dr. Carter rolled her on her side and cleaned her off while Dr. Talbot grabbed an oxygen tank and strapped the mask over Katrina's face. She gave them a weak thumb's up.

"We've got to get out of here," Vara said.

"But the others."

"Don't worry about them. A shit-ton of weresharks are about to breach that water, headed straight for Galveston. We need to be out of their way."

Dr. Carter ran for the controls and turned the engines on. The *Westenra* was just starting to turn around when he saw the first shark fins emerge from the water.

Dozens of sharks leaped out of the Gulf. They breached as gloriously as great whites hunting fur seals in South Africa. Then one of the weresharks landed on the *Westenra*. Vara de Moses attacked the monster, stabbing it with one of his last silver harpoons. The wereshark fell back overboard.

"Get us out of here, doctor! *Fuera! Fuera*!"

The doctor pushed the engine into full throttle as hammerheads began reaching for the low-railed gunwales. Dr. Carter was thankful for the silver coating that kept them from climbing onto the research vessel.

Suddenly, the vessel heaved to starboard, dipping into the Gulf and pulling on water.

"Look!" Dr. Talbot shouted over the rush of waves, pointing to the outrigger. A wereshark had grabbed hold of the outrigger. It was now dragging the boat down.

"I'll get him," Vara said. "You just get us out of here."

The shark at the end of the outrigger was another great white. It was a terrifying creature, all jaws and mouth and death. The wereshark bit at the outrigger and pulled at it. A second great white joined the first. Vara crawled along the outrigger, his harpoon gun in hand. He shot the first Great White in the side, wounding but not killing it. The great white released the outrigger but glared at him as it sunk down into the water.

Vara knew he was dead before the third great white broke the water. He saw death in its face as it charged the surface. Vara had no chance of survival. The shark's giant mouth was wide enough to swallow him whole. It was the biggest damn monster he could imagine. But as the great white shot out of the watery depths up at him, another body hit it. Slammed into it like a wrecking ball. Something like a giant, black-coated corpse covered in spines was suddenly attached to the side of the great white. The shark breached the water beside Vara, then landed back in the water, shaking its body, violently trying to escape the urchin monster attached to its side. As the giant shark shot off in another direction, Vara saw what was attached to it and could only pity the damned thing. There was no getting rid of a grindylow.

The other wereshark continued to reach for the outrigger and drag it down. Vara reached behind to his quiver and pulled a harpoon out of the bottom. He loaded the harpoon and aimed his rifle. This time, he hit the great white right in the eye. Or he would have, if the shark hadn't held its hand up to block the harpoon. It yowled with pain, but continued pulling the outrigger down while Vara reloaded.

He shot again. This time, the harpoon hit the shark in the head hard enough that the shark's head jerked backward. Dying, the wereshark turned human as it sunk into the water. The last thing Vara saw of the beast was something that looked like a person with a giant mouth for a head, and no eyes, ears, or nose.

But the lycan gave one last tug before dying, and the outrigger snapped behind him. The research vessel tipped in the other direction, and Vara found himself flying into shark-infested waters.

Up onto the boat Belén pulled herself, gasping for air. The vortex of teeth had risen to the surface. The vessel was surrounded by dozens of large predators.

Belén saw her brother holding on to the outrigger while the sharks circled him. She ran to the side and stretched out her arm, reaching for the outrigger.

In the water, one of the fins swam so close to Vara that he could have reached out and grabbed it. He saw the horrible stripes along the back of the young tiger. Trying not to panic, he pulled himself gently up onto the remaining outrigger.

Belén crawled onto the other side of the outrigger, a large bull shark bit at her. "*Mijo*," she cried out. Just as a shark was about to grab her, Dr. Talbot pulled her back onto the *Westenra*.

She wanted to jump out to her brother, but Dr. Carter and Katrina held her back. Out over the Gulf, a shark grabbed Vara by the foot and jerked him back into the water before letting go.

Tears in her eyes, Belén shouted her love over the water. "I love you. I am so proud of you. You have held the Treviño name well. You are the best fighter I ever met."

Tears bulbed from her eyes. She had fought alongside him for so long. She couldn't imagine a world where he did not exist, but he could not be saved.

A shark struck Vara. He could feel his essence draining out of him.

"Belén." His voice was weak. He reached out to her with one arm while he tried to tread water with the other. It wasn't going so well. He couldn't feel his legs anymore.

"*Te amo, mi hermano*," she gasped. Then she made the sign of the cross. She began the last rites for Vara, saying, "May the Lord Jesus protect you and lead you to everlasting life. Amen."

Tears in his eyes, Vara thanked her. Then he turned into one of the sharks that was circling him. He brought his hands together. There was a tattoo on either palm. Put together, they formed a crucifix. Vara spoke one last time in the language of the baptized dead.

The shark fell below Vara as all water disappeared in a straight line from Vara's hands. He lowered his palms toward the sharks. The water parted. Fish and sharks and weresharks plummeted through the air and down to the bottom of the Gulf. He could see the derricks, and he could see the Mother and Martha. And then another wereshark came up behind Vara and tore his arm off. Vara fell down into the waters that were rushing back together in a massive collision.

There was no time to mourn. Another wereshark, a large blue, had climbed onto the deck. Dr. Carter, who had stopped the trawler when Vara went overboard, pushed the engines back to full throttle.

Belén pulled out her harpoon gun. She was wet, covered in Chrism, and she were exhausted both physically and emotionally.

"For Vara," she said.

But then Emily jumped on board between Belén and the wereshark. She hissed and showed her teeth and spines. The wereshark towered over her, palms smoldering from where it had grabbed the gunwales, but Emily refused to give up any ground. She showed the wereshark her long, bony claws. The shark bit at her. She cut through the wereshark's skin like scissors through paper. The monster balked, then jumped back into the water.

"Thank you," Belén said to Emily.

Down below, Yig realized she was looking through cold eyes, and her skin felt smooth, and her hands were clawed. By taking the katana, she had not only pushed out the Mother, but she had taken control again. She was bewildered. She'd never been cognizant in this version of her body. She thought it was impossible before, but now, more than ever, she realized Martha was another identity, not a wereshark. They were all the wereshark.

Suddenly, the water around her disappeared. She could feel air against her scaly skin. Fish and monsters were falling down from above. She looked up but could not make out what had happened.

She looked at the Mother. She was as confused as Yig. Being pushed out of Yig's head had taken its toll on her, if only for a moment.

Yig saw the tooth, *her tooth*, gleaming in the moonlight. While the Mother was distracted, Yig grabbed her tooth from around her neck and yanked it. She could feel a blast, as if some hold on the world had given out. Water had returned, and she was rolling with the wave. She righted herself in the dark and swam for the boat.

All around her, sharks were dispersing. It was like somebody had set off an electric bomb in the water, and it was wreaking havoc with their senses. They wanted to get as far away from it as possible. Even the weresharks were fleeing. They appeared in the dark like sudden, speeding banshees ripping through the night water. And then as quick as they appeared, they were gone again.

Yig wasn't quite sure where to go. Even in wereshark form, she was confused. Up and down were backwards, or inside out? She wasn't sure. There was too much blood and fear in the water. It was hard to get a read on anything. But then she heard the little pulse beacon that Dr. Carter had set out. It was faint at first, but it grew louder as she swam to it.

Yig came up for air next to the outrigger. In the last seconds before she emerged from the water, she had returned to her human form. The shark tooth, her shark tooth, was in her hand. She climbed naked up on the deck of the *Westenra*, her hand burning. Her grindylow family was there, as were the members of the Carfax Society. She saw Belén, but not Vara.

"Did you get it?" he asked when he saw her. "Are you okay?"

"Yes, Dad. I'm okay." She showed them the tooth.

Then the Mother of All Sharks leaped out of the water and jumped on top of the boat's cabin and looked down on everyone. She was all teeth and black eyes.

"You ruined everything!" she wailed. "You are the worst!"

"Sorry," Yig said unapologetically. She shined her black eyes and sharp white teeth.

"No," her father said. He turned to the wereshark. "This is my daughter, not yours."

"You can have her after I've finished killing her. I'll leave enough to bury. Or drink."

The grindylow flew up to her, all spines and teeth. Yig's father was an old and powerful grindylow, but she was the Mother of All Sharks. She flung him over her head. He hit the boards on the other side of the boat and was impaled on a wooden pallet. He couldn't move.

Yig climbed up on the top of the cabin.

"Now we're talking," the Mother said. "We're going to get us an old-fashioned girl fight. Come on!" But Yig wasn't interested in the Mother's talk. She bull-rushed the Mother, and they both fell down into the water and disappeared.

CHAPTER THIRTY-TWO: ALL THINGS WITH THE TIDE

The *Westenra* pulled up to the dock. Dr. Talbot and Dr. Carter saw Oscar and Emily off the boat. While Emily went to her car, Oscar tarried. "Thank you for helping us," Oscar said. A bandage was wrapped around his arm, where he'd been impaled.

"I'm sorry about your daughter. She was a very unique individual."

Oscar paused for a moment, like he was trying to swallow down something. Then he said, "Don't give up hope on my daughter just yet, Doctor. As you said, she is a very unique individual. In all my years, I've never heard of a grindylow/wereshark/human hybrid."

"But if she is gone?"

"Then I will mourn her when the time comes."

"And our agreement?" Dr. Carter asked. He handed over the vial of grindylow blood back to Oscar.

"Keep it. There's enough of my blood on your boards now. I'd hate for you to get a splinter trying to soak up my blood." He looked at the boat and laughed.

"Thank you, Oscar." The grindylow and the head of the Carfax Society shook hands then. "I hope, if nothing else, this leads to a new era where the Carfax Society can work in unison with the island's dark creatures."

"You know, for a long time, people thought we grindylows were vampires."

"Really?"

After Oscar left, Belén and Katrina came off the boat next. Katrina looked pale, but could walk.

"She is going to drop me off at UTMB," Katrina said. "I'll blame this on a freak boating accident."

"Freak lawnmower accident," Dr. Talbot said, raising his stub.

"And then?"

"Back to Pennsylvania for me. Then back to hunting. There are more lycans than you think, doctor. Hiding in plain sight. Don't forget that. They look just like you or me."

"Thank you."

He stopped Belén. "And thank you. I'm sorry about your brother. He was a great fighter."

Belén nodded as she held back the tears. "He's in a better place, but I'm not sure about me."

Dr. Carter put his hand on her shoulder comfortingly. "If you need me, I'm only a call away."

"I'm the last of the Malleus Maleficarum in Galveston."

She walked off with Katrina.

Lynne and James returned to the boat. As Oscar predicted, they spent the rest of the day collecting all evidence of grindylows and lycans. They sent everything to the Carfax Society's North American headquarters in New York City.

Somehow the evidence disappeared mysteriously. The Harkers were blamed.

Alone in the dark, a small shark's fin appeared near the beach. The shark moved back and forth like it was caught on a line. Then the tide rolled the poor beast up on the sand and away from her precious water. The shark gasped for water, its mouth opening and closing beseechingly. Between gasps, a hand emerged from the shark's throat. The hand pushed through the mouth. Then a second hand appeared. The fingers were like the legs of a large spider or crustacean trying to escape the jaws of the shark. The hands pushed outward. Searched for a precipice but all they found was sand. They clutched at the sand and pulled hard. Skinny arms were pulled from the shark's mouth. And then a head looked out from inside the shark's mouth. The woman pulled herself out of the dead shark's jaws. She turned around, reached into the dead sharks' jaws, and pulled out a black shark's tooth. She got to her feet and walked away.

THE END.

THANKS FOR READING

If you enjoyed Shark Toothed Grin, please leave a review on Amazon. These reviews not only help others select books, but also help authors to be seen.

I am also the author of the Severed Press books Dominion and Kaijunaut, as well as the Cadaver Dog series. If you enjoyed Shark Toothed Grin, please check them out.

My books can be found on Amazon at:
http://www.amazon.com/Doug-Goodman/e/B00IHF1I8S/

My website is www.douggoodman.net.

 SEVERED**PRESS**

CHECK OUT OTHER GREAT DEEP SEA THRILLERS

PREHISTORIC BEASTS AND WHERE TO FIGHT THEM
by Hugo Navikov

IN THE DEPTHS, SOMETHING WAITS ...

Acclaimed film director Jake Bentneus pilots a custom submersible to the bottom of Challenger Deep in the Pacific, the deepest point of any ocean of Earth. But something lurks at the hot hydrothermal vents, a creature—a dinosaur—too big to exist.

Gigadon.

It not only exists, but it follows him, hungrily, back to the surface. Later, a barely living Bentneus offers a $1 billion prize to anyone who can find and kill the monster. His best bet is renowned ichthyopaleontologist Sean Muir, who had predicted adapted dinosaurs lived at the bottom of the ocean.

MEGALODON: APEX PREDATOR
by S.J. Larsson

English adventurer Sir Jeffery Mallory charters a ship for a top secret expedition to Antarctica. What starts out as a search and capture mission soon turns into a terrifying fight for survival as the crew come face to face with the fiercest ocean predator to have ever existed- Carcharodon Megalodon. Alone and with no hope of rescue the crew will need all their resources if they are to survive not only a 60 foot shark but also the harsh Antarctic conditions. Megalodon: Apex Predator is a deep-sea adventure filled with action, twists and savage prehistoric sharks.

CHECK OUT OTHER GREAT DEEP SEA THRILLERS

HELL'S TEETH
by Paul Mannering

In the cold South Pacific waters off the coast of New Zealand, a team of divers and scientists are preparing for three days in a specially designed habitat 1300 feet below the surface.

In this alien and savage world, the mysterious great white sharks gather to hunt and to breed.

When the dive team's only link to the surface is destroyed, they find themselves in a desperate battle for survival. With the air running out, and no hope of rescue, they must use their wits to survive against sharks, each other, and a terrifying nightmare of legend.

MONSTERS IN OUR WAKE
by J.H. Moncrieff

In the idyllic waters of the South Pacific lurks a dangerous and insatiable predator; a monster whose bloodlust and greed threatens the very survival of our planet...the oil industry. Thousands of miles from the nearest human settlement, deep on the ocean floor, ancient creatures have lived peacefully for millennia. But when an oil drill bursts through their lair, Nøkken attacks, damaging the drilling ship's engine and trapping the desperate crew. The longer the humans remain in Nøkken's territory, struggling to repair their ailing ship, the more confrontations occur between the two species. When the death toll rises, the crew turns on each other, and marine geologist Flora Duchovney realizes the scariest monsters aren't below the surface.

CHECK OUT OTHER GREAT DEEP SEA THRILLERS

LOCH NESS REVENGE
by Hunter Shea

Deep in the murky waters of Loch Ness, the creature known as Nessie has returned. Twins Natalie and Austin McQueen watched in horror as their parents were devoured by the world's most infamous lake monster. Two decades later, it's their turn to hunt the legend. But what lurks in the Loch is not what they expected. Nessie is devouring everything in and around the Loch, and it's not alone. Hell has come to the Scottish Highlands. In a fierce battle between man and monster, the world may never be the same. Praise for THEY RISE : "Outrageous, balls to the wall...made me yearn for 3D glasses and a tub of popcorn, extra butter!" – The Eyes of Madness "A fast-paced, gore-heavy splatter fest of sharksploitation." The Werd "A rocket paced horror story. I enjoyed the hell out of this book." Shotgun Logic Reviews

TERROR FROM THE DEEP
by Alex Laybourne

When deep sea seismic activity cracks open a world hidden for millions of years, terrifying leviathans of the deep are unleashed to rampage off the coast of Mexico. Trapped on an island resort, MMA fighter Troy Deane leads a small group of survivors in the fight of their lives against pre-historic beasts long thought extinct. The terror from the deep has awoken, and it will take everything they have to conquer it.

www.ingramcontent.com/pod-product-compliance
Lightning Source LLC
Chambersburg PA
CBHW031947170626
46807CB00006B/2380